The Flayed Man

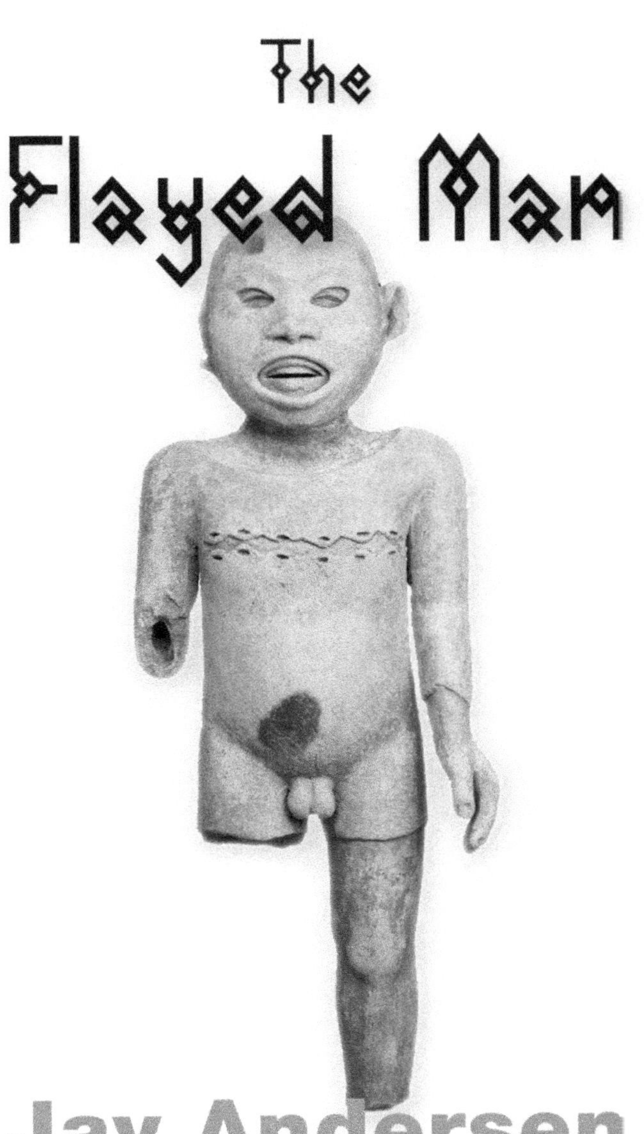

Jay Andersen

The Flayed Man

Print Version - ISBN: 978-1-7376308-9-0
E-Book Version - ISBN: 979-8-9862681-0-1

Published by

40274 Diamond Lake Street
Aitkin, MN 56431

218.851.4843

www.riverplacepress.com
chip@riverplace-mn.com

DEDICATION

For Tamera

Chapter One

Summer 2001

In Minnesota the state troopers wear a khaki shirt with maroon trim on the pocket flaps and epaulets. The sheriff's deputies dress similarly, except their shoulder and pocket trim is brown. Game wardens wear green trim. Sometimes the officers will wear tapered pants in the darker color, sometimes with a stripe down the leg seam. Wellingtons or western boots are the standard footwear. Small city officers wear similar shirts in two shades of blue, often with dark blue pants and black boots.

Today, Police Chief Paul Tharp wore a pair of New Balance running shoes, faded jeans and a black John Fogerty "Centerfield International Tour" tee shirt. I bought the tee shirt in the used clothing shop at the county recycling center for a dime. It has a bleach flash on the bottom hem, left. Maybe that's why someone recycled the shirt. Maybe they didn't like Fogerty anymore. Maybe they got fat. It was, after all, leftover from the '80s.

I also wore a dark blue mesh visored sport cap with a machine embroidered silver shield in the center with the words "Cache Harbor Police" in the same color wrapped around the insignia. My light blue short sleeve shirt with the contrasting dark blue epaulets and pocket flaps was draped between my holstered .357 magnum and my basket weave black leather service belt. I'm not a slob, the temperature was pushing 90 degrees in a town where 75 is considered downright tropical. And it was only 8 am.

I was eating breakfast at the Outpost Café and making believe that if I didn't actually have on my service shirt and badge, I was off duty. It was early August in what had turned out to be the hottest, soggiest summer in North Shore history. The man seated across the booth from me claimed that I kept my shirt off at breakfast because I liked my eggs sunny side up and I had only two changes of uniform in case I dripped yolk down my front.

"Eggs done like that aren't even dead," he said.

I made no response and kept eating the thin yellow centers characteristic of mass-produced eggs, mixed with the last of my greasy hash browns.

"Scrambled eggs are dead eggs," he continued, "you know you aren't going to run across a partially formed beak if they're scrambled."

I stopped chewing and looked at Reefer Carlson for a second, then continued to mop up the remains of my eggs with a piece of raisin rye toast.

"We go through this every morning I order number three," I said. "I'm a chicken cannibal. I like undone baby chicks. You can't gross me out. There are people who like hard centers, over easy centers and runny centers. Scrambled eggs are for people who want to avoid the philosophical question of white and yellow duality in chicken eggs. In other words, Reefer, it's only eight in the morning and already you're ambivalent about something as important as eggs."

Carleton "Reefer" Carlson chewed on the slice of orange provided with his scrambled eggs and ham and listened to yet another in my long line of explanations for liking runny egg yolks. Reefer was a tall man, taller than me, and slightly younger. He was dressed casually in light slacks and a golf shirt. He kept raising his white eyebrows over his dark glasses during our conversation and wrinkling his brow up to his pale red hair. He was editor and publisher of the Cache Harbor County Telegram-Herald and ate breakfast with me just about every morning except Sunday when he would drive eighteen miles up the hill for brunch with his parents. Reefer had lived all his life on the shore and known me for the five years I'd headed up the two-man department. I knew that he knew that I knew that his keeping tabs on me was good journalism. I also knew he was a friend and we trusted each other. He knew that too, otherwise why would he be sitting across the booth from me watching me eat runny eggs at least three out of six days a week?

On the days I scheduled myself for night duty, Reefer ate breakfast with my deputy, Mel Swanson. Mel was arguably more earnest than me, definitely married and certainly expecting. Mel also doesn't have my sense of humor. He still has the rough spots left on the edges of his personality, not polished off by the grit of cynicism. He hadn't arrested the same punks, drunks and abusers time after time…the same fourth degree felonies and misdemeanors year after year. I was forty and fleeing a big county deputy sheriff's job ten years in the festering. Mel was twenty-three and didn't like runny yolks. What can I say?

"You ever notice Marie always has the top two buttons on her blouse open when she serves you?" Reefer switched the conversation to his other favorite topic. Women. Food and women, then somewhere farther down the list of important points of conversation came the newspaper, drinking, other people's feelings and social consciousness. "No, I mean haven't you noticed that all the other waitresses here keep their blouses buttoned, but Marie always has those two open for you?"

"Marie's a nice kid. She's also half my age. Maybe she keeps those buttons open because it's hot and humid in here."

"No way! I've watched her for a long time. She's got the hots for you."

"Bullshit"

"Look, to prove my point, I'll signal her for more coffee. She'll scoot on over, hardly look at me and stoop a little lower than necessary when she pours your coffee." He paused for emphasis. "If that's not love, I don't know what is."

Marie tossed her mass of long mahogany hair, swept a plastic insulated pot from the counter and glided over to our booth – all in one incredibly smooth motion. She stooped over a little lower than was necessary while pouring my coffee, set the pot down in front of Reefer without so much as an acknowledgement and left us the check.

"Thanks." I looked into the white skin of her throat where the yellow blouse met the top yoke of her amber uniform jumper. The color of her skin did not at all remind me of Lisbeth Ann.

"Have a nice day," she said bouncing away from our booth with more energy than she should have had at the end of the breakfast rush.

"If that ain't love," Reefer reiterated, "I don't know what is."

I dumped two half-ounce dollops of synthetic cream from their plastic containers and stirred them into the coffee. "How old is Valerie?"

"Twenty-four."

"And how old are you?"

"Thirty-seven."

"That's a thirteen year difference."

"So? You're almost forty-one, and I'll bet Marie is…let's see, third year of college…twenty-one, maybe twenty-two. That's…" Reefer counted on his fingers, "twenty, maybe nineteen years difference. My daddy always said he was going to trade my mother in at forty for two twenty year olds."

"Did he?"

"Not yet."

"If I'd have gotten married when Angela Sue Lipscombe wanted me to, our kid would be Marie Craske's age, and I don't want to go around unbuttoning someone the same age as what could have been Angela Sue's and my daughter." I didn't exactly mean that, but I was single and had always been, whereas Reefer had been married twice and would always view that institution serially. Besides, I had a need to needle him about his sex life. Reefer's first marriage ended at age eighteen. His second ended officially six months ago. The twenty-four year old with whom he was currently keeping company was his one and only reporter, Valerie Hackney. Hiring Valerie put the finishing touches on his marriage to Blanche. Reefer's only real regret was his estrangement from Nancy, his twelve-year old daughter. He made up for his marital and familial pain and suffering by "nailing", as he put it, Valerie Hackney every chance he got: her place, his place, the office, the beach, his new mini-van — sometimes all within an astonishingly short span one from the other.

It wasn't that I hadn't had my share of love affairs, they just didn't fit the job schedule. That's a problem with career cops, even if they're only chiefs of police in towns of 1,500 people. Currently I was seeing Lisbeth Ann Sarstadt, Cache Harbor public librarian. Like Reefer, her marriage ended about six months ago, but unlike Reefer I'd only been what you'd call "intimate" with Lisbeth Ann twice in the month and a half we'd been seeing each other. It wasn't easy for Lisbeth Ann to get unmarried. It wasn't easy for me to push her.

With all of this sliding in and out of my head on a hot August morning, I drifted off into looking out across the increasing sea of vacation-colored clothing. I can usually tell the tourists from the locals and the salesmen and the other passers-through. Especially the retired ones. The old guys in Bermuda shorts, wing-tips and dark socks with clocks embroidered at the ankles, their colorful short sleeved shirts pulled tight across their settled bellies; wives in their polyester pants and flower print tops. The cock-a-poo waits in the Lincoln Continental, panting for air and water, love and affection as well as a place to piss.

Mel Swanson jerked one of our two city squad cars to an authoritative halt in front of the large, fly-blown café window. He stopped at the yellow no parking line right on the corner where Reefer and I could see him. He slammed the door and nearly vaulted over the hood on to the curb, then slowed his pace as he entered the café, so as to not give the customers the impression there was anything wrong in paradise. Marie watched him as he threaded his way toward me through the maze of crowded tables. She put away her menus when she saw he wasn't going to stay for breakfast. He slipped in the booth beside me, looked at Reefer for a moment, then on my nod, decided it was all right to talk.

"Looks real bad, Paul." Mel Swanson's eyes were stretched wide open, there was a thin film of sweat on his upper lip. He was swallowing too much.

"What looks bad?" asked Reefer, looking for a story more exciting than the impending annual summer town celebration.

"Gertie found a dead guy in the old Palmer barn," he said to me, ignoring Reefer. "Only it's more than a dead guy. It's like nothin' I ever saw before."

I reached in my wallet and tossed seven dollars on the table, pulled my two-tone blue shirt from between my holster and gun belt. Reefer made a move to follow but I held him back with my hand as I slipped on the shirt. "I'll call you if you need me." My turn of phrase to keep distance between official accuracy and a printed press release. I flipped some additional change on the table for Marie. She watched Mel and I weave our way through the toast and jelly, bacon and egg crowd. Once outside I motioned that I would drive and slid into the driver's side. Before getting in the passenger side, Officer Swanson placed one hand on the silver painted light post at the corner of Superior Avenue and First Street, bent over toward the gutter and threw up everything he had eaten in the last several hours.

Chapter Two

"One Zebra One to dispatch."

"Go ahead One Zebra One."

"Ruthie, we've got a possible ten-fifty. I'd like you to alert One King One and the coroner for a standby."

"What's your ten-twenty, Paul?"

"We're headed north on County 47 to the village limits, the old Palmer place. ETA is five minutes."

"Ten-four, Paul. Who is 'we'?"

"Uhh, Ruthie, 'we' is One Zebra One, One Zebra Two and One Zebra witness."

"Roger, Paul. One King One is in Ely, but I'll give One King Two the alert. Call is in to the hospital. We'll cover city while you're ten-seven. Cache Harbor dispatch oh-eight-fifty-three. Out."

Lotta goddamn numbers and codes to learn just to talk to someone on a radio. Everyone with a scanner knows what you're saying, anyway. Big secret. I slowed the squad behind a pulp truck laboring up the hill at the edge of town. No use in wasting lights and siren on this one, whoever was in Palmer's barn was long dead. Mel hadn't posted the site as a crime scene, but it was far enough off the main road so it was unlikely anyone would have entered the premises in the twenty minutes it took him to drive in and us to get back.

One third of the "us" was Gert Bushmiller riding in the back seat behind the mesh that kept our drug-dogs from climbing into the front seat, and drunks from trying to do the same. I hadn't noticed Gert when Mel pulled up at the café. Likely she was scrunched down so no one would see her in a squad car. Funny duck, that one. She had flagged down Mel as he drove past the side road that leads to the Palmer place. Told him there was a dead man in the barn and it looked like he'd been "skun alive".

"You OK now?" I asked Mel, as we turned off the highway on to the road that led to Palmer's drive. He was still pale from vomiting but managed to nod and apologize for losing it on the curb.

Gert leaned against the mesh and firmed up her dentures with her thumb. "Don't feel bad Sonny. I liked to barf m'self when I seen him. 'Course I seen lotsa dead animals when Ragnar and me was together at the Slave Lake camp. Still and all, when Ragnar skun out that bear, we both commented on how it looked like a man. This fella looks just like that. Just like the bear Ragnar skun out at the Slave Lake camp back in the fall of '47. You boys was too young to be of much use in '47, I suppose."

"Yes m'am." I slowed the squad as we rounded a sharp curve.

"I always remember that skun bear because it wasn't three months after in…oh, I guess November…that Ragnar drown in that damn lake. Ice was thin, ya know. Thin right there in the bay where we had the camp. Married for a year come Christmas, we was."

I braked at the two-track that lead off the road and up into the overgrown Palmer place.

"Man in the barn, there, looks like Ragnar's bear."

I drove in a near circle through the long grass in front of the barn and stopped at the side entrance where Mel said the body was.

"One Zebra One to dispatch. We're ten-eight at the scene."

"Roger, Paul. Cache Harbor dispatch, oh-nine hundred."

Gert was all for going right back in the barn, grisly as the scene apparently was. Mel wasn't exactly moving in that direction. I guessed she wanted to be sure the body in the barn really did look like Ragnar's bear, but I didn't want any more feet scuffing up the place than had already been in there messing up my crime scene. I also guessed Mel was in no hurry to deal with the "skun" man.

"Hold it, Gertie. Mel, here needs to take your statement while this whole thing is fresh in your mind." He looked relieved at that but Gert sort of got her back up.

"I wasn't doin' anything I should'na been. I always cut through here on my way to town. It was the flies."

"The flies?"

"The flies. All that buzzin'. I thought there was a hornet's nest in there. Tourists pay good money for a hornet's nest…'specially one on a twig."

"The flies."

"Oh, yeah. The flies in there are real bad." She wrinkled her nose. Mel turned away and looked out over the alder brush that once had been Palmer's front field. Couldn't grow shit in this rock. Trying to killed old Palmer long before he actually died.

"Well, you stay here with Mel."

"Could be my memory'd jog some if I saw that fella again. A woman my age, she sometimes gets forgetful. Wouldn't wanna miss any details, would ya?"

Gert wanted to assure herself the man in the barn really did look like Ragnar's bear. That was the only memory she wanted to jog. Long-dead Ragnar and no Christmas anniversary at the Slave Lake. Couldn't blame her, but no.

"I'll look for the details, now, Gert. You give Officer Swanson all the facts you can remember about this morning, and I'm sure that'll be a great help."

"I know what you're up to. You just want to keep this pup from havin' to go back in that barn and puke all over again."

"Gert! That's enough."

"Maybe so." She squinted at me and then at Mel as he took out his pocket tape recorder. "We don't get many killin's around here, do we?" It was more a statement than a question, but I agreed. Few to none, in fact. But until there was an investigation underway, I still wasn't willing to say there had been a killing. That displeased Gert.

"Man don't skin hisself alive, Chief." She said it with a finality I couldn't argue with. If it had just been the ranting of an eccentric old bag lady, I guess I'd have been more skeptical, but there was no reason to doubt Mel Swanson. His breakfast lying on the curb in front of the Outpost Café, and all. So now I'd have to see for myself, but I already knew the rest of this day was going to be a mess. Probably the rest of the month. Just as big a mess as the man inside Palmer's barn.

Gert began babbling into Mel's recorder as I turned and walked to the side door of the barn. The weathered planks were nearly closed, but stuck open a crack on the raised corner of the cement step. I could hear the flies buzzing as I pushed open the door.

"The fella's in a stall at the northeast corner of the ground floor," Gert yelled at me from across the yard. I raised my hand to let her know I'd heard, and went through the door.

I'd been in the sagging old barn once before, chasing out teenagers who were using it for a massive after-prom drunk. With exception of the flies it was quiet, now. No swearing football players and their screeching girl friends, half in and half out of their expensive party dresses. The beer cans were gone from the floor. So were the condoms. Dust motes flickered in the shafts of early sunlight forcing itself through the cobwebs and dust thick on the windows. Old deep yellow straw heavy on the floor and in the long-since abandoned feed bins. Moldy oats in the corner. Smelled like old, very old wood. I looked up through the open trap into the haymow. More cobwebs, this time hanging in long old lady gray- haired strands, swaying slightly in the morning breeze. The ceilings were low because lumber was expensive and the log joists were hard work cutting and fitting. People were shorter, too. Enos Palmer had been a little man, they say, no more than five-four. The log stanchions were smooth from cows rubbing. He built the farm before the turn of the century and the barn was meant to last through cold winters and damp lake-wind driven summers. He hand peeled the pine logs, squared them off to fit, rabbeted the joints and secured them with maple pegs. The cement gutters were washed clean of manure and a wooden hay rake hung crooked on the east wall, escaping vandals and treasure hunters all these years.

The family left the place a good two-dozen years ago after Enos died. They had expected some enterprising young farmer would soon buy it. The offers came and were rejected. Surely the farm was worth more than that. But it wasn't. There were no more farmers here by the lake. No one wanted to break his body the way Enos had. Can't grow shit in this rock. Mrs. Palmer died. The sons looked for low bid. No one bid. The tourists all wanted cabins on one of the thousands of lakes that dot the wilderness from the edge of town on up through Canada and beyond. I wonder where the sons are now and who knows where to turn if someone actually wanted to buy the place.

I stopped at the last stanchion in the northeast corner of the barn. It was surprisingly cool. The air smelled faintly of iron and the flies dispersed in a cloud as I stepped toward him. The skin on my neck and shoulders prickled and sent little waves of electricity across my scalp and I could feel the roots of my hair tingle. There was a salty taste sliding from the glands on either side of my jaw.

[Oh-nine-ten. Gert Bushmiller. Tape one of one. "OK, so this is the way it was, you understand. I wasn't trespassin' or anything. I was just stoppin' by the place to see if it was all right and to see if anyone had been out here for a picnic or anything and left something. You know, something I might use. I never take anything from these old places, you know that, Mel. I just pick up things that are valuable to me. Things other people throw away, things nobody else wants. Well, I rode my bicycle down from the cabin on County 47 and took the logging cutoff just above the city limits. Of course I had to walk the bike because them damn trucks have chewed up the road somethin' awful. I don't own a watch, but I'd say by sun time it was between a quarter to and seven when I got here."]

I walked around the wooden feed box, dragged to the center of the last double stanchion. The man was lying on his back, one leg was partially tensed in a bent position and the left arm stuck straight up in the air; the hands and feet were missing. The genitals had been removed in the process of skinning. I noticed that the musculature of the body had a sheen to it, probably as a result of coagulating fluids. There was a great deal of dried blood on the northeast wall and on the straw around the wooden feed box that had been used as a skinning table. It may also have served as an alter. A long, jagged cut extended from the middle of his chest down into the abdomen. The gash had started to pull back from the skeletal structure as the raw flesh dried in the morning air.

["I seen there had been a car here lately, so I parked my bicycle over there by that little maple and started looking around for – you know, anything of value. I seen over by the pump where a lot of water had been drawn and dumped out on the gravel path to where the house used to be. I can't see too good, but it looked like the grass and dirt was kinda – I don't know – kinda pinkish color. It was still damp on the wooden well cover, like someone had done a lotta washing there…like their car or something, only there was a pinkish cast to the ground. Then I figured someone had poached a deer in that north pasture, so I went into the barn, because that would be a good place to hang a deer if it got to be daylight too quick and you wanted to come back for it after dark. Ya oughtta hang venison anyway, at least for a couple days. Ragnar used to hang it for a week, because that made the steaks taste better."]

Without touching the body, I squatted down on my haunches and peered into the gap of the chest cavity. I hadn't thought to bring a flashlight, but the position of the body caught the sun forcing its way through the windows. I couldn't be absolutely sure, but maybe ninety percent, that his heart had been cut out. I set my hands on the tops of my legs, like you do, and pushed myself up to standing. After you turn forty, you creak more than at thirty-nine. The man I was looking at may never have reached thirty-nine, the creaky age. He appeared to be short and thick; it was hard to tell his exact height, with the feet missing and the chest spread open and all. It made him look stockier than he may have been. His face was a mass of muscle bundles and only the lips and eyelids remained. Thank God the eyes were closed. I only hoped that they had been long dead before the fate of the body that housed them had been so terrorized.

["Not much else to tell. Your Chief knows the rest of it by now. I just walked in the barn, started scrounging around, saw some blood on the straw and sorta followed my nose to that end stanchion. Can't say I ever saw anything quite like it. I seen men burned and even lose a leg when me and Ragnar lived up north. Like I said, I seen plenty dead animals. I never seen no human look like that. Ragnar's bear. That's what he looked like. But not like that either, exactly. Not without the hands and feet. I liked to barf, Mel. I wish I had. Woulda got some of that poison outta my system. I know you're embarrassed by it, but you got some of the poison outta you by throwing up like that."]

I noticed a door that led off of the end of the double stanchion. I figured it had once been a milk cooling room. I walked around the stiffening corpse and pushed open the whitewashed door with the toe of my shoe. It swung easily on its old hinges. The floor was concrete and there was one window facing north...it barely let in the light through the fly tracks, cobwebs and thirty years of encrusted dust. On a decaying cement block in the middle of the floor, I saw the burnt remains of what I suspected was the dead man's heart. The smell of burnt flesh still hung in the air of that small room. I remember a fireman once telling me that you could always tell if a person had died in a house fire, even if the body wasn't discovered for hours afterwards. There was a smell of pork in the house, he said. But I left the milk house before the odor had a chance to make an impact on the glands that again began to act up on the sides of my jaw.

Finally, I stepped out of the barn into the sunlight. The air would eventually settle into a hot, humid afternoon. Gert was still talking to Mel, but I could see by the position of his tape recorder that her statement was over and that she was now regaling him with tales of her former life...the one before she became the Cache Harbor bag lady. Her wild hair stuck out from under a greasy blue bandana; her torn sweater covered layers of shirts and undershirts. She wore blue jeans and knit leggings under her full print skirt. As the day wore on Gert would remove her layers of clothing and place them in one of the paper grocery bags she always carried in her bicycle basket. Last August about this time, one of the local gossips reported Gert was riding on County B with nothing on but a pair of cotton bloomers. It was never confirmed, but the image of mad Gert cycling down the road, hair flying in the wind, pendulous breasts flapping from side to side as she furiously pedaled to escape the clutching heat, dominated more than one morning coffee conversation at the Outpost Café.

I took a soiled handkerchief from my back pocket and tried to wipe away the growing image of the dead man in the barn as he encroached upon my eyes, covering the image of the old bag lady and my officer. The raw flesh, the gaping mouth, the reaching arm with its amputated hand, all crowded into my mind and stayed imprinted on the insides of my eyelids. I remembered hearing someplace that a man is born hard and lives hard but to die hard on top of that is just too damn hard. I stood there in the slowly spreading sunlight hoping the man in the barn had not died as hard as it looked, that he hadn't been skinned alive, or aware that his heart was being cut from his body. A cop can handle natural pain and suffering, death and dying...there's schooling for that. But torture and maiming makes my skin crawl.

I walked over to where Gert was still filling in Mel on the tribulations of the Slave Lake timber camp. I thanked her for her cooperation and asked that she not discuss the matter with anyone until I had a chance to file my preliminary report. Useless request. Gert will head straight for town as fast as her old bicycle will carry her and by noon everyone from the Canadian border to Duluth will have the gory details. The town may view Gert as the local crazy, but this story was going to put her square in the spotlight. There was something to it, it carried the timbre of truth because, after all, weren't the cops up there right now? Wasn't the coroner on his way? Wasn't it the most fascinating and gruesome thing you could ever imagine?

I called in dispatch and put all of these things in motion, including a call to Reefer Carlson. I needed him to take photographs. One of the failures of a small department...having to use the press for your documentation. No secrets. While I waited for Ruthie to confirm my calls, I watched Gert Bushmiller ride a wobbly bicycle with determination down Palmer's drive to the paved highway. Mel was stringing a yellow and black plastic crime scene banner around the barn and pump area. It's times like this I wished I still smoked. God knows how long it will take to clean up this mess. To die hard is just too damn hard.

Chapter Three

Reefer Carlson changed the batteries in his electronic flash unit and continued taking pictures as I directed him this shot and that. Reefer'd never covered a murder, so he wasn't much help as I tried to remember what photographs I'd need based on the only two previous homicides I'd ever had anything to do with. So far we'd shot the well and pump, all angles of the corpse and were finishing up in the cooler room. He was taking more pictures than were probably necessary...and taking them faster than usual, hoping some of them would turn out and he could get away from what he was calling "the fucking slaughterhouse". Naturally he'd brought along Valerie Hackney, a move that irritated me. I don't usually have a problem with the news media – if that's not too big a definition for the local fish wrap – but Valerie sometimes acts as if she was a Pulitzer Prize winning reporter for the New York Times. She isn't, and maybe I acted a bit curt with her this morning by not allowing her inside the yellow and black ribbon that marked off the investigation area. I could tell Reefer didn't like it either. But we could argue that point after the pictures were taken.

While Reefer and I moved into the barn, Valerie tossed her mop of blond hair, fumed a little at the two of us inside the crime scene tape and pranced along the perimeter furiously writing down everything she could that might have the slightest relevance. Had to admit she was pretty enough, petite, well dressed and sporting a larger than average dose of self- assurance. Valerie took good care of herself. She also wanted to go places in journalism but was apparently smart enough to realize that big metro papers chew up reporters faster than college programs turn them out. She considered herself a good writer, but rationalized her lack of fierce competitive spirit by swearing to anyone who'd listen that she really loved living in a small town. On the other hand, I didn't think she was much of a reporter at all and what's more I don't think Reefer did either.

My guess is that Valerie was lucky to have the job she did, making up for the salary by opting for the security of bedding down with the boss. Valerie was essentially a gossip. Coasting. So was Reefer, coasting. Pretty sexist attitude, I know. Shit, truth happens.

A juicy murder could bring out the sleeping tiger in us all. I'd wait and see about that.

Reefer was unloading his camera and disconnecting his flash unit as the coroner approached.

"Can I stay and listen to this," he asked. I told him I figured he'd seen everything about the dead man there was to see, so he might as well hear about it, too. Dr. Ed Loetz wouldn't move away from the corpse no matter how much I suggested we take the air outside. He wanted to show examples and generally re-create Rembrandt's anatomy class painting in the east stall. Me, I'd had enough anatomy for one day.

"Look, Eddie, that thing is gonna start smelling real soon if we don't get it out of here. So if you're finished, we're finished."

"S'matter, Paul, you and Reefer don't have the stomach for this kind of work?" He signaled the two paramedics who had driven him to the scene. "Body bag him and put the burnt offering in separate plastic." He turned to me, "You want to outline the body or should I have Al do it?" In answer, I took a wide felt-tipped pen from my pocket and tossed it at Al. Neither paramedic Al nor his partner looked especially happy about handling the body.

"So what do we have here," I asked as Al outlined the body on the feed box top and we moved back through the dusty barn.

"You mean the official cause of death?" Loetz flipped open his metal covered clipboard box. "Heart failure, I suppose." He chuckled for a moment. "Maybe severe trauma to the cardiopulmonary region, maybe atypical myocardial infarction. I don't know exactly what to call it. The guy had his heart cut out."

"How un-medical a conclusion", Reefer weighed in on the conversation.

Loetz flipped though his notes, reading from his observations. "The chest and abdominal area was cut from a point midway at the sternum in a line straight down through the rectus abdominis muscle to just above the navel. Transverse incisions were also made generally along the line of the rib cage. Let's see," he adjusted his glasses, "the pericardium was ruptured and the heart was removed by cutting or tearing – and I'm guessing, here, until we crack the chest – cutting or tearing the right innominate and pulmonary veins and the innominate left common carotid, left subclavian, pulmonary arteries and the inferior vena cava."

"In other words," Reefer butted in, "someone cut him open, reached in there and jerked that puppy out."

"It's remarkable how you journalists have a knack for simplifying complex situations," he smiled. "Of course, there was other damage done to the immediate area, but you'll get a complete analysis after the autopsy."

I watched as the two paramedics hustled the body bag past us through the door to the yard and waiting ambulance. "What about the rest of it?"

"Well, he didn't die of having his skin removed, that would have been done afterwards. There's really no way to skin a man alive – I mean as completely as this one was." Loetz pondered as we stepped into the sunlight and the paramedics slid the body bag into the open ambulance gate. "It was a fairly neat job, too. Not probably done with the same instrument used to open him up."

"How so?" I squinted at the orange ball of sun and knew it promised to be a scorcher.

"The incisions were rough and it took a couple of tries to open the cavity. The skin removal was probably done with a large curved butcher's knife. I can't tell you which one was used to remove the heart, but probably the one that opened him up." He paused. "That's the way they used to do it."

"The way who used to do what?" I asked.

"The Aztecs." Loetz closed his clipboard with a loud snap. "If you ask me, this was a ritualistic sacrifice patterned after the Aztecs. I don't know much about that sort of thing, of course. They don't give you time off in med school for anthropology, but I must have read about it in some undergraduate class I had to take." He sighed and stowed his clipboard and medical bag in the front seat of the ambulance. "Anyway, we had a poster hanging in one of my surgery classrooms – something about quick and easy cut-rate heart transplants. Pretty funny at the time. It showed four Aztec priests holding down this naked guy on a big stone while a fifth priest cut out the guy's heart by what some joker titled "the Barnard method".

"Was the guy dead?" I could feel my jaw glands working again.

"The guy in the poster was alive, I assume that was part of the joke."

"No, I mean our guy in the body bag. Was he alive when his heart was cut out?"

"No way to really tell, but I'd say it was unlikely unless there were five of them in that stall. You really can't cut out the heart of a conscious man unless you've got four strong guys holding him down." He slid his butt onto the ambulance seat. "I suppose he could have been unconscious at the time. There did appear to be a trauma to the semispinalis capitis muscle. If that was severe enough it could damage the occipital bone that covers the cerebellum. Without a closer look, I really can't tell if the area was damaged by a blow or in the skinning process. But, no – I'd say your guy was not aware he was being operated on."

Al the paramedic had returned to the ambulance carrying the charred remains of the victim's heart in a plastic Ziploc bag. He held them at arm's length. I was relieved by Loetz's explanation of probable death. At least we weren't dealing with an outright sadist. Reefer kept returning to the Aztec angle.

"Don't know anymore," said Loetz, closing the passenger door and rolling down the window. "I sure as hell don't know any more about the skinning part of it. All I know is Aztecs used to sacrifice people by tearing out their hearts. They did that a lot, I understand. Of course, you really can't exactly tear out a human heart. You'd need to make some incisions first, unless you were extremely strong."

"Or a maniac whose adrenaline was running rampant." Reefer's imagination was also running rampant.

"Thanks, Reefer," I said. "That's all I needed," letting my imagination wander off into the realm of public panic and hysteria.

"Well, if that's so," Loetz reached in his pocket and pulled out an old encrusted pipe, filled with tobacco, "his adrenaline, as you call it, would have calmed down quite a bit afterwards. It must have taken a good hour or more to do that skinning job, careful as it was." He lit up the pipe. "Somebody wanted that fella's hide awful bad to do that careful a job of it."

I stepped back from the ambulance window as Loetz blew out a noxious cloud of blue smoke. Valerie Hackney had spotted us and Reefer walked over to talk to her. She stayed on the other side of the yellow tape.

"One other thing you might want to know," Loetz added as he buckled his seat belt. Al the paramedic was in the back of the ambulance with the body bag looking uncomfortable and slightly pale, his partner slipped into the driver's side of the van with Loetz. "The victim was probably an Indian."

"You're not telling me he was an Aztec?"

"Hardly. But by the general size and shape as well as some of the facial characteristics, I'd guess he was Indian of some kind. Also, there were the lips and eyelids. They were pigmented in such a way as to suggest someone other than Caucasian or black. Some Asians have a dark coloration like that. Maybe we'll know more after the autopsy."

The driver started the ambulance and Loetz leaned out the window.

"By the way, I'd get a hose on that stall as soon as possible or it's going to get pretty gross in there."

"Just as soon as I make one last tour in case we missed anything. When do I see your report?"

"As soon as Mrs. Jackson has her twins and I convince Trudy Kastner's little boy he shouldn't put any more dried beans up his sister's nose. Probably late tomorrow." The ambulance made its way out of the yard and down the drive as Mel Swanson untied the yellow ribbon to let them pass. Loetz had come to Cache Harbor shortly after I took the Chief's job. Takes a special kind of person to take on doctoring in a small town at an understaffed hospital and tiny clinic. Loetz shared those responsibilities with three other MDs and an irregular host of visiting specialists. No one had wanted the coroner's job, and Loetz being low man on the pole, pulled the duty. It had hardly ever interfered with the rest of his personal or professional life...not like it was now going to interfere with mine.

"Ed Gein, that's what it reminds me of." Valerie pulled out her reporter's notebook the minute she saw me heading in her direction.

"What about Ed Gein?"

"You remember back in the late '50s, the crazy old codger in Wisconsin who killed and cut up women, made lampshades out of their skin and…"

"That's enough, Valerie. Don't let your imagination run away with you."

"Well, I need a perspective on this so the readers…"

"And for the time being, I'd appreciate it if you don't refer to this as a maniac killing, Reefer, like you did back in there with Loetz."

Reefer stuffed his camera into a fancy nylon carrying case. "Time to muzzle the press, honey," looking at Valerie.

"C'mon, Paul," she persisted, "you can't seriously believe this was done by some perfectly sane person who just didn't like that fellow in the barn. I mean, people just don't go around skinning other people and jerking out their hearts no matter how much of a hard-on they have for the victim."

"You two have got a skip in your disc player. I keep hearing the same song over again. 'Nobody sane would do this, nobody but a maniac would do this.' I don't even know who the fuck this guy is and you want the whole town locking up their kids and turning off the lights. Whatta ya say we identify the victim first. That might provide a clue. Then we go looking for the bad guys. But let's not speculate there's wildmen running loose in the woods carving up the population for lampshades. Print this shit and you'll have tourists as well as locals fleeing Cache Harbor in droves."

"Maybe they should be careful. Maybe it's not safe in Cache Harbor."

"Listen, Val, this story is going to get picked up soon enough by the metro media, and those assholes never get it straight. They sweep into town, talk to a lotta people who don't know squat about the facts, steal what they can from reporters like you and dish it up with breakfast for a two-point-five million market just slathering for something sensational to take their minds off the boredom of suburbia."

"Why don't you have an attitude about this, Paul?"

"It just seems to me your responsibility is to get the story right before everyone else gets it wrong."

"Now, back off, you two." Reefer stepped between us absorbing the daggers we were shooting at each other's eyes. "We'll get the facts right and print them straight. But you can't expect us to just sit back and not try for as much information as possible."

"I just don't want to be the one who's scooped."

"This is major murder Paul, and we wouldn't be doing our job if we didn't follow up on it."

"I'm not trying to muzzle the press, Reefer. You know me better than that. All I want is to keep the speculation to a minimum and be the first one you share any new facts with. As soon as Gertie Bushmiller hits town on her bicycle, there'll be enough Ed Gein stories floating around to fill six newspapers."

"There's nothing that says I can't pursue this story on my own, Paul." Valerie put her notebook back in her handbag.

"There's nothing says I have to give you any information either. If you want to play hardball, the only thing you'll get from me is a fat 'no comment'. It's a crime under investigation, Valerie. Print a bunch of crap, force a change of venue...costs the County money and pisses off the county attorney, not to mention me and Mel."

"God knows I wouldn't want to piss off you and Mel," she threw back in a voice so wet with sarcasm I had to let it dry before I could scrape it off my shirt. She turned on her heel and pranced back to Reefer's new minivan. I maintained he bought that rig so he and Valerie would have yet one more place to grab a nooner. He keeps telling me what a wonderful and understanding woman she is. She just basically told me to go to hell. Maybe grisly murder brings that out in some people.

"Don't worry about Val," Reefer shouldered his camera bag. "She smells a big story and I guess I can't blame her for wanting to go after it. Hardly ever happens and this may be the only chance she has."

Sure, and I get these chances every day. Touchy Paul, that's me. I'm always out there solving murders, especially one where the perp makes an overcoat out of the victim. I don't get this right, some slick attorney fucks me all over the courtroom. Besides what the hell have I got but a dead body with no skin, no heart, no hands, no feet, no dick, no identity. Who is he, where'd he come from, who did him, and how'd he get in the east stall? All my so-called clues were soaking into the ground around Palmer's well and I got an officer who barfs just thinking about it. Shit, a bullet would have got this John Doe just as dead.

"Mel and I have to go over the place one more time, so I'll see you later." I squinted up through the trees at the sun to avoid the glare from

Valerie Hackney. It was getting hot and sticky already. We'd have to work fast before the whole place started smelling like the dump. Probably piss off the BCA for washing down a crime scene.

"I'll have the pix ready for you this afternoon," Reefer got in behind the wheel of his minivan. "Don't worry, I won't print any in next week's paper." He started the engine, leaned through the window and spoke in a stage whisper. "Ed Gein – wasn't that the guy made belts out of women's nipples?"

Chapter Four

It was nearly noon before I finally got in my two-by-four office at the back end of the fire hall. I'd sent Mel up to the county law enforcement center, which has an office and jail attached to the courthouse. Cache Harbor is my town but it sits in Sheriff Ashley Tucker's county. Ash likes things kept neat and orderly through out, even if we all know he doesn't do much of the work himself. The reciprocal arrangement between the county and its municipalities – known as a joint powers agreement – had been instituted a few years ago in a spirit of cooperation. It also served as an insurance policy for high-risk public employees. The police departments of the county's five little communities and the sheriff's department all interact with one another through the exchange and sharing of equipment and personnel. This one-for-all-and-all-for-one attitude means that when Ash wants to pull one of his famous 4 AM raids, he can use his own deputies as well as the local cops and the liability to men and equipment is shared. It can work the other way, too, but I don't pull many early morning raids. Not my style. So what I get out of the deal is use of county facilities and manpower, such as the dispatcher, which was where Mel was headed.

We'd gone over the scene at Palmer's with as fine a toothed comb as our combined experiences allowed. Finally in the end I decided not to hose down the place. There was the sheriff and the state Bureau of Criminal Apprehension to consider. Best to let them weigh in first. Mel dusted the pump handle for prints but drew a blank; same thing on the door handles and everything else that could carry a print. No footprints, either. If there had been a vehicle, it left no tracks or impressions on the grass. We even spent the better part of an hour sifting through straw in the stanchion. Found a corroded penny and four pull tabs from beer cans left there before the Legislature banned them for environmental reasons. So much for the morning's work.

The City doesn't give me a secretary. I can understand that, there's no room in the office or in the budget. They don't provide me with an answering machine either, which I can't understand, so I bought one myself. All the message says is call 911, but if you insist, wait for the beep and I'll get back as soon as I feel like it. There were four calls on the machine: three hang-ups and one guy who muttered something about the lousy condition of the city streets and that no one would do anything about them anyway because everyone in town government was on the take. I erased the messages and turned down the speaker. All I wanted to do was keep myself scarce until I listened to Gertie's taped statement and had time to prepare a news release, call BCA and get the paper flow started.

I cranked up my computer, which is left over from the Civil War: Windows '48. The screen is small and fading, the keyboard is brown with finger smudge and there's a greasy gray film all around the once-white monitor. I heard Mel drive up in the squad as the old beast hummed to life.

"Nothing on the dispatch of any importance," he said dumping the mail on my desk. "Deputy Dog says Ashley won't be back from Ely until tomorrow, late. He got him on the radio, though and Ash says he hopes you have everything under control because it doesn't sound like anything he wants to mess with."

"Do tell." Nothing in the mail except a flyer for handcuffs.

"Deputy Dog also contacted BCA and they said that unless the sheriff wanted to take a look at the scene, it was OK with them to hose it down as long as we had all we wanted."

"Saves me the call."

"Ash doesn't want to look at the scene, but Dog does, so he's going out there now. When he's finished he said he'd have the fire department hose it down."

"What's with Dog?"

"You know Dog. When Ashley quits running for office, Dog wants the job. That means he wants to know everything about everything, so in case one of us screws up he's got something to hold over our heads."

"You mean, in case one of us wants to run against him, he's got something to hold over our heads." Chief Deputy Billy T. Dogget was a bastard most of the time, even though I had to admit he was a good cop. No nonsense. Dog was always right, always by the book and one of those people you just had to learn to live with because they out-ranked you. With Dog on the scene and paperwork on my desk, I sent Mel home to his wife Judy who was expecting their first child at any moment.

Once Mel was gone, and with the message machine turned down, I began listening to the Gert Bushmiller tape. I'd forgotten that I'd asked Mel to stop by the Outpost and order me lunch du jour to go. So there was Marie Craske standing in the doorway with a large styrofoam sandwich pod, a paper cup of coffee and the two top buttons of her blouse unfastened.

Marie had the easy grace of a woman much older in years. What was it Reefer said? Twenty-one? Maybe twenty-two? Third year in college? She was not a very tall girl, but taller than the diminutive Valerie Hackney. Her long, mahogany-black hair was pulled back and fixed at the base of her neck with a leather clip. Her skin was fair, full lips, big eyes, the usual stuff that sends male hormones in a spin. She pretty much had it all. Unlike most of the other waitresses, she looked good in her blouse and jumper uniform; maybe because she was younger and thinner. A lot thinner. Not many years sampling the mashed potatoes and gravy back in the kitchen, the fries or the pies.

She made conversation while I ate my grilled cheese sandwich. She had a half-hour off for lunch. She thought it was silly, a half-hour right at the peak of the lunch rush. She said she was off at 2:00, but generally she stayed through her lunch break to help. Didn't need lunch, snacked through the morning. Went home most days a half-hour early because of staying through. I suggested she tell the cooks not to put the sliced kosher dill in with the potato chips. Makes them soggy. She smiled and didn't say anything and I smiled and didn't say anything. Saying nothing around women is a habit of mine. Lisbeth Ann says that makes our relationship awkward. I guess saying nothing is still better than talking about fishing and law enforcement to women who aren't interested in either. Hard to work fishing into dating conversation and talking about the job is bad policy. Marie didn't seem to mind the silences. She went on to tell me she was graduating in art next year from the University, that she lived at the east end of town in a small cabin with her roommate

Emily Baxter. Emily was never home and forever out of town, out of state and sometimes even out of the country, since she was Canadian by birth. Emily didn't have to work to go to college. Marie didn't have to live in Cache Harbor, either, but she liked the north and had worked at the Outpost for the past three summers.

"What are they saying at the coffee shop?"

"You ought to be asking what they aren't saying." She wrinkled her nose and squinted her brown eyes. "I've never heard such gossip. All of it, probably way off base."

"In left field, I'm sure." Coffee was finished and I wished I had more and something to do with my hands.

"As near as I can tell, Gertie stopped at Dickie's barbershop first, because she has a crush on Dick. Then she headed straight for us at the Outpost. Gertie left hours ago, and it seems everyone who comes in has a different version of the story...but they must have heard it from her."

"Gossip multiplies geometrically. Plus I'm sure Reefer and Valerie are not exactly silent on this."

"That may be. Gertie just walked into the café and said to the first person she saw – which was Ben Clausson, I know because I was serving him – she said, 'Did ya hear about the dead guy at Palmer's?' Just like that in her screechy voice."

Marie did a passable Gertie imitation and we both chuckled over it. She was animated and slightly flushed as she talked and it dawned on me that we were having a good time being friendly over a bad situation. I started digging in my billfold to pay her before we got so chummy I'd forget. She was missing tips by being in my office and now she'd have to work until 2:00.

"So, what was the latest version you heard before you came over here with my sandwich?"

"Well," She perched on the edge of my desk and I could smell the hamburgers in her hair. "By putting all the stories together, it seems a short Indian man who was probably a spy for the Castro government, was found cut to ribbons and skinned alive in Palmer's barn. The police suspect an international ring of drug smugglers, gunrunners and ex-CIA agents. The dead spy had been horribly tortured by either a fanatic Shiite Moslem hit squad or by a demented old man who used body parts for household decoration and danced by the light of the full moon in other people's skins." She stopped and leaned forward. "How'm I doing so far?"

"You're right, the guy's dead." She pouted a little and sat back on the desk.

"Some people are saying there's no danger any more because the killers got rid of the traitor and just happened to dump him in Palmer's deserted barn. Others – those who believe in the demented old man version – are locking their doors and keeping the kids in after dark tonight."

"This would be the Valerie and Reefer influence."

"You, of course, already know who did it and have been on the phone to Washington all morning..."

"I have a fan club."

"...but will probably issue some stupid non-committal statement to cover it all up because it involves some pretty important people high up in the government, and you'll more than likely get paid to keep your mouth shut."

"I don't have a fan club, they all talked to the crank who left a message about the city streets."

"What message?"

I shook my head, dismissing the question and whistled softly. "I'd say we've got us quite a case on our hands. What do you think about all this?"

"Me? I just wait tables and listen to the conversation." She got up from the edge of my desk and straightened out her uniform, picked up the money and made a move toward the door. "I don't take much stock in any of the gossip and only about half of what Gertie said." She paused and smiled faintly. "But if you do have a flayed man with his heart cut out, it sounds to me like the someone who did it is a copycat Aztec."

The room got about half again as small the minute I stood up. I could reach out and touch her and not only could I smell her, there was a ringing in my ears that hadn't been there before her last sentence. I dumped the styrofoam pod in my wastebasket along with the handcuff flyer.

"That's just what the coroner said. You been talking to Eddie Loetz over lunch?"

"He doesn't eat at the Outpost."

"I suppose I could start tracking down the Aztec angle by checking out a library book. The history of ancient Mexico is not one of my strong subjects."

"I'm sure Lisbeth Ann would be a great help in the card catalog." That little smile again. "Or, you could talk to Dr. Vollmer about it."

"I already talked to one doctor about it and it appears they don't know much about anthropology."

"This doctor is a PhD in Pre-Columbian studies at the University. He was part of an art history survey I took. If there's anything Aztec about your murder, he'll be able to help."

"Does he teach at the U during the summer?"

"No." She opened the office door and let in the gasoline and oil smells from the fire hall. "But he has a summer place up the hill near the end of the trail, and he was in for lunch just a couple of days ago. He even remembers my name from class."

Chapter Five

From roughly the Continental Divide to the shore of Lake Superior, the land drops over 1300 feet in less than fifty miles; from over 1900 feet of elevation above sea level to 600. The major roadways, called trails, plunge from the bedrock of original Mother Earth, through layers of glacial deposits back to the base of ancient lava flows long since uncovered by the cold and merciless waves of the Great Lake. Rock nearly three thousand million years old brackets the drive from top to bottom. Granite and basalt outcrops jut immobile above the trails near the Divide and the Canadian Border. Here the waters drain to Hudson Bay, while only a few yards down the trail they flow to Superior. The boreal forest grips the thin, inconsequential layer of soil with spreading tendrils and twisted taproots looking for anchoring cracks in some of the most ancient rock on earth. Scoured out and wedged between the bedrock are thousands of deep, clear lakes left there by the countless advances and retreats of glaciers. This is the new rock, the traveled rock brought by the ice mountains and left in eskered piles and ribbons only a mere few thousand years ago. When the great ice finally melted and the glacial sea retreated down the hill puddling into a much smaller Lake Superior, shale sea bottoms were left behind, rippled and layered one on the other for sometimes over thirty feet thick. Here the forest changes to birch and other hardwoods. Finally the entire epic concludes in massive sheets of dark, quartz-lined rock rooted to the earth's very magma core: the shore, where small pebbles tumble and flatten in the waves and the herring gulls bob along on the cold and rolling swells.

I began my drive down the hill near the Divide where Dr. Doyle R. Vollmer had his summer home. Professor Vollmer had all the answers a person could legitimately want about Pre-Columbian culture. But I really didn't need to know that Cortez landed in Mexico in February of 1519 in order to figure out who killed the man in Palmer's barn. True, says

Vollmer, but on the other hand we only have the word of Cortez and Bernal Diaz del Castillo on Aztec culture, because the conqueror and the priest were the only ones to ever set anything down on paper. Apparently the Spaniards put an end to the Aztecs and about 1500 years of their culture by the following February. Vollmer thought Cortez and Bernal's accounts of Aztec barbarism were a bit out of focus. He said that seen from the Spanish point of view, the priests and politicians were bloodthirsty despots who regularly and ritually murdered hundreds of their subjects. As a matter of fact, Vollmer admitted, they did all that, but it was as a result of a perverse interpretation of their long-inherited religious beliefs and their desire to stay in power. To me, that still sounded like the priests and politicians were bloodthirsty despots and Cortez had them pegged. One of the reasons the conqueror got on so well with the emperor was that he impressed Montezuma by rounding up 6000 Indians and slaughtering them all at a place called Cholula.

So much for history and the benevolent spread of Western ideals and Christian morality in the New World.

I pulled my truck over at a wayside rest. Time to take a leak. As I stepped into the woods out of sight of the road, three thoughts crossed my mind. The heroes in adventure movies never stop to take a leak. Life is much duller and slower than what we see on television. And, Dr. Vollmer wasn't telling me everything he knew about the case, just everything he knew about Aztecs. Sometimes I have my sharpest insights taking a leak.

Out of force of habit I checked the truck before climbing back inside the cab. The department only has two vehicles. The squad Mel was driving and my four wheel drive pickup with the permanently mounted canoe rack on the topper roof. The aluminum canoe was always lashed to the rack, the paddles and fishing tackle always in the back of the truck just in case life got duller and slower paced than I expected.

By the time I reached the turnoff to the County airport any thoughts of fishing were gone from my mind. On my way up the hill to question Vollmer, I'd stopped at the airstrip office. If the dead man came to Cache Harbor in a car or truck, an abandoned vehicle hadn't been reported yet. He might have arrived by plane. But the airport manager told me there were no unaccounted for private craft on the field and a quick check of the three charter passenger manifests from the last five days turned up only names of tourists who flew out Sunday evening after a weekend at one of the more expensive wilderness lodges. One of the private planes that had flown in was owned by Dr. Doyle R. Vollmer.

Aside from his obvious confidence in his own knowledge of ancient Mexican history and culture, Vollmer had been less sure of why he was being interviewed by the local cop. I could understand that. Even I wasn't sure I knew why I'd made the fifty-mile trip up the hill. Vollmer wasn't a suspect, just a source of information. Yes, Aztecs did indeed kill their human sacrifices by cutting out the victim's heart. Yes, there was a ritual flaying of the sacrifice for one of the gods. The heart was often burned on an alter. And the method? An ornately decorated obsidian knife, very sharp, very effective. Did Vollmer have one? Yes, several, although one of the finest examples was missing from his collection. Did he think someone took it? Yes, he did, but hadn't reported it because it only just happened. A group of his students had visited earlier in the month; maybe one of them had borrowed it for analysis in a paper, and just forgot to mention it. He was sure it would turn up. Vollmer had a lot of artifacts in his house: idols, statues, carvings, wall hangings. Quite a museum.

As I hit the city limits it struck me that Vollmer was a bundle of facts and the picture of poise when he talked about the early Mexicans. He wasn't quite so poised when he answered questions about himself, his collection, or who the dead man in Palmer's barn might be. He stressed the fact that Aztec sacrifices like the one I was looking at, were done purely for religious purposes. The Sun needed the human heart to continue its daily round of life-giving light and heat...which is why the ancient priests cut out so many. Flaying was symbolic of shucking off the old earthly dress for the spiritual dress of resurrection. Rich men paid to have slaves killed and flayed on their behalf, to insure a safe place for their own souls in Aztec heaven. I'm sure that made the slaves feel better.

I turned at the Lutheran church corner and wondered what the congregation's good-natured pastor would make of an Aztec catechism. Vollmer had thought it was slightly sacrilegious to cut open and flay a man unless there was a spiritual motive behind it. He couldn't come up with one under the circumstances, nor did he have any ideas about who would be practicing such a faith out here. So, he concluded it was some nut who read a book on the subject. So, I thought I'd check out one of those books to see if I would reach the same conclusion. It also gave me the opportunity to check out Lisbeth Ann Sarstadt. Since it was pushing five o'clock, I'd stop there first before going back to the office where I'd do nothing but listen to phone messages and write the official news release...neither on the top of my "to do" list.

"There aren't any books on the subject."

"Then you've got a dumb library here, Ms Sarstadt."

"No, actually we have quite a collection on the subject, I only meant they have all been checked out by Valerie Hackney. However I have a large, glossy book on Pre-Columbian art in my personal collection if you'd care to look at it after dinner."

"What are we having and at what time?"

"Shall we eat Mexican at 6:30?"

"I'd rather eat Chinese at 7:00."

"I agree to both. How did you know I was a whiz at stir fry?"

"You told me last week. Besides tacos wouldn't settle with some of the other Mexican things I know about."

"Whatever."

I liked to watch her move, Lisbeth Ann. She wasn't very tall but moved light and graceful. When she was happy she radiated all the charm and good spirits a man could ask for. When she was dark, the clouds rolled in and there was no penetrating her shield. She had more than her share of darkness since her separation and divorce from Dick Sarstadt. For my money, the match had never been made in heaven, not with Dick's over-the-road lifestyle and Lisbeth Ann's need to stay at home and in charge of her small, literary domain. Besides, she was smarter than Dick – never an easy thing for some men to accept, and no small point between these two. Lisbeth Ann never flaunted her brains, at least not to me or anyone else I knew. There are just some people blessed with native intelligence and the knack of knowing how to use it. Then, there are those who struggle to get past the sports section. It's never easy to break up the dream, but in their case, the dream turned nightmare. No kids, thank God. That was Reefer's personal ulcer and it gnawed at him constantly. He could not divorce his daughter Nancy no matter how much he tried to forget his wife Blanche.

The blond heavy-chested image of Lisbeth Ann kept swimming around in my head as I drove back to my fire barn office. Her large eyes tilted upward and her full mouth could as easily spread to a great rejoicing grin or a deep pouting frown. A date with Lisbeth Ann was always an adventure. I could only hope tonight would bring the grin not the frown. I had enough frowns weighting down my day so far.

My answering machine was blinking at me when I walked in. Three general calls, another bitch about the streets – as if I paved in my spare time – but the next call was from Judy Swanson. I could see by the paperwork on his desk, Mel had checked in the office while I was playing games with Vollmer.

"Damn this answering machine! Mel, Mel if you're there, I think it's started. Fifteen minutes apart ever since you left. It's four-thirty and I'm calling the hospital when they get to be less than ten minutes apart." Click!

He must have heard her plea. He was gone and no note. This was their first and I for one would be glad when it was history. The sixth call was from Eddie Loetz. Nothing new. The twins had been delivered and he had performed the autopsy. First impression confirmed. The victim was Indian, but probably not a local. Had Eddie mentioned this fact to anyone? Otherwise how was it the gossip included information that the man was Indian? Gertie didn't know. I hadn't told anyone. That left Loetz or the killer.

The last message was from Marie Craske.

"Paul. Sorry I made that crack about Lisbeth Ann and you this morning. I really am. My roommate Emily has some books on Pre-Columbian culture. If you want to look them over, I'm sure she won't mind. Neither will I. I have to pull Karen's shift tonight, but I'll be off tomorrow morning. Please call. My number is..."

I wrote down the number on my pad. What crack had that been? Oh, yeah. Lisbeth being a great help to me in the card catalog. No big deal, Marie. Reefer was right. Marie was wearing her top two blouse buttons open for a reason. I'd have to think about that. I cranked up my computer and opened my standard news release form file. It was time to compose 'for immediate release murder one'. I already knew what Reefer and Valerie would think of the effort, and I'm sure it would just confirm the suspicions of the gossips down at the Outpost: the Chief was in a cover up to his ass. I closed my eyes and tried to concentrate on non-committal, non-information. The raw, red figure of the flayed man was still imprinted on the insides of my eyelids. I wondered if they'd still be there if I was lucky enough to close my eyes during a long, languid lovemaking with Lisbeth Ann. Or would the image be there if I happened to close my eyes kissing Marie Craske. For that matter what was the image behind Reefer's closed eyes, or Valerie's?

And who did the flayed man see just before his eyes grimly closed forever?

Chapter Six

"Clothes." Lisbeth Ann tugged at her own blouse to emphasize the point she was making to me. It was one of those over-sized affairs, her blouse, with large sleeves and she wore it with a woven belt. To me it looked like without the belt, we could both fit inside. That'd be OK. It was a light amber color and I couldn't help thinking about how good she looked in it, and in the shorts, sandals and bangly jewelry. She spoke summer all over. "Clothing. You didn't find any at the scene. The man wasn't killed with his clothes on…not that way, he wasn't."

"Gotta point." The body had been completely unclothed, skin and all. That was not mere nakedness, the absence of a shirt and pants. That was something more than naked.

"Clothing serves an important symbolic function. People choose it carefully and protect it, which means whoever the murderer is, has some pretty gross looking clothing of his own to get rid of."

Lisbeth Ann rinsed off the last of the dinner dishes. She had made something that sounded like maw googuy pan. It was good, though. Chicken, mostly, with mushrooms and pea pods. So was the white wine, good. Not something I normally drink, but I took my refill into the main room of her small house and sank heavily into the davenport. She followed and sat next to me, but not too close. She was still very interested in the murdered man. Everyone was.

"I mean, if your clothes are all bloody, you can't just leave them lying around, or send them to the cleaners or take them to the laundromat." She edged closer and took a sip of her wine. "Clothing is important enough so other people notice if we do something unusual with it. Buried or burned or even thrown away or concealed, signals other people that something is wrong. Besides, clothing is really not all that easy to get rid of. Maybe someone has seen some clothing someplace that looks out of place."

"There does seem to be a kind of careful planning to all of this. Someone took a lot of time to do what they did to the victim. They also spent some time cleaning up...the site and themselves. Very deliberate."

"Exactly. The killer removes all the clothing from the victim, stacks it neatly and carries it off after the deed is done. No evidence. No identification.

"Then why leave the body?"

"What do you mean?"

"Why go through all this careful rigmarole, including a time consuming ritual and then leave the body for the rest of us to investigate? Why not just haul it off and dump it in the woods? Could stay hidden for years out there before some camper stumbles on it."

"Maybe the whole thing took too long. Not enough time to move the body and clean the barn. Got rid of as much evidence as they could."

She had a point. The man had not been dead that long before Gert Bushmiller found him. Sunrise would have cast an entirely different light on the murder scene. Panic could have changed the plan.

"The detergent people haven't invented something that takes out blood stains, have they?"

"Usually if you get to it right away, you can get most of the stain out with cold water before it sets, then regular washing will usually finish the job. That could explain all the water you found at the pump."

"Or, maybe the killer wasn't wearing clothes either. Washing blood off skin is a whole lot easier than getting it out of clothing."

"That's bizarre, Paul. That really conjures up a picture of some maniac carving up bodies and dancing around naked in the moonlight."

"Ed Gein all over again."

"Never mind. It's the Valerie Hackney theory you were talking about. But face it, some people aren't sleeping well tonight. Brings to mind those movies where the madman grinds up half the high school graduating class in a blender."

"Neither of us believes that. No, someone was trying to make a point by going to all that trouble and leaving the body to be found...on purpose."

"Let's get back to Valerie Hackney for a minute." She dribbled a little more Chablis in my glass. "She checked out every book in the library on ancient Mexico, Aztecs, Mayans, the whole shot."

"I think she thinks this is her big chance for investigative reporting. She was pissed off this morning because I wouldn't let her run all over the crime scene. I'd hoped Reefer would settle her down, but it doesn't look like it. She'll be up half the night."

"She's got a few days to work on it. Monday's their deadline and it's only Wednesday."

"How long before it turns Thursday?"

"About four hours."

"Got any plans for the rest of the evening?"

It hadn't been difficult to help Lisbeth Ann out of her amber blouse with the big sleeves. Or her shorts. It felt like a commitment night and that felt just right at the time. It had been a while and we started out urgent, went at it in earnest and finished quietly, even peacefully. The flayed man was not behind my eyelids, mostly because I kept them open to watch Lisbeth Ann. Even in the end when the pleasure squeezed my eyes shut, the tiny explosions of light did not illuminate his grotesque and bloody image.

When I finally pulled into the driveway it was just after midnight. I carried in the book on Pre-Columbian art she had loaned me. Inside my little rented house was a large orange juice and six hours of much needed sleep.

Chapter Seven

"So that's it, then?"

"That's it."

"Not long on words."

"Not long on information, either, I'll admit that."

"Val won't like it."

"Tough shit." We were back in the Outpost doing breakfast again. Me and my sunny side ups, because I like them that way and because it leaves Reefer slightly queasy.

"Val is really into this case, Paul. I've never seen her so intense."

I mopped up some yolk. This was Reefer playing apologist for his girlfriend and cheerleader for his newspaper's bid to solve the murder. I wasn't buying either.

"For chrissake, she's checked out every goddamn book on Aztecs in the library. I had to borrow an art catalog from Lisbeth Ann just to get a look at a sacrificial obsidian knife. I had to drive a hundred miles to talk to a Pre-Columbian scholar about what he calls Mezo-American culture. I have other people digging up materials on the same subject for me all because Valerie has the local market cornered on information. It comes damn close to interfering with an investigation, if you ask me." I was overstating the case, I knew that. But Reefer needed to know I wasn't going to get sloppy about this investigation, I wasn't going to tolerate nosey reporters and by the looks of the news release I wrote, I wasn't about to get chatty with the facts, either. Enough said.

"Easy, Paul. Val asked me to ask if the two of you might have a few minutes together after breakfast. She really does want to help, you know."

"I'm supposed to see somebody else about more Aztec stuff."

"Listen, I'd like to see this thing wrapped up, too. Soon as possible. Val is obsessed with it." He leaned in closer over his hash browns, "It's interfering with my nookie."

"Your nookie!"

"Shh! Not so loud. This place is full."

"They all know you're scoring Valerie."

"Not anymore, I'm not. She spent all last night curled up with those library books. My sex life could be ruined if you don't solve this case."

"I'm supposed to fight for truth, justice and the American way just so you can get laid?"

"All I'm trying to do here is inject a little humor into the discussion."

"I've got a dead man in the morgue, Reefer. It ain't funny to him."

"OK, OK. Don't get tense." He handed me a thick packet of eight by ten black and white photos and read my news release back to me while I finished my coffee. " 'On the morning of August 12 at approximately 8am, the Cache Harbor police department reported an apparent homicide. The victim is believed to be an adult male of unknown age, race and identity. According to Police Chief Paul Tharp, the man may have been the victim of a ritual killing. The matter continues to be under investigation.' How long did it take you to write that? Eight seconds?"

"It took longer than you think. I chose every word carefully." I flipped through the photos even though they didn't help settle my breakfast. "Has Valerie seen these?"

"Instead of grossing her out they piqued her interest even more."

"That's the way it is with some women."

"You bastard."

I picked up the bulging envelope and left a tip for Karen, who had switched shifts with Marie. It was Marie I wanted to see this morning... only for her roommate's books, I told myself. But I guessed I could accommodate Valerie for a minute, and then maybe stop by the hospital to see Judy Swanson. I had called the hospital last night somewhere between the first glass of wine and dinner. A seven pound eight ounce baby girl born at six fifty-seven pm. Since it was Eddie Loetz who picked up the phone, I also learned that he had told no one except me that he thought the victim was Indian. Now that he was certain of it, it seemed to matter more because it was a part of the original rumor and should have been locked up with just three people: Eddie, me and the murderer.

Valerie sat across my desk from me and told everything she knew about Aztecs. I gave her a copy of the news release.

"Until I know more about the victim and get better information on a possible motive, I don't know that I can spend any more time on ancient Mexican theology."

I'll give her this; she really tried to explain how a better understanding of the sacrificial procedures would help in the discovery of motive and even lead to the killer. It wasn't that I disagreed, but what I had in the flayed man file to this point hardly merited a scholarly discussion on dead civilizations. Vollmer could give me that anytime I asked, and he had. What Valerie was giving me was old news.

"OK, so who did it?"

"I suppose that's all that matters."

"That's what I get paid to do. Find out who did it. Then why. Then sometimes if it matters to the prosecution, the under-the-surface-'why'. I'm not a psychiatrist. All I need is motive, not the deep motivation. I need things like love, hate, greed, sex, fear, power. The usual suspects."

"I don't necessarily agree, but I told Reefer I'd try to stop acting like a jerk. I'm bucking, Paul. I'm bucking for a good story, my name in syndication. You may as well know that. I promise to play fair and not get in your way. The last thing I want is to antagonize your investigation. That's not any better journalism than just sitting back and printing the official explanation." She pushed my news release back across the desk. "You tell the official story the way you think you have to and let me do the interpretation. I'm after readers and you're not."

My opinion of Valerie went up a notch or two. It's always been easier for me to know where people are coming from than wondering if I'm going to be blind-sided down the road. Maybe if I'd stop viewing her as competition...no, more like a threat. How worried was I about my image? Was I getting defensive while swearing I wasn't? She'd turned my crank because I thought of her as a wannabe, not a professional. Well, maybe when you work in a small town at the end of the road, that makes us all wannabes. She wants a syndicated story. I wannabe a hero. Piss on it. Why does a man do this kind of work, anyway?

She was getting ready to leave the office when I heard Mel's squad pull into the fire barn. Daddy at work again. He barged into the office not realizing Valerie was occupying part of the space, nearly knocked her over, then stumbled through an apology as he set a large grocery bag on my desk.

"Congratulations, dad."

"Thanks. She, I mean Shelly, was seven pounds…"

"I know I called last night. Why aren't you taking the day off?"

"What's to do? The delivery went fine. Mother and child are OK; they'll be released tomorrow. Judy wants to rest and get to know Shelly. God knows we cleaned the house six times last week to be sure it would be all set when they come home from the hospital. All I'd do is get the place dirty by hanging around." He smiled at Valerie and looked like he had something more to say but didn't know if he should. He shot a quick glance at me, which of course Valerie picked up.

"And?"

"Oh, yeah. Late last night I got a call from Tommy Plaiser at Moose Horn Lodge. We, that is I didn't exactly know where you were, so I went up there this morning, early."

"I was around but not exactly around. What was on Tommy's mind?"

"When he was shutting down the kitchen last night, he found a bunch of clothing in the outside dumpster." Mel held out a plastic bag. "This was in the jeans."

The Ziploc held a regular man's black billfold, the kind you'd wear in your back pants pocket. Nothing fancy, just worn leather at the rounded corners. No money, no photos, credit cards, license, ID. Stuck in the corner of the divided concealed bills pocket was a folded voter registration card. Jorge Ricardo Ponce y Cuevas-Portilla.

"All right! Now we're getting someplace." Valerie edged past Mel to look at the card.

"Val, we're looking at evidence, here."

"Are you going to throw me out?"

"Nope. I'm going to do us both a favor and openly discuss this information in front of you." She'd dig it out anyway, so in the interests of not chewing my cud twice, I let her stay. Cuevas-Portilla was thirty-one years old and had a Calexico, California address. Mel pulled the road atlas out of a file cabinet and the three of us crowded around southern California. Mel smelled like cigarette smoke, Valerie smelled like sandalwood. I probably smelled like Juicy Fruit gum to them. Calexico, it turned out was a small border town directly across from the much larger city of Mexicali.

"Tommy checked the lodge register," Mel offered, "but there was no one by this name staying there, or even answering a Mexican description." He reached into the grocery bag and pulled out a pair of black jeans, a madras short-sleeved shirt, a pair of white jockey shorts, white crew socks and a pair of expensive reptile hide cowboy boots.

"Lucky find." Valerie reached for the clothing. "Can I touch this stuff?"

"Might as well, everyone else has." I looked through the billfold again. There was a little concealed key holder, but it had never been used. "Clean. I'd say a very lucky find. Maybe too lucky." I tossed the registration card on the desk and headed out the door. "Call the Calexico PD and get what you can on Cuevas-Portilla. I'll be back in an hour." When I glanced back, Mel was reaching for an area code directory and Valerie was scribbling down label information from the dead man's shirt. I knew I'd be reading his boot size and brand names of all his clothing in her story next week. I'd left the windows rolled up in my truck and the cab felt hot and airless as I slipped behind the wheel. Maybe she'd also report Cuevas-Portilla had left skid marks in his jockey shorts.

I drove east out of town and turned on County 2. Marie's cabin was the farthest one on a dead end driveway running along the Lake Superior shore. I hadn't bothered to call ahead. I'd just smile and thank her for her phone message, take whatever books her roommate had to offer and then get back to Cuevas-Portilla. But as luck would have it, she came to the door dressed in a soft purple bathrobe, bare feet and tousled hair. Her face had a freshly scrubbed glow. I stammered through an apology for getting her up early after forgetting she had worked the late shift last night.

"That's all right. I'm glad you got my message. It was wrong of me to be catty about Lisbeth Ann."

"Not to worry. I wanted you to know we got some more information on the victim and I'll have to spend the rest of the day checking into it."

"Will you have a cup of coffee?" She opened the door wide for me to come in and to catch the line of her body in the bathrobe. I declined the coffee, but there was one question I could ask. It wouldn't hurt to stay a minute. Did her roommate have any information in her textbooks about Aztec artifacts, say obsidian knives? As it turned out Marie had just happened to be looking through the stack of books she'd set aside for me and found a catalog of small objects, including knives. They all seemed to be owned by museums. I told her I thought there was some law between the United States and Mexico about keeping national treasures at home. She offered me a chair but we both continued to stand. I mentioned that I'd followed up on her suggestion and went to see Professor Vollmer. The visit probably saved me a lot of dry reading. She accepted my thanks and we kept standing there neither sitting or moving toward the stack of books. I said I'd noticed he had quite a collection of Mexican things himself and wondered if he'd ever mentioned to his class how he came by them.

"No, he just said he was a collector. I never thought anything of it. Maybe Emily could tell you, but she's in Toronto."

Marie broke the tension and reached down and picked up the stack of five or six books waiting for me on the footstool. Her bathrobe managed to stay closed. Just. She'd gotten together everything she could find. Three art history books and a couple of antiquities catalogs. The page markers were not hers but had been left there by Emily. Little smile. Keep them as long as you like. I took the stack from her, but managed not to break our eye contact. Marie was one of those people who always made eye contact when she talked to you. I wasn't used to that. In my line of work most people prefer not to look you in the eye. She smiled again and fumbled with a thin woven gold chain that hung around her neck, but made no effort to close the deep purple 'V' of her bathrobe. I thanked her and made toward the door. She wished me luck. I stepped out on to the small cabin porch and finding no further reason for staying, got in my truck and drove off. I was sure she was still looking at me when I got to the corner where I had to wait for three large double-bottom logging trucks as they labored up the hill. I glanced down at the top book in the seat next to me and leafed through the pages to the first marker Marie had said was left there by her roommate.

It was a black and white photograph of a glistening obsidian knife. There was an inset in the picture, a drawing of a similar instrument being used to cut out the heart of a hapless slave. Four leopard-cloaked priests held down the victim on a carved sacrificial stone. The caption said it was an excellent and rare example of Toltec influenced Aztec carving. As the last truck lumbered by I read the small photo credit line. 'From the Doyle R. Vollmer Collection. Photo used by permission.'

During the summer months you could usually find the old flower peddler set up in front of the video rental store. No one knew exactly where he came from and he certainly didn't have a license to sell on the street. I'm sure there was an ordinance somewhere on the books prohibiting that kind of thing except during the week of the annual town celebration. Voyageur Days was next week and I didn't care about some obscure ordinance prohibiting an old man from selling happiness and beauty. I bought a bunch of cut flowers on my way to the hospital to visit Judy and new little Shelly Swanson.

Judy looked radiant. That's what you're supposed to say about new mothers. Little Shelly looked red and a lot like Winston Churchill, but then again all babies look like that. I was sure she'd improve.

Back at the office, Mel looked tired. His long night and early morning was catching up with him. I glanced through the mail as he finished his phone conversation. There was a pattern to the mail. Mondays were jammed with flyers and free shopper newspapers as well as all the leftovers from the previous week's work. Tuesdays were nothing special. Wednesdays the local paper showed up along with a fair amount of mid-week mail. All the work that should have been done on Tuesday got finished on Thursday and showed up in mail slots across the country Friday morning. Saturday's mail carried all the communications the bureaucrats and lazier office workers should have sent out for Friday delivery. Mel hung up the phone.

"Saw Judy and little Shelly. Nice way to start a family. Good looking wife, fine looking daughter. The husband could use a little work."

"Long night. That was Deputy Dog checking in. He didn't find anything up at Palmer's either. He had the place hosed down late afternoon and figures that after six volunteers spent an hour up there with a fire hose, the gossip should take on a much more graphic tone. Words like 'slaughterhouse', 'gore' and 'gouts of blood'.

"Dog reads too many detective stories, besides Valerie will have all three of those in her lead paragraph."

"And, Ash is back and wants to have a meeting with all the local law enforcement personnel this afternoon at two to discuss patrol and security for the Voyageur Days celebration."

"Four big days this year instead of three." I hate Voyageur Days.

"I got through to the Calexico police. A Sergeant Ordonio should call back around eleven."

"Which is right about now. Does he know we're on Central Daylight?" The phone rang. It was Sergeant Harry Ordonio, Calexico PD.

"I understand someone finally got to Sparky Portilla."

"Sparky? The ID we have is for – I think I'm pronouncing this right – Hoarhay Ricarrrdo Ponsay ee Cuayvas Porteeya."

"That's Sparky. He picked up the nickname when he was a kid. He and his brothers burned down a vacant building, only it wasn't so vacant. There was an illegal alien family of five holed up in it. It's been all down hill for Sparky ever since. He's got a rap sheet long as your arm but damn few convictions."

"Any guess why he should turn up here? Especially dead?"

"Portilla probably has more enemies than there are parishioners in your local Catholic church. According to my files he's been involved one way or another in robbery, assault and smuggling. About the only thing he hasn't done is assault little children. Yet."

"Nice guy to have visit our fair community."

"Do you know who shot him?"

"What makes you think he was shot?"

"Nobody in their right mind would get close enough to him to do it any other way."

"Someone did. They apparently bashed in the back of his head, then cut out his heart and finished the job by skinning him like so much pork."

"That was not Minnesota Nice."

"A little atypical, I agree."

"Couldn't have happened to a nicer guy. I'm glad it's your case. I been watching this sleazeball sneak back and forth over the border for years with everything from truckloads of weed to cases of booze, even archeological contraband. The desert is too big and Customs has too few officers. I'd like to think one less Sparky Portilla makes the job just that much easier...but some other asshole will just take his place."

"What's archeological contraband?"

"We run across that kind of smuggling a couple times a year. When the heat turns up on illegal aliens or the Feds get worked up over cocaine, guys like Portilla supplement their incomes by trafficking in what the Mexican government calls national treasures."

"You mean Aztec artifacts?"

"Aztec, Toltec, Mayan, you name it. The scientists haven't dug up all the places where you can find this stuff. A lot of people across the border have authentic Pre-Columbian art pieces in their families. When money gets tight they sell the stuff to guys like Portilla. This isn't junk or replicas, it's the real thing and the Federales get very pissed off if they catch you booting it out of the country."

"Portilla could have a regular network of buyers on this side, then?"

"He wouldn't be selling them on the street corner, I'll tell you that. Listen, I'll send up his file by courier express, you should have it in a day. There's photographs and mugs and all kinds of shit. Whoever killed him did us a favor. When you catch him, read him his rights and then thank him for me."

Chapter Eight

I leaned against the old Compugraphic typesetter Reefer kept around to remind himself of what life was life before computers. Valerie was at her terminal and I was eating a ham sandwich for lunch. There was an open peach yogurt container on her desk. I had a favor to ask of Valerie and Reefer had already turned me down without listening. I argued it was the editor's job to make requests of his reporters, not the police. That didn't cut it. Reefer was getting even. I needed to ask her myself. OK, I can keep score.

"I've got a favor to ask." She gave me one of those looks. "But it's not a one-sided deal." Another look. "Let's treat each other like professionals, OK? You trust me like I know what I'm doing and I'll treat you the same way. No small town shit between the cops and the newspaper."

"Fair enough."

"Good. The Calexico police called back on Portilla. I'll have his file tomorrow. I understand it's a doozie."

"I figured he must have done something to merit enemies that would kill him like that."

"I'll go over the file to see what's confidential, if anything. I'll also have to think about what the county attorney will have a shit-fit over if it's made public. But I guess after that, there's no reason why you can't look it over before your deadline."

"I appreciate that, Paul. What can I do for you?"

"At this stage of the game everyone's a suspect." I knew it sounded corny like an old Monogram movie script, but given Portilla's background, there was one person I wanted to talk to first, before Valerie got on the trail. I didn't know if Portilla's file would bear me out, I didn't even have a thing but a hunch and I wanted to be the guy who played that hunch first.

"You can shut me out of an investigation anytime you want."

"If I have a suspect. I don't have a suspect, I have a hunch. This is a very public crime and I don't expect to be the first person talking to everyone who might know something. I'm OK with that. I know I can't just dribble out the information as I see fit. But neither do I want us to be in a horse race, you and me."

"In other words you have a 'maybe'".

"That could be too strong a word. I've got some observations from a Calexico cop and I'm starting to link up some people based on those observations, even before I see the file. What I'm doing here is setting up the ducks before the shotgun shells arrive."

"Who's the duck?"

"You'd get around to him soon enough, as soon as you knew he's an expert in Pre-Columbian civilizations and lives at the end of the trail."

"Dr. Vollmer. He's on my list, but I thought he taught at the University."

"He does, but he spends his summers flying into Cache Harbor and talking to his collection of artifacts up at his Birch Lake place. I was up there yesterday."

"I probably do want to talk to him about Aztecs."

"I already did that. I might want to talk to him about other things as well. Too many people paying attention to him, he might get spooked if he has anything to hide."

"So if Portilla's file is such a doozie, do you think there's a connection between he and Vollmer?"

"Could be, maybe not. I don't know. I'm just covering my ass by asking you to hold off talking to him until I see the file and maybe drive up to visit again."

"I've got a couple days until deadline."

"Thanks. I'll do what I can for you with the file."

"Is this your way of saying we're working together on this case?"

"That's one way of putting it."

"Thanks."

I hit the wastebasket with the waxed paper from my sandwich. Valerie polished off her yogurt. She told me the former editor would have buried the story on page six next to the recipes and dress patterns. It would have been bad publicity for the town and the advertisers would scream about driving away business. Reefer was talking page one, and while the Telegram-Herald was still no award winning watchdog sheet, some guts was better than none. And who knows maybe the advertisers won't scream.

I left her stroking her keyboard. She always dressed well, always looked like she was ready for a party. Today she was all business. I tried to picture her between Reefer's sheets and the signal wasn't coming in clear. Maybe the story she was working on changed her; maybe she really wasn't the person Reefer made her out to be. Maybe the links in my head between Portilla and Vollmer weren't so real either. But the good doctor had a large private collection of things the Mexican government preferred left in Mexico; Portilla was a small time smuggler, and he was dead in Vollmer's backyard. I didn't think that was too long a stretch. Don't have to hit me over the head with a two by four to get my attention.

The two o'clock meeting in Sheriff Ash Tucker's office was the usual Voyageur Days bullshit. Extra duty for all the cops in the county, but Ash gets to ride in the parade. All the officers agreed that town celebrations brought in thousands of people and thousands of dollars. That meant that traffic control was a pain in the ass, the beer garden was a pain in the ass, the parade was a pain in the ass and Ash Tucker was a pain in the ass. A duty schedule would be worked out. It would be fair and the Sheriff thanked you in advance for your voluntary cooperation in making this year's Voyageur Days celebration the safest and soundest in years.

Three o'clock. The hours were going to drag until I had my hands on the Calexico Portilla file. And it was hot again. High eighties with enough humidity to drown a cat. So it was back to the office and paperwork; three traffic accidents all coming to trial, one felony sexual misconduct and a gross misdemeanor DWI. The note taped to my phone told me Mel was checking out yet another fender bender. I paged through some of the stack of books I'd gotten from Marie. I'd let Valerie Hackney become the Aztec expert, let her fill up the front page with obscure facts and innuendo. I'd play hunches instead. I'd seen what I needed. Vollmer's collection even made the textbooks, and it wasn't blood lust priests who did in Portilla like they were doing in the slave in the textbook photo. I didn't need to know any more about Aztec ritual than that there was someone in the county who did. What was biting me was waiting. I could just hop in my truck and drive up to Vollmer's place and pop the question. 'You're a collector, Portilla was a supplier, you're an expert, he's a crook, he tried to pull a scam, you saw through it, your knife's missing and he's dead. Big lotta fucking coincidences.'

Instead, after an hour of my kind of speed-reading, I packed up the books and put them in my truck. Or was I just looking for an excuse to see Marie, the dark haired girl in the loose fitting purple bathrobe?

Her gray Ford Escort was still parked in the driveway. I stepped up on the porch and knocked on her door. No answer. I walked around to the back of the cabin and looked toward the lake. Down the long length of pebbled beach I could see her stretched out on a large blanket baking in the sun. Her long black hair was spread around her head and shoulders. The two-piece bathing suit she wore was red and white candy-striped and from a distance it looked to me as though it was hardly there at all. I set the stack of books on the concrete blocks that served as steps to the back door, and walked down the beach toward the candy stripes.

It was a little cooler by the lake, but still hotter than people around here could ever remember. Days were growing noticeably shorter and once the sun tipped below the rim of tall trees to the west, it was good to have a light jacket handy. There were no trees on the shore of the big lake to interfere with the sun. Marie would have a long time baking before the cooler evening would raise gooseflesh on her pale, exposed skin.

She turned her head toward me as I crunched my way along the pebble littered beach. No quiet approach here. On the Wisconsin side there were miles of pale creamy sand, but here on the north shore there was only acre upon acre of small, flat stones rubbing and sliding together for eons creating only a rough gravely sand between them like unmortared cement. She patted the edge of her beach towel as an invitation to sit beside her. The bright high sun reflected off the barely rippling water. It was blinding and I slipped on my sunglasses. The day was going to be too hot for my uniform. Shoulda known. If I took off my shirt would I really be on duty? Would it look funny to Marie, the first thing I did was remove part of my clothing? What I really wanted to do was get into my cutoffs and a tee shirt, load up the canoe and go fishing. Who was I kidding? What I really wanted to do was slip into my shorts and a tee and drink beer next to Marie on the pebble beach. But that was a dumb idea, what with Lisbeth Ann and all. This kid next to me was all slicked down with sunscreen and would slip away inside a month and slide two hundred miles south back to school.

"I brought your books back." Having made that statement I realized there was little to keep me there. I could leave that minute, thank her and be business like about the whole thing. Get back to work, crime solving. Her glistening pale skin seemed to dare the sun to burn. She patted the towel again. Seen from a distance, someplace from outside my body and far down the bay, it would appear threatening – a cop in uniform standing over a young, near-naked girl sunning on the beach. I could imagine the whole scene would change the minute I sat down, seem more benign, friendly. Tossing stones in the water.

"Do I make you nervous, Paul?" She squinted into the sun at me as I eased down into the pebbles.

"No, I just realized I was blocking the sun." Of course you make me nervous, you've got a great body and I can see most of it, and besides this is all being done on purpose...the beach, the towel, the bikini.

"I don't tan very easily. Maybe it's because I don't get much time in the sun. This is the first full day off I've had since I started work this summer. Even with most afternoons free I never seem to get around to lying out for more than an hour. They say you shouldn't spend much time in the sun, but I've been out here since one. It feels so good to cover myself with sunscreen and just let the sun bake away at me. Maybe that's the reason, too much sunscreen." She was fully stretched out on the towel; she wiggled her toes to the rhythm of her own speech. A thin patina of oil and perspiration coated her pale wheat colored body. The red and white striped bikini glared at me. "There's at least another good hour of sun, why don't you just knock off, kick back and cook away your worries."

I didn't really have anything that pressing. The rest of day and evening was going to drag until tomorrow brought the Portilla file. All I needed was one or two little indications from Calexico that I was on the right track and hunches could turn into probabilities. If Vollmer was into this, he was being careless.

"You don't say much, do you?" She shifted to her right side; the movement left the top of her bikini struggling to do its job. Her black hair fell over one shoulder. Her eyes were a dark graybrown, set wide apart from her small, slightly sharp nose. Her mouth turned up at the corners with a little curl and there was a small suggestion of a dimple at her chin. I remembered a similar scene that took place years ago when I was maybe sixteen. It was also a hot summer afternoon and I sat on the lawn of a friend's house staring down at a young girl who I thought was the most beautiful and exciting creature I'd ever seen. She lingered in the sun, mouth parted and eyes closed, short blond hair flashing in the light. Her swimsuit was not as brief, but crisp and yellow. I never kissed her and that probably ended our relationship. It was a gold-plated chance to carry off my first real kiss and probably a feel or two as well. I couldn't do it and I lied about it afterwards to my buddies.

Marie reached over and touched my arm where the short sleeve ended just above the elbow and asked if I wanted anything to drink, like iced tea. Down the beach and several hundred yards away three little kids ran out on the pebbles and began pelting the water with skipping stones. She said it was a universal sport, stone skipping.

"No matter when I'm out here, some little kid is down the beach skipping stones. The tiny ones just stand there in the water with their diapers hanging down around their knees throwing handfuls of stones into the water trying to be like their older brothers and sisters." She shifted position to her knees, which brought her face to the same level as my own. She had tucked in the bikini top straps to avoid leaving a tan line on her shoulders. I thought it wouldn't stay in place, but it did. I glanced away at the three children as they furiously threw stones into the water. When I looked back I could see a fine film of perspiration dotting her upper lip. Her left arm reached out and touched the back of my neck. Her kiss was light and full on my mouth. Then she pulled back slightly, looked me in the eyes, suddenly stood up and announced she was going to shower. "Bring the towel with you when you come up to the cabin, will you?"

She slipped on a pair of clogs and walked down the beach. I was watching her against the sun's glare. She turned and let her bikini top fall to the beach, then lightly stepped out of the striped bottoms.

"Bring the sunscreen, too." She glistened in the sun and her tight butt shone whiter than her lightly tanned back as she continued down the beach. I dug the heels of my running shoes into the loose array of pebbles. Their colors were pale red and gray, black and brown, white and many speckled variations. Most were rounded and slightly flat, but occasionally there was a jagged reminder that time and the lake's waves had not begun work on this one.

The water was virtually flat still. Tenochtitlan had been built on a lake. The city of the Aztecs had three causeways leading from the shore to the island itself. Eventually that was how Cortez brought the people to their knees, by cutting off the causeways and starving them out. But centuries before the Spaniards came the Nahuas and their descendents farmed the rich Mexican valley, mostly in peace and harmony until the Chichimecas came.

About the time of the beginning of the Christian era, another prophet and teacher arose among the Toltecs. He was a man-god who dressed as a feathered serpent and brought enlightenment to the people of the shaking earth. Under the watchful eye and moral strength of Quetzalcoatl the people mastered herbal medicines to cure their ailments, became expert stoneworkers and builders of complex temples and cities. They wove bright and exotic designs, potted elaborate ceramics and learned the values of precious stones. The man-god taught them painting to express their lives and home; he patiently instructed them in the art of featherwork, making cloaks and mantles and religious adornments. As carpenters, they built strong homes and as craftspeople they filled their homes with objects of beauty and function.

Above all, Quetzalcoatl taught them the movement of the stars and brought order to the round of their days. The gods they worshipped were for the most part benign; their sacrifices were symbolic and few. And the man-god taught them metaphor. They became great interpreters of dreams, devout guardians of the culture and unsurpassed orators.

After ten centuries of a civilization only known to parts of the American continent, the dreaded Chichimecas made their move. They were a mass of nomadic people ruled by the magic of Malinalxochitl, sister to four hundred brothers and daughter of their mother Coatlicue. At some time, and no one knows exactly when, Coatlicue was visited by a crown of feathers floating down from the heavens. She hid the crown beneath her skirts and she conceived. Her daughter was furious and rallied her mass of brothers to kill their mother. But in Coatlicue's womb, fully grown and armored, waited Huitzilopochtli with hummingbird feathers on his left leg and a snake of fire in his hands, his face striped in blue. He sprang from his mother's body, struck his sister a killing blow to the head and slaughtered his four hundred brothers.

The warrior god Huitzilopochtli, the hummingbird of resurrection, spread his people throughout Mexico and eventually to the city of Tula where they overran the peaceful thousand-year kingdom founded by the feathered serpent. There they settled and began the long process of fusing and melding, intertwining. intermixing, intermarrying. Finally by the time Cortez lead the westward lust for gold, the people of the hummingbird and the people of the serpent were one: Aztecs.

When the hoards of nomads protected under the wing of the hummingbird swarmed into Tula, Quetzalcoatl saw there would be a change, foresaw the blending of the people, foretold the end of the era when the planets would rule and men would vanish. He took as his sign a cross of negative space and told his people the base of all creation was found in the union of opposites: the spiritual and the material, the flowing and the solid, the enigma of the burning water. He then buried his treasures, burned his houses and at Teotihuacan, city of the gods, he consumed himself in flames. He told them that in that spiritual form he would sail the eastern seas to the ancient land and one day return to the west with his disciples to once again lead the people of the shaking earth.

While the feathered serpent was away, the beliefs he founded and the knowledge he had given was adopted and adapted by the flexible Chichimecas. But it was also changed to reflect their fierceness, their magical roots. The sacrifices became real and slaves by the thousands were butchered in bloodstained temples. It took the blood of a sacrifice to raise the sun each day. These Aztecs spread their kingdom from coast to coast and to the northern deserts and the southern jungles. All the Nahuatl people lived in fear of the Aztecs and they gave up through tribute and in battle hundreds of their youths and untold quantities of food and booty to sustain the rulers who lived on the island in the lake city.

When Cortez and his troops touched their majestic ships on the western shore, the watchers for the feathered serpent knew their god had returned. The illusion did not last long. The subjected and tortured people of the valley took up arms and ran with the armored gods who rode great four-legged beasts and carried a cross like the quincunx of Quetzalcoatl. In a year it was over. For all their brutality and scorn, the Spaniards were better masters than the Aztecs; but the ancient glories died with the conquest of the hummingbird; the cities were ruined and the people dispersed. The natives who once only had death on the sacrificial stone to look forward to, now farmed again in peace. The beans and the corn and squash bloomed in the valley watered not by blood, but rain from the mountains.

I'd read it all in one of Marie's books. It made me melancholy like the approaching mackerel sky waffling over the sun. It would rain this evening. I picked up the towel and sunscreen, brushed off my jeans, walked the beach to the remains of her bikini, collected them and dropped everything by the pile of books I'd left on the concrete block step. Inside the cabin the shower was running and Marie's naked body was wet and would be slippery cool to the touch; her kiss would be longer, more consuming.

I opened the truck cab, slipped inside and switched on the engine. The ride back to town was slow and empty. I stopped at the video rental store, then drove home to cold pizza, brandy in orange juice and two adventure movies.

Chapter Nine

The file from Calexico PD confirmed everything Sergeant Ordonio had told me by telephone – and more. Sparky Portilla was not the sort of person I'd expect to find hanging around Dr. Doyle Vollmer, but then again, looks can be deceiving. Among all the other assorted misdemeanors and felonies that peppered Sparky's file was a solid conviction for burglary which netted him five years in the slam. He spent twenty-eight and a half months in a California prison before he was released to his parole officer, and considering his checkered past, he was on a short string. Apparently Portilla knew the next time he took a fall, it would be big time lock up and throw away the key, so he was faithful to his parole officer every time he left the state. He listed his occupation as import/export sales rep for F.L. Gutzman, S.A., at an address on Aveneda Juarez in Mexico D.F. Apparently the folks at Calexico station weren't buying the story that Sparky sold decorative glazed tiles, which was the main line at F.L. Gutzman. Someone had penciled 'bull shit' next to that entry in the file.

The parole officer's records showed that Portilla had, in the past fourteen months, traveled on business to Denver, St. Louis. Des Moines, Chicago and Minneapolis – three times to Minneapolis, but not once to the address on Aveneda Juarez. Sergeant Ordonio was kind enough to include a hand-written note explaining that the population of Calexico was only about 13,500, but Mexicali directly across the border weighed in at nearly half a million and most of them wanted to be in Calexico. There are no iron fences in the desert, he wrote, not like in the city. We assume Portilla has crossed the border many times, was his conclusion… unchecked and unrecorded. He added that all the cities on Portilla's itinerary listed stops at colleges and universities, leading him to believe F.L. Gutzman was selling a lot of hand-painted decorative bathroom tiles to mid-America's institutions of higher learning. Sharp deduction.

"But there's nothing in that file to show a solid connection between Portilla and Vollmer." Mel Swanson pointed the squad up the hill toward the professor's summer home and I settled back enjoying the drive. "All pretty circumstantial."

"True enough, but Vollmer doesn't know that." I was looking out the window at the passing pine trees and rock formations, we were only a few miles from Vollmer's home and we hadn't bothered to call ahead. I figured I'd take my chances not finding him home rather that tip him off by telling him I had a few more questions. Vollmer wasn't real happy answering the first batch and he sure as hell wasn't going to like the second. "If we act like we have something concrete that links the two of them, we might get lucky and Vollmer'll crack right away and save us all some time."

"So you really figure Portilla had connections in all those cities and he was selling pretty tiles to some people while dealing illegal antiquities on the side."

"Melvin, my man, F.L. Gutzman's files are going to show Sparky made all sorts of contacts in all those cities. But the only place the universities are going to show up are in the parole officer's file, because he would be the only man watching Sparky that close."

"Is there that big a market for hot idols?"

"Who knows what he was delivering? I asked Lisbeth Ann to check the colleges in those towns to see if there are any more Vollmers out there. If that doesn't pan out, maybe Sparky was pushing Mexican Red on campus between calls on tile dealers." I didn't like that scenario as well as the first one, but Portilla was a multi-talented crook and after all a peso is a peso. I also didn't like pulling Mel away from town on the day his wife and new baby were coming home from the hospital. But look at it this way, two cops are better than one when you're trying to make an impression. It was early and with any luck I'd have Mel back in town shortly after lunch and give him the weekend off. Not that I have such a big heart, but with Voyageur Days looming in the near distance, time off wasn't much of an option.

I knew I was pulling on the Portilla-Vollmer connection, but I'm always suspicious of coincidence. I mean, after all one's a collector, the other is a supplier, so what's the big mystery? It was a good hunch. The idea had merit. It wouldn't do for a court order, but hardly anything did these days. And then there was the body. I just knew it had been left to be found, ditto for the victim's clothing. On the other hand, the professor was an expert in things Pre-Columbian, not an expert killer, so maybe he was clumsy that way.

Vollmer had an old beater station wagon that he kept parked at the airport to ferry himself back and forth when he wasn't flying down to the Twin Cities. He wasn't exactly a fixture in the local community, where people identify you by the vehicle you drive. I doubted many people would be familiar with Vollmer's mode of transportation. The airfield employees would recognize the wagon driving in and out and so would the owners of the small general store-laundromat-gas station on the trail above Vollmer's house, but that would be about it.

My chief suspect was finishing his breakfast on the deck and watching us approach over a cup of coffee. He was cordial and curious. He offered us café con leche, explaining in most Latin American countries they drink a stronger brew than in the US and generally start the day with a fifty-fifty mix of milk and coffee. As the day progresses, the milk decreases until the drink is straight up at supper. He didn't tell us how these people managed to get to sleep at night with all that caffeine knocking around in their systems.

"I'll get right to the point, Dr. Vollmer. I think I have reason to be disappointed in our conversation of the other day."

"Oh, how so?"

"How well do you know a Jorge Ricardo Ponce y Cuevas-Portilla?" Mel's Spanish was about as good as mine. We both did well on the 'ee' sound of the double 'l' in Portilla.

I can't say that Vollmer was floored by that question. He wasn't having any show of feelings for us. I guessed he was a man used to being put on the spot by smart-ass grad students whose major recreation was trying to trip up their professors. This left a look of implacability all over his face.

"So the man in the barn was Sparky Portilla."

"Seems so. Dental records will confirm it." I had to remember to ask Eddie Loetz to request those records as well as get a list of next of kin from Sergeant Ordonio.

"Sparky Portilla, as you no doubt already know, was in the import/export business…painted tiles, I believe." He poured himself the coffee I'd declined and he didn't add much milk.

"Portilla exported more than hand painted tiles. We have reason to believe he was relieving certain Mexican citizens of their family treasures, probably in payment for a shot at crossing the border. We think he then, quote, 'exported', unquote, those objects to buyers in the States."

"You mean collectors, experts or appreciators of Pre-Columbian culture. You mean people like me."

"We're not accusing you of anything," Mel was always handy to have along at questionings because he remembered the little details I was apt to forget – like badgering the witness and reading them the Miranda warning.

"I'm not so sure of that, officer, but I freely admit to having known Sparky Portilla. In fact, he was well known to several of us who are interested in Meso-American art."

"He's also known to the Calexico police, Customs and the Feds as a sleazeball smuggler, among other things. He has a rap sheet a mile long and a record of university stops all across the Mid-West – Denver, St. Louis, Des Moines, Chicago and Minneapolis. Does that last one include you, Professor?"

"I'm not aware of a collector in Des Moines, but the other cities would be correct. There have been times in the past, yes, when I collected with a bit more avidity than I perhaps should have. That is to say, it may not have been perfectly clear whether or not the Mexican government would be upset with my owning a certain piece. Now, since I travel freely to that country to visit dig sites, there is no question of my dealing with a man like Portilla."

"But Portilla has visited here three times in the last fourteen months. Most recently in June and obviously again within the past few days."

"I shouldn't have thought Sparky was that concerned with documenting his whereabouts."

"Sparky wanted to stay out of prison, and letting his parole officer know his whereabouts was the reason – just like the court ordered."

"And you think I'm one of these 'whereabouts?'"

"If you were in Minneapolis at those times, I'd say it was a pretty good bet. That's why I'm disappointed in our last conversation. I think you knew there was a good chance the man in the barn was Portilla."

"Are you accusing me of killing Portilla?" Vollmer's Teflon was rusting. He set down his coffee cup a little too hard on the glass-top deck table and pushed away his wrought iron chair.

"No, I'm not. Right now all I'm saying is that you were less than forthcoming with me Wednesday." He rose from his chair and took a step closer to me. He was a tall man on the thin side and in his early fifties, quite athletic looking and poised on his feet.

"I'll tell you one or two more things, Chief, and then I'm afraid you'll have to talk to me through my attorney. You never asked me anything directly about that body on Wednesday. You said you wanted to know about Aztec sacrifice and the ritual of flaying. Frankly, my first thought when you told me of the way the man was killed, was that someone was trying to set me up."

"You told me you thought whoever did it was performing a kind of sacrifice."

"I have my ass to cover, too, Chief. I also told you one of my obsidian knives was missing. I needed some time to see if someone was playing a bizarre joke. The flayed man could have been some drunk who died from his own stupidity and then the whole sacrifice drummed up to discredit me."

"If that's true, you have some awfully rough friends or some very nasty enemies," Mel weighed in on the confrontation.

"Do you have enemies like that, Professor?" His threat of calling in an attorney was pushing me to the line, which would either work or queer the beer. "Enemies who would find a drunk who died of alcohol poisoning, or fell down a flight of stairs, drive him up here to Cache Harbor, skin and gut him just to make a point?"

"No! Of course not!" Vollmer flailed his arms around and paced the deck as he talked. His coffee was long cold. He was at a loss to find a good reason outside of himself that explained the flayed man in the old Palmer barn. Everything was pointing his direction. "What I mean is, I don't think so. I can't imagine why or who would do such a thing." I could see he was wondering if indeed he did have those kinds of enemies and would they come looking to do an appendectomy on him. "But I did not do that, that killing. Portilla."

"When was the last time you saw Portilla?" Mel again going for the facts. Vollmer had apparently forgot about his attorney, which was fine with me. I don't generally like getting people upset but when getting them upset gets me someplace, that's another matter. We were getting someplace.

"All right. I saw him in June. You know he was in the Cities." Vollmer sagged a little and sat back down. "He tried to sell me an inconsequential idol of Olmec origin. I knew right away it was contraband. I declined and I believe his other collectors had, too. Then last week – Friday, it was – he got in contact with me again. This time he had an exquisite piece of Toltec feather work. I knew something similar was in the possession of a collector in Denver. At first I thought there was no question of its being contraband or even stolen. Feather work from this particular period cannot survive without special treatment and I wasn't aware of anyone de-accessing their collection. On the off chance it might be legitimate, however, I wanted to check my catalogs and records, but they are all kept here when I'm not at the University. He told me he had some contacts he needed to make for his export firm and would be around for a couple of days. I flew up here Saturday morning and determined that the piece was indeed legitimate and available. I flew back to Minneapolis Monday morning, but Portilla never called me. I was disappointed, however I doubt I could have afforded the piece. After waiting I came back here Tuesday evening. I believe they can substantiate that at the airport."

"Portilla was killed Tuesday night, Wednesday morning," Facts from Mel.

"Gentlemen, I'm not creating an alibi, I'm simply telling you what happened. There are people who can verify I was in my office, there are people who can tell you when I flew in and out of here. There are even people who can probably tell you that I bought milk or bread or something at the Trading Post store up the road." He was gaining his confidence back again and I could sense he was ready to play the call-my-attorney card. "But I doubt anyone can confirm any of our whereabouts – including yours – late Tuesday night or early Wednesday morning. That's when people are usually asleep." Sure enough, he stood up, collected his coffee cup, placed it on a lacquered tray and prepared to leave the deck. "I really cannot say anything more. If you persist in this questioning, I'll have to call my attorney."

"One more thing, Professor." He scowled but stopped. "What was the feather work worth?"

"In my opinion objects like that are priceless. I can't imagine why Robbie Perrine wanted to sell it and why he wanted to deal through Portilla. Robbie is the Denver collector. It was suggested he would need something into five figures, but never specified an exact amount. That was one of the things we obviously would have discussed had he gotten back to me Monday. Now if you'll excuse me I have to pack."

"Are you leaving the area?" Mel nailing down the facts.

"I have a lecture at the University this evening. Am I not allowed to leave?"

"Not at all. We'd just like to know where you'll be if we need to ask any more questions."

"Any further questions will have to go through my..."

"Or add anything to your allegations that someone might be trying to purposely link you to a crime where no link exists."

Applause, applause for Mel. He handled that very well. Vollmer told us he'd be back the next morning, Saturday, for what he hoped would be an extended time of relaxation before going to the University for fall quarter classes. He wished us luck in finding Portilla's killer, maintained again it was not he, no matter what we thought. I wasn't thinking much in that direction, only that when it comes to possessing valuable stuff, some people no matter how much 'Kultcha' they have can get down in the ditches with the rest of us.

We stopped outside of town at Cache Harbor Municipal Airport to check Vollmer's story at this end. The field manager told me a young mechanic named Larry Biederman had been on duty over last weekend and might be able to confirm when Vollmer flew in and out of Cache Harbor. Mel re-checked the passenger manifests I'd looked over earlier, while I talked to the mechanic. Biederman confirmed that Vollmer arrived in Cache Harbor last Saturday morning and that he flew out Monday morning. He hadn't worked Tuesday night so he couldn't say when the professor returned and there didn't seem to be any written record of it.

"You're pretty sure of Saturday and Monday, though."

"Oh, sure. I remember they flew in Saturday."

"They?"

"Oh, sure. The professor lotsa times brings students up for the weekend."

"How many?"

"You mean how many times does he bring up students?"

"No, how many on Saturday."

"Oh, sure. Lemmie see. I guess a couple. Maybe."

"But you're not certain."

Biederman shook his head. "One or two, probably.

"What about Monday? Did they leave together?"

"Oh, sure, but like I said, I saw them fly out but I didn't see Professor Vollmer exactly or the others either. I just saw the plane leave."

"But you didn't do a head count."

"No."

"Anybody else around who I might talk to about this?"

"Oh, sure, probably Teddy."

"Teddy."

"He's the ground crew for Quetico Charters, those two rigs in the south hangar. They usually do business with fishermen."

"Know where I can find him?"

"He flies in out of Kenora usually for the weekend."

"That's Canada."

"Oh, sure. I know. He'll likely be here today sometime."

"Will you have him call me soon as he lands?"

"Oh, sure."

I found Mel in the office. Vollmer had filed a flight plan for last Monday, but no one was in the office when he did it, and even if there had been, chances are the others, if there were others, would not have filed it with him. One more little conversational oversight on the part of the good professor.

I asked the airfield manager to call me when Vollmer flew off to his lecture and to have Teddy call me when he flew in for a weekend's work. Covering my ass was what Vollmer called it. The man was more Teflon than

I was giving him credit for. Now he had company over the weekend – maybe. I can't say Biederman was a great lot of help, just enough to confuse the issue. Vollmer often brought students up for the weekend, so Biederman assumed he did last weekend as well. They always left together, so Biederman assumed they did this time, too. But do you think Vollmer would offer that piece of news on his own? The professor was getting under my skin. I'd like to ground him, just to give him a lecture of my own. That is, if the weather didn't ground him first. Clouds were roiling in from the east and it smelled like a summer thunderstorm in the making. Then there was always this Teddy person from Kenora.

"What do you suppose Vollmer and his students do on all these weekend jaunts?" Mel pointed the squad out of the airfield parking lot as fat rain drops started hitting the windshield.

"Drink and fuck." Well?

Chapter Ten

By the time Mel dropped me at the office, the rain was getting serious and so was the thunder. The tourists would be sitting on their balconies looking at the lightning display over the east bay and sipping something tall and cool to drive away the humidity. The campers in the Boundary Waters would be huddling in their tents, sopping up leaks with dirty clothes from their stuff sacks. I sent Mel on his way. It was time to bring home Judy and Shelly from the hospital; time to start a new phase in their lives. If love and luck were on their side, they'd survive in a day and age where most marriages are measured in years not decades and there aren't the silver anniversaries there used to be. I guess I was wondering if I'd survive marriage and a family, knowing it was getting close to too late to find out.

Waiting for me in my office was the morning mail, the recorded messages, a styrofoam lunch pod and Reefer Carlson.

"You weren't at breakfast this morning and now it's damn near past lunchtime. You off your feed?"

"Busy." I looked over the mail Reefer had picked up for me at the Post Office. I'd decided early on after waking up I'd do breakfast at home. I was just not up to facing Marie over eggs sunny side up. I'd had an incredible opportunity to spend what could have been hours making love to a fresh and willing young girl half my age, and I didn't do it. What's more I wasn't going to tell Reefer about it. When I left Marie's bikini at her doorstep, I figured I was turning down the opportunity for at least two good reasons. The first was Lisbeth Ann, whom I truly cared for, and the second was getting involved with a twenty year old. I mean, how wide was that gap going to get after the initial roll in the hay?

By the time I'd watched the two movies I'd rented, eaten all the cold pizza in the house and had three stiff drinks, I wasn't buying those two good reasons anymore. I blew the chance of a lifetime. Shit! Forty-year-old men hardly ever have twenty-year-old girls practically drag them off the beach and force them into sex.

With echoes of 'you're a stupid dickhead, Tharp' ringing in my ears, I finally went to sleep. When I woke up I'd had yet another change of heart. This time I had no idea at all how I felt about what was becoming known in my head as 'the Marie problem'. Rather than confusing the situation further by stupidly staring at her over breakfast, not to mention listening to Reefer's usual comments about her buttons, I chose to start the day with cold cereal. That's never enough for me, so now I was staring down at a white pod on my desk with both ends of the guest check taped to the lid. I guessed right away this was not a list of charges for what was inside the pod. She'd brought me a note with lunch and I was not feeling comfortable about reading it. I looked over at Reefer who had his feet up on the corner of my desk, reading the Duluth newspaper.

"It was there when I got here." He looked at me over the comics page. "Marie must have brought it over for you. I don't think she does that for just anybody." He folded the newspaper and waited for a reaction. I opened the pod and took off the guest check. "I didn't come over here just to watch you eat, ya know. I came to snoop."

"I figured that. What do you want to know?" *(Dear Paul – please forgive my forwardness yesterday. I'd still like to get to know you. Can we begin over again? Marie)*

"Oh no. You'll just answer the questions I ask. If I ask the wrong questions or fail to ask the right ones, I'm the worse off for it. I've been around the block with you before."

"Ask Valerie star reporter. She knows all, sees all and will probably tell all in next week's paper." Marie knew my favorite lunch was a grilled cheese sandwich.

"Talking to her like you did gave her a helluva lift."

"But did it help your love life?"

"That too."

"Tell me something, and I'm perfectly serious about this. Do you two screw as much as you say you do?"

"More."

"Be serious. I'm not prying, I just want to know if I'm somewhere in the normal sex life ballpark."

"Who says we're normal. Normal people do it maybe twice a month."

"And you do it twice a day, or is it twice an hour?"

"Paul, your sex life sucks air. You know it. I know it. Lisbeth Ann is a nice lady, but she's going through the just-divorced stage. On the other hand you've got a terrific little number who would like to get all over you like ants on candy, and you won't give her the time of day."

"That doesn't answer my question."

"No, we don't do it as often as I make out, but if you tell anyone, I'll break your kneecaps. I want everyone to think my losing Blanche was the best thing ever happened to me...especially Blanche. Pisses me off. There. That's the truth and I hope you're satisfied."

"I'm gratified you told me. Maybe I can be as honest with you some time."

I finished off my sandwich and thumbed through the Calexico file. I pulled out a couple of sheets and handed the rest of the folder to Reefer. "I promised this to Valerie. Have her make copies of what she wants and get the originals back to me ASAP."

"So tell me more."

"Like how much is off the record?"

"Tell me as we go along."

I walked over to the coffee maker in the corner next to what passed for Mel's desk. It wasn't much of a desk, just a folding table from the courthouse basement, but the chair was as nice as mine, with good casters and a comfortable seat. I scooped out some coffee and turned on the pot.

"For the record, Valerie has most of that already. Add to it what's in that file and presto! That's it. Portilla was a crook, but a careful one. He told his parole officer when he was leaving town and where he was going. He was probably offering five or six collectors smuggled ancient Mexican artifacts. One of those contacts was in the Twin Cities and we are checking on any possible connection at this time. The matter remains under investigation and Chief Tharp reports no arrests have been made."

"Now, what's off the record?"

"A lot of circumstantial stuff that can't be printed. Mel and I made another call on Professor Doyle Vollmer at his elegant summer home up the trail. He's had dealings with Portilla in the past, and had one pending as recently as a week ago. Portilla shows up with a Pre-Columbian bauble on Friday and asks for a load of money. Unlike a previous visit in June, Vollmer figures this time the goods are legit."

"So they've seen each other twice this year."

"Right, but here's where things start to go astray. Vollmer hops in his four passenger on Saturday and flies up here to check authenticity records, then pops back down to Minneapolis on Monday, satisfied the goods are good. But no Portilla, so Vollmer flies back up here on Tuesday evening."

"That's when Portilla was killed."

"Or early Wednesday."

"The ME's reports aren't always to the minute."

"True, but Vollmer may have had company interfering with that scenario. A mechanic at the muni field thinks Vollmer had students up visiting, but that's yet to be verified."

"Maybe Vollmer took the kids home on Monday and flew his smuggler buddy up here Tuesday, got into an argument over the price of that bauble and bumped him off."

"Possible. That's a lotta flying around, coincidence and circumstance. Vollmer has no alibi for Tuesday or Wednesday, but it seems funny he'd go to all the trouble to cover his tracks and then not have an iron clad for the night of the murder."

"Therein lies the conundrum."

"I thought that was another word for a rubber."

"I didn't hear that."

"Anyway, Vollmer has a different take on this. He thinks there's a strong possibility someone is trying to set him up, or point clues in his direction."

"C'mon, you mean someone went to the trouble of killing and skinning Portilla just to pin the rap on Vollmer?"

"I'm just telling what he said. I know it sounds far-fetched, and he can't come up with any names, but it's not exactly out of the question."

"You mean like other collectors. I suppose if he was dealing with a guy like Portilla, he could have beat out some collector in Pittsburgh, who then got pissed at them both, kills Portilla and makes it look like Vollmer did it."

"We're checking on it."

"Are these collectors that vicious?"

"I don't know, but I've heard archeology is filled with double dealers and other nasty folks."

"In the meantime, what's with Vollmer?"

"He says he has a lecture obligation scheduled for this evening at the University. He was going to fly down, return tomorrow and then stick around here for the rest of the summer."

"In this rain?"

"That's what he says."

"So you wait around here while your only suspect flies around the countryside. Isn't that a little risky?"

"I haven't anything I can use to detain him. He'd just scream for his attorney and be outta here in an hour."

"So you're banking on him showing up back here tomorrow night."

"Gotta have faith." The phone interrupted us. It was the airfield manager. The rain had let up some and Doyle Vollmer flew out just a few minutes ago. I guessed this was where the faith kicked in.

After Reefer left, I cleaned off my desk and dumped out the untouched coffee. I wanted to stop at the FoodCity store to speak with the manager about two youngsters suspected of shoplifting. Part of cleaning off my desk was sending a wire to F.L. Gutzman, S.A. in Mexico City: 'Regret to inform you, sales representative Jorge Cuevas-Portilla died here under suspicious circumstances Wednesday, August 12. Death under investigation. Would appreciate details of recent sales reports victim may have filed with your office over past eight months. Contact this office or Calexico CA USA police.' Another part of cleaning off my desk was leaving a message for Sergeant Ordonio to forward a list of next of kin and to be on the watch for a possible response from F.L. Gutzman.

I knew the two juveniles the FoodCity manager suspected of lifting cans of Franks N Beans and Mini Ravioli. I agreed they were little bastards and would bring it up to them the next time I saw them skateboarding illegally on the sidewalks downtown. In the meantime I advised the manager to keep his eyes open and collar them for prosecution if he caught them lifting again. Then I drove over to the library.

Mertha the library aide was short and dumpy and always smirked when I came to visit Lisbeth Ann, as if I couldn't be there to check out a book or anything. This afternoon Mertha was in the Kiddie Korner trying to keep a second grader from winding out eight million feet of tape from an audio cassette of Winnie the Pooh stories. The kid was bored with summer. Lisbeth Ann was in her office and I slipped in unnoticed by the suspicious Mertha. One long look at Lisbeth Ann further confused my feelings about women – the feeling I had about the one in my life and the one trying to get into my life. Lisbeth Ann smiled at me; her blond hair was drawn back from her face and fixed at the nape of her neck with a black bow. She wore small pearl earring posts and only a suggestion of makeup. Her eyebrows were pale brown and flattened over blue eyes. Straight nose, sculptured upper lip, full lower, broad cheekbones and a smallish chin. She looked fresh as first thing this morning in crisp monogrammed blouse and full blue skirt tied at the waist with a blue and white sash. She told me she had what I wanted and I agreed. She smiled at my double entendre.

What she had was a list of Pre-Columbian experts. There was only one known collector that fit the description in each of four cities regularly visited by Portilla. They were all employed by large universities. Vollmer had been right; no collector in Des Moines, so Portilla had other business in that city. I looked over the list of names and addresses and made special note of Robbie Perrine in Denver, the man with the valuable feather piece. I'd call him first. I wanted all of their opinions on the smuggler from Calexico and on Vollmer, if they knew him.

"Listen, I have a Library Friends meeting tonight at seven; why don't you drop by the house around ten and we can have a nightcap."

"And spend three hours talking about the flayed man?"

"I promise not to."

"Thanks, but I'm bad company; it's the only thing I'm thinking about. I'm just not sure I'm doing the right thing with Vollmer."

"What about him?"

"Well, frankly he's a suspect...the only one I have and not a very good one at that. I've kinda let him out on a string now, and if the string breaks and he flies the coop, I could end up mopping out latrines at the bus depot."

"Maybe two nightcaps?"

Right then I was sure I'd made a good decision leaving Marie's bikini and beach towel at her door. Three hours later when I answered the door at my own cabin, I wasn't as certain. Marie stood outside in the pouring rain; a small umbrella shielded her black hair from the steady downpour. Her graybrown eyes shone in the reflected light from my living room lamp.

"Will you be in for breakfast tomorrow?" She asked it as if it was the most serious question posed all week.

"Sure." My mouth went dry and I struggled with the words to ask her in from the rain, but they never came out.

"Great. I'll see you then." She smiled and turned away into the streaks of silver rain tearing against the black August night.

And the telephone rang. It was the municipal airfield.

"Chief Tharp? This is Teddy LaFavre. From Quetico Charters? Larry Biederman said you wanted to talk to me. Yeah, he kinda filled me in. Sorry it took so long to get back to you, the rain kinda slowed things down. Well, anyway me and Larry was talking here a minute ago and I think maybe he was thinking of some other time. I mean about them students flying in with that Vollmer? Yeah, he flew up with students a lot, for sure, but the time you were talking about? Yeah, last weekend, well, we...Larry thinks this way now, too since we discussed it and all... we don't think there was kids with that Vollmer. The guy was too old for that. Yeah, one guy kinda stocky and dark. Oh, I seen him before for sure. Come to think of it maybe back in June. Slick Indian lookin' fella he was. Yeah, anyways it was him with that Vollmer on Saturday. I got a better look than Larry did. He was in the hangar and I was workin' outside on a prop. It was that dark fella all right. Remembered him from earlier on. Wore lizzardy cowboy boots, pointy toes and them under slung heels, not dogger boots for sure. Yeah, but I don't recall seein' him leave when that Vollmer flew out on Monday. I normally don't stay over Mondays, but I had a gummed carb on the one Cessna. I'm pretty sure that Vollmer flew out Monday by hisself. Larry, he don't remember, but I'd remember all right. Yeah, I'd remember them fine lizzardy boots, I would."

Chapter Eleven

Even though it had rained most of the afternoon and evening, it was still August hot outside. The windows in Lisbeth Ann's little house were open and I could hear the rain finally letting up. I guessed it was about one-thirty in the morning, but I couldn't move my arm to check the time on my wrist. She had fallen asleep in my arms and was resting quietly, softly in the envelope of receding rain sounds and my own warm body. Our lovemaking had been urgent again; Lisbeth Ann had presented a budget to the Library Friends and the going had been tense. Give volunteers with limited knowledge but limitless interest an opportunity to run things and likely they'll run them into the ground. The dumbest thing any American President ever said was George Bush's comment on the nation needing a thousand points of light. The points of light I needed came when Lisbeth Ann and I came together. Still, there was the jolting image of Marie standing at my door in the savage silver rain. Still, there was the image of that sheared lump of twisted bone and muscle that was once a person, no matter what kind. So, did I fuck up with Vollmer? Did I let out too much string? Was he right this minute flying to South America to escape prosecution? Why did that illiterate Canadian call me long after Vollmer flew out? Where the hell was my luck going, down the storm sewer with the rain? So all the heat, all the passion, all the panty-pulling, nipple sucking, thrusting and release still amounted to this: Sparky Portilla was imprinted to the insides of my eyelids, bright red with blue veins and so was Marie Craske imprinted naked in the shower, as if I really knew what that would look like.

Now here we were, images of the flayed man dancing through my mind, red and blue tendoned mass slowly shifting shape into a stocky square Mexican, shifting again to the blond pliant women in my arms, shifting again to the black-haired young woman with the soft smile molded on her lips, robed body standing easy in the cabin door. The images continued to scroll through my mind until I finally drifted off into a short, fitful sleep. It was three o'clock when I finally awoke. The rain had stopped and I slipped silently from Lisbeth Ann's bed and covered her with a light blanket before I left. I doused the light and checked to be sure the door would lock behind me. Most people in Cache Harbor never bothered to lock their doors, whether they were inside or not; but perhaps there were people afoot in the night with motives for harm I could not understand. I wanted her to be as secure as if she were still in my arms.

Starting the truck, I supposed there would be talk about the policeman and the librarian and how I never went home Friday nights and left her house God-knows-when early Saturday morning. I pulled out of her driveway; the neighbors can suck a fart for all I care. Within a half hour I was washed and asleep.

By the time the Japanese alarm on my wristwatch stopped playing three morning choruses of Beethoven's "Fur Elise" managing to wake me from an exhausted sleep, Barnie Droogsma and Tim Sievertson had been on South Apple Branch Lake fishing muskies for at least half an hour. By the time I scuffled into the bathroom to take a leak and brush my teeth, Barnie had hooked on to something that wasn't a thirty pounder and it wasn't a log or a rock either. They had been fishing in close to shore where the big cabbage floated and the fish liked to be early in the day. By the time I'd finished washing my face and combing back my hair, Tim was reaching along Barnie's twenty pound test monofilament trying to grab hold of the eight inch Pikey Minnow lure that had dug its treble hooks into something on the bottom. By the time I'd finished shaving and slipped on a clean uniform shirt before walking out the door for breakfast, Barnie Droogsma and Tim Sievertson had discovered what the muskie lure had caught.

"Godfuckindamnsonofabitch if I'm not going to give up eating breakfast altogether. Every time I try to eat something, somebody finds another goddamn body and feels compelled to tell me about it." I pounded my fists on Deputy Dog's dashboard and finally settled back in his squad as we raced north up the trail. Well, I was pissed. I had enough on my plate.

"Fuckin-A, man. I do you a favor and all you do is bitch." Dogget flipped on his siren as he drove through a construction zone. The highway department was working Saturdays to get a big, messy job done before the snow flew. A second squad was also speeding toward the public landing on South Apple Branch Lake, and Sheriff Ash Tucker was already there at the scene. Tucker liked to have me around when there was a major crime, probably because I had as much deputy time in as any of his staff. Also I knew he was bucking to have me join his crew and dump the Chief's job. Every time there was an opening he'd call and every time we failed to come to an agreement. Maybe if Dog left number two, but that was unlikely as long as Ash kept winning elections.

"Ya know, Dog, I have enough to do in the city without chasing after a body in a plastic bag. It's outta my jurisdiction."

"That's what you've got Melvin for and besides this body is in two bags, not one." Dogget pulled his screaming, flashing squad into the US Forest Service public access road doing at least fifty. He slammed on the brakes behind the Sheriff's car and gave Ruthie his ten-twenty at the scene. When I baled out of the squad, I saw Ash and three other deputies huddling over Barnie Droogsma, Tim Sievertson and the two heavy duty silver plastic trash bags that had been tied together with twine and attached to a boat anchor.

Sievertson was telling a deputy how they snagged the bags, while Droogsma was looking sick to his stomach. Dogget and I walked over to a grassy area where the deputies had removed the trash bags from the body. It was hard to tell her age, but she was unclothed, had reddish hair and was maybe somewhere in her twenties. Her body had been cut in half above the pelvic girdle and each part had been stuffed into a trash bag. The bags had then been fastened together around a small boat anchor and dumped into South Apple Branch Lake. There had been some damage done by turtles or fish, but by the looks of it, I'd guessed she hadn't been dead long.

"Cold water kept her pretty good." Dogget leaned over her face and tried to remember if he'd seen her before. "Anybody know who she is? Seen her before?" The deputies responded with a headshake 'no'. "She musta blown in to shallow water after that last storm we had. That's probably when the bags tore and the little fishies got in there with her."

"You seen her before, Paul?" Ash stood at my side, fat, old and sweaty.

He couldn't keep up this work for that much longer, not in his condition. I shook my head 'no'. "I know you're busy with that butcher job at Palmer's but I asked Dog to drive you up here to see if there was any possible physical connection between your murder and this one. Usually folks go off and shoot their wives or boyfriends. Nice clean .38 to the head. Two killings like these ain't natural. Makes you think some guy's out there with a butcher knife practicing for meat cutting school."

I remembered when I was a kid reading the ads in the back of Popular Mechanics: 'Learn meat cutting and earn big money.' I walked around the severed body trying to make the connection Ash had suggested. The flesh at the cut was ragged and white like the underbelly of a dead fish. Her legs were cocked apart and there was very little pubic hair between them. Some flesh had been gnawed off the lower part of her left calf. I looked over at her head and trunk; the arms were folded across her breasts and appeared to be locked there. Her face was sallow and puffy, but she had been an attractive woman with short auburn hair and a nice mouth.

"I'd say she was cut in half because she wouldn't fit in one garbage bag. If someone wanted to cut out her heart like they did Portilla – that's my dead guy's name – they went about it wrong. They would have had to reach all the way up through her intestines when it would have been easier to cut at the breast bone."

"Jesus Christ, you guys." Barnie Droogsma was choking back his breakfast. "Can't you shut up about her and put her back in those bags… you're makin' me puke." Ash signaled a deputy to move Barnie away from the body, something the young deputy was more than willing to do.

"There's a little brandy in my glove compartment," Ash motioned toward his squad. "See if that'll fix him up. I'll need to question him later and I don't want barf all over my office."

"Eddie Loetz said it isn't easy to remove a heart, so I'd guess any dummy who wanted to would figure out a better way than go through the stomach and everything. I guess I'd wait for the autopsy to be sure, but unless the heart is missing – and I don't see how it could be – there doesn't seem to be any connection on the surface other than the one you mentioned."

"What did I mention?" Ash squinted at me against the morning sun.

"Meat cutting."

On the way back down the hill, Dog and I met the ambulance speeding Dr. Ed Loetz, coroner, to the South Apple Branch scene.

"Eddie'll have fun with that one." Dogget sucked on a breath mint. "That makes two in less than a week. Jesus! I just can't see how them Docs can dig around in dead people, especially after they've been dead for a while. Makes my backbone chilly, Pauly."

Before I could agree, the county dispatcher broke in with a message for One Zebra One. Dr. Doyle Vollmer just landed at the Cache Harbor Municipal Airport. Shit! I'd gambled and won that round. Vollmer was no runner which meant either he was innocent – and there went my only suspect – or he was way too confident, and that made me mad. I hate being underestimated.

"Keep pluggin' away, Pauly. There are damn few professional killers in the world and those who aren't can't live long with the knowledge of what they done. Something will turn up, just like something will turn up with that two-part Jane Doe."

"Was Ash just dying for my expert opinion or is he banking on the two murders being connected?"

"Well, you've got to admit they got a certain brutality about them that makes 'em stand out."

"So if they're connected, then it's finders keepers. I get them both because I caught the first squeal."

"Ash is funny that way. He likes continuity."

"He's lazy."

"That, too."

Dogget said something would turn up. What turned up was a phone message on my office machine from attorney J. Bently Prudhomme representing Dr. Doyle R. Vollmer and would the Chief kindly ask no more questions of his esteemed client without Mr. Prudhomme in attendance. I wrote down the number, dialed and decided to follow Dogget's other advice, 'keep plugging.' Vollmer was my only suspect, so in the words of Bruce Springsteen, 'no retreat, baby, no surrender.'

OK fuckhead, get your hundred dollar an hour butt up here because I've got a witness who saw double last Saturday, had single vision on Monday and identified the dead man on Friday late afternoon. And while we're at it, what if the two-part Jane Doe turns out to be a University student, as Sheriff Ash Tucker so fervently hopes?

"Law offices of Butler, Buchanan, Fielding, Schloss and Prudhomme."

"J. Bently Prudhomme, please."

"I'm sorry, sir, the attorneys are not in on Saturdays; we're open for messages only. If you'd care to call back Monday…"

"That won't be necessary, Ma'am. Just tell Mr. Prudhomme that Chief of Police Paul Tharp called from Cache Harbor and requests the presence of his fat ass together with that of his client Dr. Doyle Vollmer in my office by 11AM Monday morning or he'll have to bail out the good professor on Wednesday. Got that?"

"Yes sir, I'll see Mr. Prudhomme gets the message."

"Thank you. You have a nice day now."

Chapter Twelve

"That's really gross!"

"It's horrible, Honey. I can't imagine such a thing."

I was glad to see Valerie was calling Reefer 'honey' again. It probably meant things were back on track between the two of them.

"And you don't think they're connected?" Reefer looked at me as he ordered more coffee. It was well after lunch and after the three o'clock coffee klatch, but before the Saturday rush of tourists dragging in their hungry kids for obscenely large orders of glopped-up burgers and baskets of salty fries. We sat in a booth, Valerie, Reefer and me. Mel was making one last sweep around town before going home to his wife and baby. I was due to stay on until eleven or so and then call it quits. The only on-sale liquor license belonged to Tubb's Pine Inn, and that rarely posed a problem. Mel Swanson lived just a quarter mile from Tubb's, so it was his regular beat.

"Right now there doesn't seem to be any connection." I sipped my hot coffee. "Of course that doesn't mean there isn't one we can't see."

"But she was cut in half and the Mexican was also cut up." Valerie made a face at the thought. "At least there's that connection. How was the woman killed?"

"Don't know. When Eddie has the autopsy, you'll know what we know. I'm just glad this one belongs to the sheriff." I didn't half believe that. If there was a will there was a way for Ash Tucker to dump them both in my lap.

"I'll bet he's pissed off at that." Reefer looked up as Marie brought more coffee. When she finished pouring, she slipped into the booth next to me.

"How come you're still around?"

"Karen's sick again."

"What's with Karen? She doesn't need the money?"

"Promise you won't tell? I think Karen's pregnant."

"Hot scoop! Hot scoop!" Reefer rummaged around in Valerie's purse and pulled out her notebook. "Write this down."

"Ha, ha, ha, boss. The kid is seventeen and runs with a dropout who lives under his street rod seven hours a day and drinks beer the rest of the time. That is not a story, but it is a tragedy."

"Were you guys just talking about the woman they found on South Apple Branch?" Marie glanced around the café to see if she was needed, but there were only two other people in the place and they were regulars who drank coffee at the counter. If they ran out, they were accustomed to getting up, going behind the counter and pouring their own. Nevertheless, they always left quarter tips. "I heard it was like the other murder."

"Nope." I finished my coffee but Marie hurried to fill it again, partly out of habit, mostly because she didn't want me to leave. "Knives are the only things they have in common."

"You should hear the gossip going around this place. People are saying there's a madman loose in the woods, that a drug ring is using this place to dump their bodies, that it's the work of a motorcycle gang...just all kinds of stuff."

"Have they gotten around to creatures from outer space?" Reefer nudged Valerie. It was time to go back to work.

"One man said laser beams could cut a person in half with no trouble at all, and that the sheriff should be looking at the high school where Mr. Paulsen has three lasers in the science room."

Valerie stood up and straightened her suit. "Mr. Paulsen is also the football coach and he didn't win a game last year. That doesn't mean he's a mass murderer."

"Cut the mass murder talk." I for one felt Valerie was way too prone toward that theory for her own good.

"For what it's worth, Paul, I tend to go along with some of the gossip Marie's been hearing. Don't discount the possibility of the weirdo in the woods. The police over in Wisconsin did that for a long time until they found Ed Gein."

I watched Valerie and Reefer leave the café. I turned to Marie. "Ya know what's gonna happen don't you?" Marie just widened her eyes at the question. "That lady is going to print a story next week that's going to be filled with wild allegations and connections about crazies in the woods practicing some kind of ancient barbaric religion on unsuspecting victims. Buried between the shockers will be a few facts. I think I was dumb to give her as much information as I have."

"There is something...I don't know, basically terrifying about knives. I'll bet when people stop to think about it, the idea of being cut or carved up is about as awful a death as there is." Marie shuddered at the thought and kept looking down at my dirty dishes.

"Easy." I reached over and patted her wrist. She curled her hand around and held on to mine. "These people weren't killed that way. They were killed, sure, and that's terrible in itself. But they were cut up later and that's terrible, too. There's no evidence any of this was done while they were alive; that would be too terrible. I don't think things like that are done in real life. Just in the movies."

"I hope you're right, Paul, but you've read the stories, too. It's happened right by the University campus last quarter, not a half dozen blocks from where I was staying. Perfectly normal looking guy – bagger for a supermarket – killed this girl and cut her up and left her in the meat freezer. She wasn't his girlfriend or anything; he just liked her and saw her with another guy and flipped out. They said she was alive when he cut off her arms."

"C'mon, enough is enough of this kind of talk. Get everyone in town worked up. Believe me, nothing like that's going on here. We've got a pretty good idea of who killed the fella in Palmer's barn. It's just a matter of time before we break him down." I became aware that I was holding her hand as tightly as she was holding mine. "Nobody's out there slicing up the public."

"Is it Dr. Vollmer?"

"That's not supposed to be part of the rumor mill."

"It's not and it won't be. Not from me, it won't."

"You're a good guesser, but so far I'm only guessing too. Do you really want to know what I'm guessing?" I intended to change the subject at that point and tried to let go of Marie's hand. She held on lightly, but firm enough to require me to make a point of pulling away. I left my hand in hers. "I guess I'm going to forget about all those bodies tomorrow and go fishing. No work on Sunday," I made a move to leave.

"Take me along."

Well, I'd not been prepared for that request. In the millisecond it takes for the brain to search all the logical and banal answers stored there just for the purposes of verbal self-defense, not one seemed capable of coping with what Marie was asking. She would simply question the credibility of whatever I came up with. As I stared back at her dark eyes I realized there was only one reason why she should not go with me and that was the last thing I was willing to admit to now. If I used Lisbeth Ann to defend my fishing alone, I'd be committing myself beyond where I was willing to go. If I did go with Marie I'd probably screw up my relationship with Lisbeth Ann...and I didn't want that either. If I didn't want Marie to come along with me, I could always make up a story about joining some deputies going off on some beer party where fishing would coincidently take place. But I couldn't make that lie sound convincing to myself let alone, look at Marie in the eye and make it sound like anything other than sheer drivel.

"It's Lisbeth Ann, isn't it." She made it sound like a statement, not a question and I guess I just blinked back at her. "Are you afraid she might be jealous if we went fishing together?"

I looked down at my knuckles and uncoupled our hands. "It might be awkward. I mean she gets a little touchy about things."

"Because of her divorce?"

"Well, yes I suppose so."

"Does she think she has a bigger part of you than she really does?"

"That's a helluva question. How do I know?"

"You've made love."

I guess I snapped back my head and looked at her in a way neither of us suspected. She pulled back slightly at the quickness of my reaction. "That doesn't mean..."

"I know what it doesn't mean." She smiled and cleared away the coffee cups. "Where are you fishing tomorrow?"

"I thought I'd drive up to Bullpen." I searched my pocket for change.

"I always thought that was a funny name for a lake. Fishing has nothing to do with cattle or baseball." She wiped away some imaginary crumbs and shook out her long hair. "Maybe I'll see you there."

I guess I slammed my office door a little harder than usual and slammed my finger into the phone pad with a little more force than was needed to make the connection. The RN at the nurses' station told me Dr. Loetz was in surgery, but I knew they had specialists who did that kind of work on live people, so I suspected Eddie was still conducting the autopsy. I suggested that to the RN and there was a long silence before I heard the familiar voice of Deputy Dogget.

"You gotta need to know, Tharp?"

"I was there, remember? You forced me to go along."

"Fuckin-A." He laughed through his adenoids. "C'mon up. Eddie's really going to town on Jane Doe. She's all strung out and he'll be stitchin' her back together pretty soon."

I could imagine the reaction at the nurses' station. Dogget made no effort to keep his voice down. They had to put up with a lot, nurses. Mostly they put up with patients in various stages of hysteria and treating dead patients like slabs of meat was not an attitude they appreciated.

Mel had left me a list of phone calls to collectors Lisbeth Ann had located in the three other cities. Robbie Perrine, Denver. Call back. St. Louis. Call back. Chicago. Call back. All the numbers had been for their university offices. The world shut down on weekends.

I put a message on my answering machine and went around the office buttoning up for the rest of the day and Sunday. Mel would handle any important City business tomorrow, and of course, Ruthie always knew where I was. It was going to be a long week coming. Voyageur Days started on Thursday and that meant driving or standing around making the place look patrolled and secure. Impress the tourists, give aid and comfort to the locals who after twenty years or more of these celebrations, still mistrust the carneys and the hawkers and even the Bermuda shorted tourists themselves who seem to love to open their pockets and let the money drain all over town.

I'd be in and out of my squad for the rest of the afternoon and evening. It made life easier because I wouldn't have to deal either with Lisbeth Ann or free time. If I was home alone would I feel obligated to call or go out with her? Would we end up in bed together again? Did she want to see me this often? That way? Did I? We human beings use so many phrases with so many multiple layers of meaning to describe our interactions. I didn't really know whether or not Lisbeth Ann and I were going together, keeping company, were steadies, lovers or were just good friends who upon occasion would screw ourselves into exhaustion. Were we close? Were we intimate? Were we in love? No, Marie was right about that; all of the above did not necessarily constitute being in love.

I parked my truck with the canoe still secured to the topper and walked across the nearly full hospital parking lot. I guessed they would start feeding the nursing home patients anytime now, then the hospital patients. Cache Harbor Community was run by lay-people and a few nuns. The administrators set policy and finances in accord with the wishes of a huge bureaucracy by the order of Franciscan Sisters. Nuns always made me nervous; there is something unreal about them, or maybe just otherworldly. I waved at the receptionist and walked back to the nurses' station. Dogget was carrying on an animated conversation with a nurse known to most area law enforcement agents as Tits Banaczek. Tits liked to score cops and it looked like Dogget was racking up points for tonight. When he finally noticed me, he broke off the conversation with Tits and steered me to a small waiting room near the O.R.

"Got something for ya," he confided. "Eddie will be finished in a few minutes, but in the meantime look at this." Dogget produced a slightly damp, rumpled and faded color Polaroid from his shirt pocket. It was a picture of the dead girl dressed in what appeared to be a gypsy costume – lots of clunky jewelry, scarves and sashes. There was a small thin man holding her on his lap. He had scraggly dark hair and a wispy beard and moustache. It looked like he was trying to dress like a beatnik or hippie of some sort. In his left hand he held a plastic jack-o-lantern and his right hand appeared to be thrust under the victim's costume in the vicinity of her right breast.

"Looks like a Halloween party to me. Where'd you get it?"

"Eddie found it during the autopsy." Dogget didn't elaborate. There are only three places on a naked female corpse where a photograph could have been placed. I suppose I rose to the bait by the look on my face when I handed him back the photo. "Gotcha! Eddie found it stuffed in the victim's mouth." He gave out with another adenoidal laugh. "We find the little guy in the hippie suit and maybe we find the killer."

But I was bothered by too many clues leading to too many easy conclusions. First there was Portilla whose condition led to someone with at least a rudimentary knowledge of Aztec religion. Then there was the neatly folded packet of clothing stashed in a place where it was certain to be found sooner or later. Now there was a dead woman with a suspect's photo in her mouth. Killers were either getting dumber or smarter all the time.

"Once we get an ID on the Jane Doe, it shouldn't be too difficult to trace this photo down. Ash is on his way to the BCA now with prints we rolled off the dead girl before Eddie got to her with his knives. Ash don't know about the Polaroid."

A hall door opened behind us and Dr. Ed Loetz stepped into the waiting room. "OK who wants the lowdown on the Jane Does?"

Chapter Thirteen

"Yes! You heard right. I said Jane Does. Plural." Dogget and I hurried into Eddie Loetz's office as he closed the door behind us with authority.

"Does that mean we have the top half of one woman and the bottom half of another?" Dog's eyes were bulging from his head at this latest revelation.

"No, it doesn't. It means we have Jane Doe and her daughter."

"Oh shit!" I kicked the closed door and popped the jamb with my fist; this was too fuckin' much. "Jesus Christ! When is this shit storm gonna end?"

"I don't make the world the way it is, I just interpret what you guys bring me." Eddie slammed the file folder on his desk and began searching his pockets for a cigarette, but never found one,

"You're saying she was pregnant, right?" Dogget had to have it mapped out for him.

"In her third month. No way she couldn't know she was expecting. From what I can make out, she was in fine shape at the time of her death."

I looked at Eddie who was looking at the file folder, then at Dogget who was still bulging and shaking his head, so it was up to me to ask how she died, not that I ever wanted to hear the answer.

"Not easy."

"I knew you were gonna say that." Dogget sat down in a lump on the oak chair Eddie provided for patient consultation. "I fuckin'-A knew it!"

"It appears her belly was slashed open with a rough-edged knife and it could have been as much as an hour later that a much sharper blade continued the cut from the frontal pelvic bones to the spine. She undoubtedly died of blood loss by then. The spine was severed fairly neatly – possibly one of those double-jointed tree limb nippers, that's what I'd look for. Her internal organs were also cut cleanly after the initial trauma."

Right away I could see where this was leading. "Are you telling me the knife that killed Jane Doe was the same edge that opened up Portilla?"

"No. But it could have been. Remember I'm looking at a wound that occurred two months ago and has been soaking in cold water ever since. It's my opinion that the slash that opened her up was made by a different weapon than the one that finished the job after she was dead."

"Two months?"

"Approximately. Sometime in late May, early June." Eddie continued to recite facts from his autopsy, but I stopped listening at June. June was when Portilla visited Vollmer. Somebody dies in June, somebody dies in August. The gash is crude, the finishing work is neat. A man, a woman, a baby.

"Paul, there's no absolute connection, you know. Not yet. Why don't you wait until Ash checks the prints through BCA. Don't jump to conclusions." I'll give him credit, Dog was trying, there was a softness to the edge in his voice. What had always been a joke about Ash Tucker foisting off cases to other departments on the thinnest hint of a connection was about to become a reality for me. It wasn't humorous, not this time, not under these circumstances. Tucker wouldn't dump this one in my lap, not without help. Or would he? We stood in the hospital corridor and I tried for the life of me to make sense of it. I could tell Dog was going through the same shit as me. Finally we walked outside into the fresh, cooling late afternoon. We'd spent the last half hour working out a terse news release for Ruthie and the weekend dispatch. Better to get something official on paper. It wouldn't satisfy the gossip junkies, it would stop them from asking questions we couldn't or shouldn't answer.

"You know if there's any connection between these two deaths, Ash is going to try to hand them both over to me."

"Maybe. I know that's his style, but if he does, it'll just mean you're the guy in charge of the investigation. He'll allow us to help out so it all doesn't fall on you and Mel. He can't take the heat that'll be generated by this one if he just passes it off."

"I moved here because I thought this kind of thing didn't happen in the north woods. I moved to get away from city rot, spreading out like cancer to the nice quiet neighborhoods and the suburbs. Somehow I didn't think there'd be as many skuzzballs here. There are and they're even worse."

"No, there ain't. Not really. You been here five years and what...? One, maybe two other serious crimes? You were doin' that work every week back where you came from. Metro Mania, don't forget it." Dog slid into his squad and slammed the door. "Besides, it makes sense. If these two killings are connected, you've done all the work so far, you oughtta be the guy gets all the glory. Backup, Pauly, it's all gonna be in the backup and Ash'll see to that." He gunned his engine and smiled at me. "Or I will."

Politics, politics, all is politics sayeth the prophet. Dogget drove off in a cloud of hot August dust leaving me with the image of his high sign in the rear view mirror. He'd probably grab a bite to eat and a couple of drinks, then chase Tits Banaczek around the bedroom half the night. I knew he was right, the Chief Deputy wasn't dumb. It had been worse, much worse working investigations in the burbs, but it damn well didn't make the same thing easier to do here. I'm really not the cynic many of my blue brethren are; I don't often use that cloak to wrap myself in, avoid the facts of life. I'd gone with a girl once years ago. She told me there were two kinds of people in the world – the assholes and the non-assholes, and once you figured out who was which, you were all set. But I guess that rule never really made it into my own 'Key to Personality Assessment'. Too bad. Axioms like that make life easier to live even if they're incorrect. Who cares about correct, it's what works that counts.

When I finally cranked over my starter and eased out of the hospital lot, most of the staff was going home and the visitors had out-stayed their welcome. The TV sets were coming to life in the recovery wing. I drove the back streets to Reefer's house.

Valerie Hackney was bending over in her front yard flower garden weeding out the offending dandelions. She was wearing a yellow one-piece sun suit and looked very nice indeed bending over the mums. Since she would probably write the story anyway, I decided to pull into her driveway and give her a copy of the news release. She waved, all yellow and sunny, her small frame wiggled its way over to my truck and she took the paper from my hand. Usually Valerie dressed like a model for the L.L. Bean catalog, but apparently when she was just being Val, it was quite a different matter. Or, maybe Bean sells sun suits that look sexier when you don't wear anything under them. I don't feature that in Freeport Maine. I'll bet every woman who buys from Bean wears panties all the time, even in bed. Reefer lived just a block up the hill, which I suppose meant he could roller skate down to bang Val whenever he wanted. I can appreciate that.

"Got a statement for you."

"What does it say?"

"Nothing."

"Does it mean I have to work my butt off over the weekend to make something out of nothing?"

"No. I'm sure there'll be more coming, but it won't meet your deadline."

"I took out my contacts. Read it to me, will you?"

I took back the sheet I'd handed her. The letterhead had the Cache Harbor County Sheriffs Department address and phone number on the heading. My sincere hope it would stay there after Ash got back in town.

"On Saturday, August 15, at approximately 8:30AM, the Cache Harbor County Sheriffs Department received information regarding the apparent homicide of an unidentified woman. The victim's body was found in a pair of plastic trash bags by two local fishermen at South Apple Branch Lake. The victim in her mid-twenties appears to have been dead for approximately two months. The case continues under investigation by the Cache Harbor County Sheriffs department, which will make further information available pending identification and notification of next of kin."

"What other information?"

"Not now, Valerie."

"Why not now?" She cocked her arms and put her fists on her hips and pouted at me, honey blond hair bouncing in defiance.

"Like it says, next of kin and a positive ID. You can't print it before her parents or husband or somebody knows."

"Paul, I know how she was found and who found her and how she was cut up and all of that."

"Use your judgment on how much you'd like her mother to read in the paper before she even knows it's her kid."

"That's crap, Paul. Nobody's been missing around here for two months, and regardless what Reefer puts in his circulation figures, nobody else but locals reads this newspaper." She took the paper from me and held it at arm's length trying to make the typing clear.

"Rules are rules, Valerie. When Eddie files the autopsy report and Ash has an ID and next of kin have been notified, then most of the rest of the stuff becomes public record."

"How about off the record?" She gave up trying to read the release and folded it in half.

"It's not my case to go on or off the record with. You'd have to ask Deputy Dog."

"So there isn't any connection between the two murders." She tipped her sharp face and looked me directly in the eye. It wasn't the same look I got from Marie, but direct nonetheless.

"I repeat. It's not my case."

"OK, I'll ask Dog, then."

I knew he'd appreciate her little yellow jumpsuit more than I. "I thought you didn't want to work over the weekend."

"I don't, but I have to check it out, don't I?"

"Good luck." I figured by now Dogget was out of his uniform and into his civvies, fueling up for his evening with Tits. I also knew that once Chief Deputy Dogget was off the radio he was as good as out of town. I watched Valerie head toward her front door. "By the way, I don't suppose I could see that story you wrote about Portilla."

"Didn't they ever teach you in cop school that reporters never do that?"

"They taught us some reporters do and some don't."

"Guess which one I am." I didn't really need to know anyway. I had it figured. I'd be prepared for the worst and hope for the best.

If life was a low budget detective series, I'd romance the reporter so that by the time we got past the second commercial break, I'd have fucked the story out of her one paragraph at a time. Life was not a TV show, so I drove myself back to my cabin and a frozen food supper. I checked over my fishing gear for tomorrow. The rest of the evening I spent patrolling in my truck watching the tourists feed the gulls.

The boredom of night duty drives me nuts, but Mel needed time with his new family and I'd promised to pick up the slack. I went through the motions mechanically and without paying much attention to what I did or saw. I kept mulling over all the little details of death and dying in Cache Harbor. Finally I shoved the whole thing into a corner of my brain and concentrated exclusively on fishing. And occasionally about whether or not Marie would actually show up on the landing at Bullpen Lake.

Chapter Fourteen

I'm a believer in the idea that if you want to catch smallmouths in the east-west finger boundary lakes, you fish the south shore. The reason is geology. When the glaciers scraped out these lakes, they left the shallow sides on the north and the deep, plunging rock walls on the south. Smallies hang off the sharply sloping underwater cliffs ready to bite in the morning and late afternoon. In the spring I throw almost anything at them that buzzes or sputters, just so long as it's not too big. They go after beetle spins and buzz baits that have those soft plastic bodies that feel like balls of snot. The summer is tougher: jigged plastic worms, small sinking Rapalas often do the trick. By the fall, smallies are back biting on the small spoons and noisy baits, trying to store up food before winter strikes in late October sending them into torpor until ice-out.

Bullpen is not a particularly long lake, but it folds back on itself with a point running down the middle almost the entire length of the water. It lays on the edge of the permit area and sees very little action from fishermen, who think all the good fish live in the hard to reach lakes. The campers want to head out into the wilderness, canoe and portage away from it all; have a quality experience in the toolies. The locals mostly fish the stocked trout lakes. I appreciate it that the Forest Service has built a nice gravel road back through the woods for nearly a mile, right to the south shore of Bullpen Lake. They placed a campsite on the opposite shore, hidden behind the long finger point of land, and they erected a small covered sign that admonished anglers to pack out their trash. Sometimes I thought I was the only guy in the county smart enough to fish Bullpen – and most of the time I was right.

Sunday morning broke cloudless and cool. It promised to stay clear and warm up to the high seventies or even low eighties. The humidity, which had been unusually high this summer, was slight and there was only a whisper of a breeze to wrinkle the lake's surface. The smallmouths were not exactly mad with hunger, but I'd managed to catch a three and a half pounder – perfect for a meal. I'd been working the southwest shore with a gold plastic worm and a fluorescent yellow jig head. For some reason, a darker combination worked on the southeast side, but they had been smaller fish and I had carefully released them back to their rocky homes.

As I made a second pass down the south shore, this time from east to west, I spotted her seated on a rock rising out of the water a few feet from the public landing. She was wearing a lightweight man's shirt – one of those blue and white striped pillow-ticking affairs and knotted at the waist, bluejeans, mocs and a very large pair of sunglasses. She waved as I paddled in close to shore.

"Hi! Need any help catching fish?"

"Sure. Where's your gear?"

"I don't have any."

"How are you going to catch fish if you don't have a pole?"

"I'll use yours. You can teach me all those tricks they write about in outdoor magazines." She stood up on the rock and hopped ashore as I nosed my old aluminum canoe on to the landing beach. I moved back to the stern and told her to climb in the bow. She had picked up a blue stuff sack from the beach and got in.

"I don't suppose you brought any lunch." I dug the paddle into the gravel bottom and pushed us off backwards into the lake. She grabbed the gunwales to steady herself against the unexpected buoyancy.

"It's in the sack with my towel and bathing suit." She held up an arm with the sack attached and then quickly put it down to steady herself.

"You'll get used to the canoe in a minute, just don't make any sudden moves or lean too far over in one direction." I headed down the southwest shore with a few strong paddles and then began J-stroking to keep us headed in an even direction. "There's a spare paddle behind you if you want to help. We'll go down to the end and anchor off that bay." She held on to the gunwale with her left hand and groped behind her to find the extra paddle.

"I have done this before, you know. Just recently, too." She proved to be a strong paddler and I ended up not having to over correct my strokes as much as I thought I would to keep us from zigzagging down the lake like novices.

My small, collapsible canoe anchor didn't have much holding power in the wind, but the air was quiet and there was little movement in the bay at the southwest corner of Bullpen Lake. After securing the anchor, I carefully climbed over the strut and knelt in the center of the canoe. I showed her how to attach a jig and plastic worm. She made a few of the standard remarks about how they feel and what they reminded her of. Then I showed her how to hold the rod with its open face reel, trigger the bail and catch the monofilament with her forefinger. I demonstrated how to coordinate her finger with her throw and how to retrieve the cast in a pulling, dipping motion. After one or two incredible snags, she got the hang of it. She also landed a nice one pounder. On my instructions, she reached down and gently grasped the variegated green body and unfastened the single barbless hook. For a moment she studied its small red-orange eye, then slowly released the fish back into the water. She rinsed off her hand in the cold water and asked if she could cast again. The remainder of the morning was spent with me helping Marie to learn all the ins and outs of smallmouth fishing.

She learned quickly. Her focus was intense when she got a strike, and she chewed her lower lip until the fish was landed. The rest of the time her laughter was light and frequent. By eleven o'clock we had worked the shore twice and I had edged the canoe to the other side of the long finger point where I knew there was also a drop-off. We tried different bait combinations, different colors, but always Marie seemed to have the natural luck of a born angler. The campsite was located just across from the drop-off on the north shore of the finger. I pulled the canoe along side a sloping rock that served as a landing spot. I'd been here many times before and told her to tie us off on an exposed cedar root just up the bank. The sun was not quite overhead, and the site was still shady and cool. Before I got the tackle box closed and the rod stowed, Marie had scattered lunch on a sunny rock. Declaring she was famished, she took a big bite of her sandwich as she handed the other one to me.

"I don't have a fishing license, you know. Is that all right?"

"If neither one of us tells the game warden, otherwise they could toss you in the brig for a year and take away my badge." She glanced at me for a moment to test my seriousness, then decided it was not possible, and laughed into her cup of iced tea. "Besides I always buy a family license."

"Why do you do that?"

"Sometimes I take kids out fishing and sometimes they're old enough to require a license and sometimes not."

"Is that how you think of me? As a kid?" She was looking at me in her way, again.

"Young, but not a kid. I was just making a joke." I looked away and concentrated on my sandwich.

"But that's part of it, isn't it? Because you're forty and I'm almost twenty-two, you think there's something wrong in our liking each other. I've seen tourists up here a lot older than you with dollies not much older than me on their arms and they aren't their daughters, either."

"I know, Marie, I've seen them too – and maybe envied them, wondering if that'll be me in another twenty years. But I've always been cautious around women. I realize it's not so usual for a guy my age to still be single, not even married once. Forgive me if I'm cautious."

"Are you cautious around Lisbeth Ann?"

"You could spoil a perfectly good day with that kind of talk."

"But you're thinking about her, aren't you? Thinking about how she would feel if she knew we were here?"

"If you mean, am I feeling guilty, the answer is no I'm not. I'd like not to make comparisons, though. I'm enjoying myself with you today, and that's the way I'd like to keep it. Nothing else, just you, me and an occasional fish." I held out my cup for some more tea. The knot in my stomach was creeping up into my throat along with the sunlight spreading across the campsite. She had a soft look in her eyes and there was a still crisp smell to her pillow-ticking shirt.

"Is it too cold for swimming, do you suppose?"

"I don't know you're the one who had her hands in the water all morning catching and releasing fish. You know, you are the luckiest person with a fishpole in your hands."

"That's just because you didn't think I could do it." She laughed and poked me with the tea canteen. "You were thinking, 'Oh God what a drag! A girl who wants to learn how to fish.'"

"No. I'm glad you came. I didn't know if you would. I should have said something more yesterday...made arrangements to pick you up..."

"That's all right. This way there's no...you know."

"Right." I knew what she was trying to say. This way there was no guilt, no reason to feel I was sneaking out on Lisbeth Ann, making dates behind her back. No reason to have an obligation, yet. She had graciously saved me the trouble of trying to figure out what I should do about the two of us. She just showed up on shore. What was there to say or do?

"It's really warming up. I'm going to try the water." She jumped up and carried off her stuff sack back into the campsite past the chained-down cooking grate and the fire pit to the other side of a flat, finely graveled area where campers were meant to pitch their tents.

"Go down the path a little further," I called after her noticing she had intended to slip into the trees behind the tent pad. "Most campers don't bother to walk all the way to the pit toilet in the middle of the night, they just leak in the woods outside their tent."

"Thanks for the tip. Are you peeking, by the way?"

"Yes." I wasn't.

In a few minutes she came down to the shore dressed in the same red and white striped two-piece that started all this a couple of days before. She dropped her clothes in a pile and pulled out a towel from her stuff sack.

"Aren't your knees sore?" I looked too long at her cream colored body, the red slashes of her suit, her beautiful face framed by a mass of thick black hair that hung to her wing bones. "I mean from kneeling in the canoe all morning."

I nodded briefly then watched her slip shivering into the dark August water. She swam with an easy grace back and forth in front of the campsite. She would hold up one arm and slowly sink vertically out of sight, then break the surface with a shout and a laugh, proclaiming how she was unable to touch the bottom. I sipped my tea and watched her perform. A sleek otter in a northern lake. I was slipping closer within her control and I didn't care. She swam into shore and stood dripping on the landing rock by the canoe. I got up and brought her the towel.

"Put it over my head and rub some circulation back into my brains, that water is cold!" She stood on the rock and bent forward as I draped the towel over her black hair, trying to squeegee water from the thick mass. I pulled the damp towel back from her face and ran my hands into the hair at the nape of her neck, stepped forward and pulled her off the rock. Our mouths touched as she circled me with her arms, tongue searching deep. She made little mewing sounds as she pressed her wet body hard against me, one of her legs moving up between mine to lock us together even closer.

No need for words. Unnecessary, even intrusions at times like this. Bodies do all the communicating: eyes, mouths, hands and undulating motions all come together in one long phrase and the phrases blend together into sentences and the sentences flow on with frequent punctuations until all the looking, touching, speaking motions end. At that point we left the metaphorical and plunged headlong into the purely physical. When it came, Marie was astride me, frantically pushing her hips down into mine, rocking and filling the silent lake site with tiny squeals of ecstasy. Her breasts danced wildly in front of me as I grabbed her hips and forced us to a shattering release. After several moments of freezing with her back arched, she slowly folded her body down on mine, gripping my shoulders and forcing her face into the crook of my neck. She swore she would love me for as long as I would let her.

Later, after her hair was dry and the shadows were lengthening across the campsite, we reached for each other again. The passion was the same as before. It wasn't going to abate. We made love again later in the evening after cleaning the fish we caught and eating our meal by candlelight in her cabin. She consumed me and I allowed myself to be consumed. I released myself to her and she accepted me, hid me in a secret place while she curled up inside of me to remain there even after the wind came up and the rains fell again. I finally drove away at dawn; Marie still curled inside of me, nestled, fetal.

Chapter Fifteen

Monday morning. I was sitting in room 17A of the Cache Harbor courthouse, feet propped up on the corner of the interrogation table. The only thing that made the table different from any other massive old oak piece in the building is that it was bracketed to the floor and there was a big steel ring bolted to the top in case it was necessary to chain a suspect during questioning. Mel was seated at the table re-reading the Calexico P.D. file on Portilla.

"What if they don't show up?" He turned over the photo of Portilla and looked at the stats on the back.

"Then we'll drive up there and drag his ass down here in cuffs." I checked my watch, it was nearly eleven and I was owly for not getting much sleep. I'd be good until three in the afternoon, then I knew I'd crash hard.

All things considered, I thought breakfast went well. I was able to move my jaws and walk in a straight line. I chatted amiably with Reefer and was pleasant and courteous to Marie, who was in turn equally pleasant and courteous to me. But Reefer had watched the two of us with his eagle eye as if he were processing and interpreting every move we made. What was the clue? Had we made such a botch of it? Had Marie almost dropped a tray of dishes when she saw me walk through the café door? Had I sat there dumb faced, staring at her every motion? Had we looked at each other too long and hard when she brought my order so that Reefer had to take the insulated coffee pot from her hand to pour his own cup? What had happened anyway? Wasn't I smooth as usual and she as gay as always or was I a stumblebum and was she tongue-tied? Whatever! Reefer kept looking at us as if something wasn't the same. I remembered when I stopped to pay at the counter, she took my money and squeezed my hand in the process, thanked me and then under her breath told me she was still in love. I guess I agreed somehow...muttered something or maybe just nodded.

In any event, Reefer was laying in wait outside the plate glass window of the Outpost Café.

"Have a nice day fishing?"

"Fine."

"Catch anything?"

"Yes."

"Anyone I know?"

"Fuck off!"

It was getting late and I was tired of reviewing what I wanted to say to Professor Vollmer and his fancy attorney, J. Bentley Prudhomme. Maybe if I had a photograph of Marie on my desk or in my wallet, I'd stop seeing her face in front of my mind and be able to concentrate on business. I'd ask for one when I saw her later that night. Yes! I'd see her then and again after that and after that and every damn minute I could until something flamed out, burned up or wore down. I heard voices in the hall outside room 17A.

"Bingo!" Mel closed the Calexico file and went for the door.

"Talk nasty to the secretaries and the message gets through every time." Vollmer entered the room first. He was still trim, but had a drawn look about him. Prudhomme was dressed in a three-piece chalk striped blue suit that probably cost three months of my wage. He was big but not fat, jowly and used talcum powder. "Gentlemen, thank you for being so prompt." I directed them to the big oak chairs with green padded seats the county provided in every room of the building. Mel offered them both coffee, but they declined.

"We're not exactly here on a social visit." Prudhomme was going to play it brusque.

"Then let's get down to it." I punched on the little tape recorder, centered it in the middle of the table and opened the Portilla file. Prudhomme turned out not to be one of those intrusive attorneys sticking objections and reservations in at every opportunity. He was as his name suggested, a prudent man. Vollmer on the other hand was sweaty and his voice was pitched higher than during our previous interviews. I kept wondering if it was because a young woman had been found cut in half in South Apple Branch Lake, or because of the photo of Portilla staring up at us from the file folder. Or both.

Mel had passed around the pictures of Portilla and Vollmer ID'd him as the man he knew. We went over the list of collectors known to deal with the victim, none of whom had bothered to call back in answer to my weekend request. We reviewed what had been hashed over previously – before I knew Vollmer and Portilla were flying partners.

"Had Mr. Portilla ever been here in Cache Harbor?"

"I really couldn't say."

"You couldn't say, or won't say?"

"What I mean is I suppose if he had been up here I would have known it."

"Would you know if Sparky was up here in June and again just a few days ago when he was supposed to be in the Twin Cities...at least according to you?"

"What do you mean by that?"

"Did you and Sparky Portilla fly into the Cache Harbor airport in early June and again just a week ago Saturday?"

Vollmer bent close to his attorney and spoke softly but urgently. It was Prudhomme who replied.

"We'd like to pass on answering that for now, if you don't mind. Possible self-incrimination and all."

"I'll say. We have a witness who will swear under oath that he saw you, Professor, together with Portilla leave your aircraft Saturday morning here in Cache Harbor. He also saw you leave the same airport Monday morning, this time alone."

Vollmer looked uncomfortable and exchanged a few words with Prudhomme, but neither offered an explanation. I let it hang in the air until we were all uncomfortable.

"You told me last week that you flew up here on Saturday morning alone expressly to check out the authenticity of the deal Portilla was offering you on a Toltec feather piece. This was where you kept your references for that sort of thing, you said. You also told me you flew out of here Monday morning, waited for Portilla to call you, but he never did, so you returned here on Tuesday evening and had no further contact with the victim." Prudhomme gave me a blank look as if to say, 'no contest.'

"Unless my witness is blind – and he did look at the same photos of Portilla you just did – there appears to be a pretty big discrepancy in the stories. He says you didn't fly in here alone on Saturday. He says Portilla was with you. He also says you left alone on Monday." Big silent pause. I was being stonewalled. "What happened to Sparky, Doc? You didn't leave him carousing around Minneapolis over the weekend, you brought him here and he never returned. He ended up in Palmer's barn without his skin. Now, do you wanna fill in a few blanks for us?"

"First of all, Chief Tharp, we have only your word that such events took place as you described them. Your witness is not on the stand and this is not a courtroom. Secondly you are concluding my client had something to do with the untimely death of Mr. Portilla."

"Not my word alone."

"I repeat, witnesses belong in court."

"What about the solo flight back to Minneapolis?"

"My client has already admitted to flying back to the Twin Cities – St. Paul Downtown Airport, actually – on Monday."

"What about June? Did you accompany Portilla here in June?"

"My client has no recollection of a visit in June or any other time by Mr. Portilla."

"That's all a crock of shit, Bentley, and you know it. Professor, you flew Portilla up here from the Twin Cities, you were seen arriving together. You spent the better part of two days here – plenty of time for the two of you to argue over price, over authenticity, past deals, whatever. You fly outta here on Monday for who-knows-what reason and then waltz back in on Tuesday night – you told me that. I'll admit I don't have a witness for Tuesday, but here you are and Sparky ends up dog food by eight o'clock the next morning. Let me put it another way: where was Portilla while you were back in the Cities?"

"We have no idea."

"Was he in your freezer by any chance?"

"Mr. Tharp! I object to that line of questioning..."

"Fuck off, Bentley!"

"Now see here, Tharp..."

"Your client flew his smuggler friend..."

"That's uncalled for!"

"...up here on Saturday..."

"You have no proof of that!"

"...and the guy turns up dead, heartless and without his hide Wednesday morning."

"If you're accusing my client..."

"In the meantime the two of them snuggle for over forty-eight hours..."

"...of murder, you'd better press charges or we're out of here!"

"...then the professor, here, flies back to the Twins, picks up a heavy who has a penchant for Aztec ritual..."

"That's conspiracy and that's all we'll stand for of this crap!"

"...and flies back in time to do the deed and meet the coroner's estimated time of death."

"Come on, Doyle. I'll stand for no more of this cheap, heavy-handed..."

"So look me in the eye and tell me I'm wrong."

"...garbage!"

"You're wrong!" Vollmer stood up and placed his hands on his attorney's shoulders easing him back down in his chair. "It's all right, Lee. I've nothing to hide." Vollmer turned to me and knotted his fingers in front of his chest as if he were about to deliver a lecture to his students. "You're right, Sparky and I flew here last Saturday morning."

"Doyle."

"His offer was most interesting and it's true I do keep my catalogs and references here at the cabin. We spent the weekend discussing price and relative worth of the feathered piece."

"Doyle, as your attorney..."

"Regardless of what that file you have may say of him, Sparky was an interesting and cultured man. It was not difficult at all to spend time with him. I enjoyed him. He was no doubt a criminal, but well-versed in what he did."

"Doyle be careful what you admit."

"All of us – everyone of the collectors you have on that list of yours – we knew who Sparky was and what he was. We substantially played the odds. We considered ourselves smarter than he was, able to tell frauds and contraband at a glance. For the most part we were right."

"Doyle, I don't think you should continue."

"He'd test us occasionally, then there'd be a long spell of straight stuff, good merchandise, honest and not smuggled."

"Watch that word, Doyle."

"What happened Monday morning?" The question came from Mel who had been closely watching the tape recorder to make sure it didn't run out.

"Simple. We had reached an agreement and I flew back to the Twin Cities to withdraw the money. Sparky, as you might well guess, wouldn't take American Express."

"How much?" Mel asked the question and Vollmer looked down at his attorney, then answered.

"Ten thousand dollars."

"That little."

"Robbie Perrine apparently had a troublesome gambling debt. I didn't ask for details. Sparky had originally asked for fifteen, so if Robbie was short of cash, he probably needed only seven or eight. Sparky almost always asked twice the price. He called it a finder's fee."

"Let's move on to Tuesday night." I let Mel continue with the questioning. I'd gotten a little out of hand and I needed the situation to cool down. However, by flying off the handle I did get Vollmer to drop the façade.

"Listen, Doyle, you needn't answer these questions."

"It's all right, Lee. I made a mistake by not coming full front with Chief Tharp last week. I wanted to distance myself from Portilla as best I could. I realize that was wrong. As I told you, and the Chief, I believe someone is trying to set me up. They are trying to make it look as though I killed Sparky. I tried to hide my relationship with him because frankly, I'm afraid and very uncomfortable with the way the finger is pointing. I honestly do not know what happened to Sparky after I flew back to the Cities on Monday. I had some work to do at the University, and actually slept over in my office that night. I believe I can produce witnesses from the custodial staff to that effect.

"And Tuesday?"

"When I came back on Tuesday evening, he was gone."

"Did he have a car?"

"There was just my wagon and that was parked at the airport."

"Was there any indication of a struggle?"

"At my home? None."

"Was he a drinker?"

"Do you mean was he a drunk? I assume so. He drank heavily, but there was no sign that he had an accident."

"When did you realize you were missing an obsidian knife?" I stood up and took the file folder from Mel. "Was it then?"

"Yes. I should not have made up that story about the possibility of a student taking one of my collection for a paper. I discovered the knife was missing almost immediately. It was worth far more than the feather piece and I suspected Sparky had lifted it and left. I don't know where and I don't know how, but the knife and Portilla were gone when I returned Tuesday night."

"I have to ask this, gentlemen." I looked both at Vollmer and Prudhomme. "Did you have any reason to suspect Portilla would be gone when you returned?"

"No."

"Did you leave in order to give him the chance to leave?"

"No."

"Did you leave in order to allow someone or some persons to have access to Portilla in your absence?"

"Doyle..."

"No."

"When you left was he alive and well?"

"Alive and drunk."

"Did you have any reason to suspect he would be anything other than alive and...well...when you returned?"

"No."

"Do you know the identity of the slain woman found this Saturday in South Apple Branch Lake?"

"What dead woman?" Prudhomme was on his feet in an instant and Vollmer blanched pale gray at the question. "What dead woman? There has been no mention of a dead woman here."

"I know." I filed their reaction in my head as Mel clicked off the tape recorder. Good timing. Maybe they would ease up and get sloppy without the recorder running. "I needn't tell you Professor, this whole matter is extremely confusing." I deliberately avoided acknowledging Prudhomme. This was just between the professor and me. "I realize all this questioning isn't easy and I want to thank you for your good will in this matter, but I also need you to understand we are somewhat at a loss for suspects. You would have to admit, were you in my shoes, that you, sir, look very suspect indeed. No one else here even knows Sparky Portilla, nor would they have reason to. I'm going to have to ask you to keep yourself available and would appreciate it if either you or Mr. Prudhomme keeps us advised of your whereabouts. In the meantime we can only assure you we will continue to check out your contention that you are being made the victim of a set up."

Prudhomme took his client's arm and made his way to the door. I guessed the attorney's reaction to the question about the dead woman in South Apple Branch Lake was due to the abrupt interrogation change. I also assumed Vollmer's reaction was due to something else. In spite of everything, he was a lousy actor.

"By the way, Chief, I'd appreciate it if you weren't quite so crude to the secretary next time you call. She's a partner's wife. Mine."

Probably Prudhomme thought he and Vollmer had won the round. I thought we'd won. Mel thought it was time to bring home lunch to Judy and Shelly. Downtown, I guess Reefer thought he had a pretty good edition locked up and Valerie probably thought she had a prize-winning story. I also figured Marie couldn't stand it another minute without seeing me, because I was having the same problem. But I also figured Lisbeth Ann probably thought it funny her amorous police chief hadn't called in a couple of days.

As I soon found out, Sheriff Ash Tucker drove into the courthouse parking lot thinking it was going to take a whole lot longer than he'd hoped to get to the bottom of the Jane Doe-in-the-lake-mystery. And right before Voyageur Days, too. Shitty luck. Turned out BCA was unable to pull prints on the dead woman. Dog had a Polaroid, but big deal. Where to start? A Halloween party? Where? Duluth, Toronto, Elk River? Timbuktu? There had to be a way to dump this thing on me. The more I thought about the blanching Dr. Vollmer, the closer Ash got to dumping it right where he wanted it.

Chapter Sixteen

"Do you have a photograph of yourself?" The cooks at the Outpost Café really couldn't manage a decent egg salad sandwich, but then again, maybe such a thing wasn't possible anywhere in the world.

"What kind of picture?" She filled my coffee cup and then tended to the dirty dishes in the next booth.

"Just something, you know that I could...have...on my desk or carry around in my wallet." I dumped in the extra cream she always brought me.

"Sure, I suppose." She wiped off the spot across from me when she saw Reefer come in the door.

"Can I have it?"

"You mean do I have one on me?" She smiled at Reefer as he slipped into the seat across from me. "I'll see." She handed him a menu and went for another cup and coffee.

Reefer made the usual suggestive remarks about the "item" he called Marie and me, remarks that were verging on statements of fact. But he soon tired of his own smarminess and launched into a dissertation on how wonderful the latest edition of the Telegram-Herald would be. It was paste-up day and the combination of computers and early advertising deadlines was putting Reefer and his small crew in their cars by the end of the workday and not in the composing room until ten at night like it used to be. As Reefer loved to say, the computer put him out of the office and into the arms of his honey before the movies came on prime time TV.

"They're gonna love it, Paul."

"Who?"

"The readers. It's murder in close-up."

"Is it factually correct?"

"Always."

"There'll be a couple of more skinnings around here if it isn't."

"When do I get the lowdown on the latest story?" He leaned closer as Marie brought his coffee.

"You have everything. I gave it to Valerie last night." I took the check from Marie and finished my coffee as Reefer ordered.

"Yeah, that, but I mean the real story. You and..." he nodded to Marie, "...you two."

"See ya." I took the check and got out of the booth, giving him as withering a look as I could, not really knowing what that would look like, but it must have looked threatening.

"What'd I say? What?" Reefer first looked surprised, then feigned indignation. He had a keen eye for detail, I'll give him that. Things hadn't been the same between Marie and me since Sunday night and Reefer could sense it, smell it or something having to do with an intuition for gossip. If the Telegram-Herald had a gossip column, I could see Reefer chuckling over his keyboard, ('Cop cuddles kid! The case of the dicking Dick. All the Norshor tongues are wagging over the cradle-robbing antics of a certain prominent police chief. It seems his little waitress is serving up more than corned beef hash after the dishes are cleared and the cop is copping the late night action.')

Marie took the check from my hand and snapped the menu closed as Reefer ordered a grilled chicken sandwich.

"You didn't say whether you wanted that on toast," she smiled "but it'll be easier to shove up your ass if it is."

At the cash register she slipped me a small photo with my change. She was standing next to a large sculpture. She told me her roommate Emily took it last fall at a student art exhibit and she'd been carrying it in her purse ever since. I took it with me and walked over to my fire hall office. In the picture she was smiling and her hair was blowing in the wind, she was dressed in a plain skirt and blouse, fastened at the waist with a colorful sash. Once inside the office I propped the photo against my answering machine. Then I moved it against a pile of manila file folders on the other side of my desk. Then I propped it up in the window. Finally I put it in a metal cubby in my desk file. Any place else and it would look conspicuously like a picture of the wife and kids. Besides it wasn't anybody's business but mine. Mel, of course would eventually see it, but he probably wouldn't care and he also probably wouldn't talk to me about it. What's on my desk is my business, goddamnit.

I punched my answering machine with authority and Lisbeth Ann's troubled voice poured out into the room.

"I thought Richard was under a restraining order." I was pacing around Lisbeth Ann's office. She was having former husband problems.

"He is...I mean he was, sort of." She was sitting stiffly at her desk and looking down at her hands. This was a private conversation and Mertha had been asked to handle the front of the library for a time. Mertha was no dummy, she knew I wasn't there again because of overdue books. "What I mean is, that after the first time he tried to come back, I asked for an order from the court to keep him away. He threatened me, but I can see now that he'd never hurt me physically. It was a temporary order. It expired months ago."

"So now he's coming back again." I would have been more upset about this piece of news a week ago than I was then standing in her office trying to look at Lisbeth Ann rather than at the catalogs stacked on her desk.

"He is back. He called me from the hotel about an hour ago. He wants to meet and have dinner. He says he just wants to keep me posted, says he has a new job."

"Is he making his alimony payments?"

"There are none, I wanted it that way."

"So it's dinner for old times sake."

"I don't know. His new job is with a television station in Minneapolis." She looked up as if she expected me to give her a good clout.

"Oh Fuck!" I realized I'd said the word too loud for a library when I saw Mertha jump back from the window that separated Lisbeth Ann's office from the reading room. Mertha had been cataloging at the desk under the window, but she probably had been straining her ears to hear our conversation. "Now they'll be all over us like flies on shit!"

"I don't know that he works in the news department. I'm sure he doesn't – he'd never be qualified for that, he'd be in advertising or something."

"I knew it would only be a matter of time. Mel told me he'd seen a clipping on Portilla in Sunday's metro papers. Now with a second murder we're sure to be in for it. Leeches! We're a long way from the major media, but when those fuckin' bloodhounds get wind of you, you're dead meat."

"Listen, Paul, if there's anything I can do..." Her voice trailed off in the echo of my anger and she clasped her hands in her lap.

"Lisbeth Ann, it's not your fault." I switched back to my concerned cop voice and swallowed my media rage. "I'm more concerned about you. Do you want me to speak to Richard? Are you concerned about your safety? Did he give you any reason to feel that it might be unwise to have dinner with him tonight?"

"No, no, none of that. I can handle Richard, even if he's still drinking too much. I just wanted you to know he was working for a TV station. I was afraid it would upset you." Big pause. "I also wanted to know how you'd feel about me and Richard having dinner together."

I guess I never thought much about it, even though it was obvious at that moment I should have been thinking a lot about it. 'How do you feel about me seeing my ex-husband especially after you and I have been fucking each other blind lately.' Oh, I don't know, has our relationship matured past that stage and into something deep and caring? 'Would you be hurt to find out afterwards that Richard and I met?' Would you feel hurt if you found out that now it's Marie and me fucking each other blind?

"I guess I wouldn't want you to find out from Reefer and his gossip monger girlfriend."

"No. I'm glad you told me. I was just thinking about that restraining order. I guess I didn't think of you two in any other way." I have a habit of digging my grave with my teeth. "What I mean is, I'm not the jealous type." However if some old boyfriend of Marie's showed up unannounced looking for a date, I'd castrate the bastard. "I don't have a right to be jealous. You and Richard, what? Ten years? Not even Reefer would make fun of that, he's going through the same thing."

"No, I guess not." She stood and turned partially away from me. As usual she was dressed nice, good looks go with good books, I guess. "Just where do we stand, Paul? I thought after the other night..." She meant after the last time we did it. "...we might have some kind of understanding. It doesn't get any more intimate than the other night...

but not even a phone call."

I was beginning to understand what hack writers call 'eyes burning into you like hot coals.' I just looked at the floor. Worse yet, I could feel Mertha's eyes burning into me from the back. I finally made a brief but perfectly honest statement. "I need some time." I'm forty years old and I've never made a commitment, and now that I could, I'm in love with a twenty year old. But I'm not so perfectly honest that I could say it out loud. Not by a long shot. Not now. I didn't want to face her, I didn't want to try and figure out if she was thinking of re-kindling with Richard. I really didn't even want to deal with the whole "Marie thing" – is it now or forever? – until all the bodies went away. The bodies had to go away and everything gets neat and clean again. Too big a mess to think, just running on fumes, just forging ahead without much thought about where to. Was it as intimate as it gets Lisbeth Ann? Was it that intimate with Marie? If it got more intimate would we fuse molecule to molecule, nucleating?

"I'll meet Richard, then." Crash. That was that. No more reverie. "We'll be going up the trail to the Moose Horn. If he makes any unreasonable demands, I'll just have Tommy Plaiser give you a call. I don't think that will happen." She made a small laughing sound. "I mean, don't sit by the phone waiting."

"Ok, fine. Call me if it looks like a press invasion from the TV station?"

"OK."

Then I left with Mertha's eyes still burning holes in my back and Lisbeth Ann's still smoldering in front. Stupid sonofabitch! You go for nearly two years without a steady and now you got two of them fuckin your brains out. What brains? It must just be your handsome good looks, that dissipated forty thing. The wit and candor of your conversation. Your foot and a half long cock and ten-inch tongue. I piled out of my truck in front of the office. Sure, all of the above. None of the above.

Mel was getting ready to start his shift. He had taken a call from the Denver collector, Robbie Perrine. Perrine had confirmed everything Vollmer contended about the sale of the feather piece.

"I didn't ask him if he was up to his neck in gambling debts; he said he was weeding out some of the more perishable objects in his collection, like feather work and weavings. And Vollmer had the pricing right. The rest was small talk about Portilla's death." Mel handed me his notes. His writing was not unreadable like my own; it was well formed, neat and almost feminine. Marie had handwriting that destroyed the meaning of the word 'cursive'. I'd heard there was an English teacher in the Cache Harbor school system who was a bear on handwriting; Mel must have been her star pupil. "Also, Deputy Dog called. The hospital would like the two corpses removed to another facility. Sheriff Tucker okayed a transfer to the Duluth morgue, but we'll need to sign off on our body."

"You do that. Our body is it? Like it'll be ours forever unless somebody claims it? What happens if Sparky doesn't have any next of kin? Do we send him back to Calexico? To F.L. Gutzman in Mexico City? 'Special Delivery, Mr. Gutzman, just sign here and be sure to keep him refrigerated. Or if you prefer, just put him in a Ziploc baggie and in about ten years there won't be anything left worth saving.'"

I slipped the yellow sheet with Mel's neat handwriting into the Portilla file. "What do we do next, Melvin?" He didn't like his full name, but I guess he realized I was using it not to ridicule, but out of a sense of frustration, term almost of endearment.

"Well, do you want to run over it again? Maybe we should have a blackboard like they do in the big city squad rooms I see on TV. Do you realize that by the time my Shelly will turn eighteen, she will have seen eighteen thousand depictions of killing on TV? I read that in the newspaper."

"No shit? I didn't know that. I'd keep her away from TV if I were you."

Together we looked at what we had and what we might have to quickly forget if one of those TV 'I' Team' crews showed up. Portilla's death was still under investigation. We agreed we'd probably have to fill in the gory details. I mean everyone in town knew about the flayed man, there'd be no sense in doing a cover-up on that. Portilla's mom would just have to find out by watching the ten o'clock news. Anyway, Valerie would have it in her story and that would hit the local post office boxes by three in the afternoon. A few suspects, but no arrests. How do we handle it if someone asks about Professor Vollmer? He's been questioned as an expert witness and an acquaintance of the victim. That's all.

"What about him claiming he's being set up?"

"Bullshit, probably. But one thing we haven't done is look for a vehicle. Assuming Vollmer is telling the truth and he left Sparky here while he flew off to get the loot, then unless Portilla was teleported from the head of the trail to Palmer's barn, there had to be a vehicle involved."

"Maybe someone saw something. We'd better check the gas stations."

"Or if the murderer borrowed a car, alert the Forest Service for a check on any dead vehicles they find on any of the logging roads. My guess is that if Vollmer was set up, whoever did it is long gone and back in Chicago playing poker with his cronies."

"What about Jane Doe?"

"What about her? Them? That's Ash's problem. Besides, he likes the lights and cameras."

"Speaking of cameras, that's a nice picture of Marie you've got there on your desk."

"Get on your shift, you little shit, or I'll haul your ass up before the city council for dereliction of duty."

Chapter Seventeen

Somewhere between the time I heard Mel leave the office and saw Valerie Hackney sitting across the desk from me, I had fallen into a deep sleep sitting with my feet propped up on the table. I couldn't remember the precise moment when the concrete surroundings of my cramped office blended into the panorama of my dream. It wasn't a disturbing dream even though it had all the right characters to make it one. It contained visions of flayed men and halved women; Marie was in it and so were Richard Sarstadt, J. Bentley Prudhomme and Reefer Carlson. I'm not one of those people who put much stock in dreams; I go nuts trying to figure them out, especially since I rarely remember most of the details. All I could remember of this dream was that I was showing some guy with a television camera on his shoulder a place in the woods where naked men and women took off their skins and danced around in the sunlight. Then their bodies changed so they were men on the top and women on the bottom and then the other way around. They all had live hearts painted on their chests.

It was at that point in the dream where Marie floated over and handed me her unborn child that was calling my name in a voice belonging to Valerie Hackney. I opened my eyes and sure enough, there she was.

"Hiya sleepyhead." She was smiling, but I wasn't. The entire chain of muscles that ran from the base of my neck to the small of my back seemed frozen in painful suspension when I tried to move. "You were getting boring. I thought you'd wake up when I walked in. Then I thought you'd wake up when I touched you. Then I thought you'd wake up when I called your name. I've been talking to you for the last five minutes. You snore, you know."

"Don't exaggerate."

"You snore, really."

"I mean about how long you've been here watching me snore."

"Swear to God."

"Where'd you touch me?"

"You'll see my initials when you get undressed."

"Don't exaggerate."

"OK, just be careful who you get undressed in front of tonight."

"You, too?"

"Me too, what?"

"Are you going to badger me about my private life?"

"Your so-called private life is getting publicer – if that's a word – by the hour."

"Somebody musta blabbed, and no, 'publicer' is not a word."

"Nobody had to do anything except addition: two and two together. I mean, you can't park a squad car at a beach cabin all night and have it go unnoticed. People will look for connections with a thing like that, watch you closer."

I made a dismissal motion with my hand and grunted while I twisted my head around on its stem to get the crunchies out.

"Believe me, I know. Don't you suppose Reefer and I were under the same scrutiny when we started seeing each other?"

"So now I'm being scrutinized by the town gossips. Just what I need."

"They finally stop. They either wring it dry or something juicier comes along to hold their attention, and pretty soon they forget you."

"Or cluck their tongues every time you walk by."

"In your case you may get quite a few clucks, after all you've given them a double dose."

"Of what?"

"Well, first there were the late nighters with our fair librarian, now there's the waitress. The man has sexual appetites we didn't even suspect."

"I'm an animal. A late bloomer. A bad example for the youth of America." I got up from my chair and looked for coffee but the jar was empty. "Reefer sent you here, didn't he? He sent you over to torment me. Admit it."

"Actually, Paul, Reefer would be pissed if he knew I was here."

"You touched me first, remember."

"Not that kind of pissed." She reached in her tote bag and pulled out a manila envelope. "One of the reasons journalists get upset when bureaucrats want to see news stories before they're published is that the journalists consider themselves every bit as professional as the bureaucrats, and not subject to pre-screening."

I nodded, gave up the search for coffee and sat back down at my desk.

"Contrary to popular belief, reporters strive very hard to be objective. However, the people they write about usually have a vested interest in being subjective. Reporters don't like tailoring stories and they don't like being told to change them at the last minute." She handed me the envelope. "But there's nothing that says in this case you can't see the story now that it's on its way to the printer. I made a copy of the paste-up."

I opened the envelope and unfolded the tabloid-sized photocopies of page one of the Telegram-Herald, and the two inside jump pages. Impressive. There was a forty-eight point headline, copy and photo above the flag, two additional photos and more copy below the fold. The photos were large and reproduced well even on the copier. One three-column shot showed the Palmer barn from the outside with squads and the ambulance in the foreground. There was a two- column shot of me and Eddie Loetz hovering over a body bag and another three-column picture of Mel Swanson and a paramedic examining the barnyard pump. The headline screamed 'Brutal Murder in Cache Harbor'. There was a box at the bottom right corner of the page that drew the reader's attention to another story inside: 'Second Victim Found in Border Lake'. Both stories were bylined by Valerie Hackney.

"Quite a spread." I looked over the inside pages she had provided. There was a photo of several deputies and an ambulance at the South Apple Branch Lake site. "How'd you get this photo?"

"Deputy Dog was still in his office after you gave me the news release. He wouldn't elaborate on what you'd written, but he did show me the photo of the dead woman and her boyfriend, and promised to send over a shot taken at the scene." She stood up, hitched her tote over her arm and moved toward the door. "It's not the greatest, but it makes us look like we're on the ball."

"You don't want to stick around while I read this?"

"You'll probably just pick at it. But remember, I'm trying to report something the way I see it and be as objective as possible, while giving the reader more than the official line in the press release. Also, remember I don't know as much about these cases as you do."

I watched her maneuver her small frame around a box of office supplies and open the steel door to the fire hall. I called her name and she turned with an expectant look on her face – the kind kids have when they think they're about to be found out. All I said was 'thanks' and that was all it took to take away that look and make her smile.

"Don't tell Reefer, OK?"

"Zippered lips"

"By the way, Harry at the variety store? He's got nice little frames on sale. One would probably fit that snapshot of Marie and look real nice on your desk."

I was stretched out on the old shag carpet that dominated her living room. My shirt was off and my feet were on her couch. I held the copies of tomorrow's Telegram-Herald over my head and tried to catch the light from a lamp on the end table. The windows were open and I could hear the waves outside her cabin. The breeze moved around the warm evening August air. Marie was in the kitchen making a chef salad for our dinner. She had put on a light oriental-looking shift over her red and white striped swimsuit; she said it was a 'hapi-coat'. It made me happy, blue and white with a big orange circular Chinese character on the back. It made her look like a target, but she said the character meant something like happiness or good fortune.

"I still can't find anything drastically wrong in this story." I'd re-read it about six times. "Gotta admit she's got the facts straight."

"What about all the information on Aztec ritual, was that necessary?" Marie had read it at least three times.

"No. But I guess I understand why she included it. Probably helps the story. My problem is I'm only looking at it from a cop's point of view and she's trying to sell newspapers." I turned to the third page and the South Apple Branch Lake story.

"Well, if you ask me, all that ritual stuff makes it sound like there's some weird sect living in the woods, especially since she barely touched on the spiritual part of those rituals."

"Where do you get that idea?" I was looking at the target on her back, she was slicing up ham into julienne strips.

"First of all, you told me Professor Vollmer said there was more to Aztec sacrifice than meets the eye. Besides, I've been reading up."

"I thought Valerie had out all the books from the library."

"Well, after you dumped all of Emily's books that I loaned you on my back step last week, I thought I was in for a long dry spell for companionship, so I started reading them. There are a lot of interesting parallels between Aztec and Christian myth."

"Do tell."

"Immaculate conception, death and rebirth, freeing the soul from bondage...all that stuff."

"Jesus, you got all that out of those books? All I saw was Vollmer's obsidian knife." I went back to reading the Jane Does' story.

"That's because that was all you were looking for. I was reading to find a motive behind Portilla's death."

I looked over at the target again, she was scattering sunflower seeds on the salad and adding the dressing. "Did you find one?"

"Maybe I have."

I looked at the photo Dogget had sent over to the newspaper. I could make out Eddie Loetz, the two fishermen and Sheriff Ash Tucker. I put down the copies and rolled over on my side. "Well, let's have it. What are you seeing that I'm not seeing?"

"I'm not exactly seeing anything you're not." She brought the salad bowl over to the small round table that separated the living room from the kitchen. "I agree that it appears very much like Professor Vollmer murdered Portilla, but you've been harping on how obvious the clues seem to be. You said it earlier when you were reading Valerie's story. Why would he kill a guy like Portilla and then go to all the trouble of ritualizing it, leaving a trail a mile wide right to his own doorstep? After all, he's the only person around here who is an expert on Pre-Columbian culture."

"Now there's you and me and Valerie."

"But that's afterwards. Valerie didn't know an Aztec from Adam's-off-ox a couple of weeks ago. All I'm saying is that the reason Portilla was killed and what happened to him afterwards don't have to fit together."

"So he was killed for all the reasons I think he was – a run-in with Vollmer over price or a past bum deal, or something else to do with the feathered amulet from Denver." I got up, bounced a couple of times on my haunches and padded across the shag to the table.

"Right. That's why he was killed. Now put yourself in Professor Vollmer's spot." She scooped out the salad into two bowls as she explained. "He's a nationally-respected scholar. Everyone in art and anthropology and a half dozen other majors at the University have this guy for at least one class in four years. And...everyone knows scholars like Vollmer live and breathe their work. He's totally immersed."

"You mean after winning the Indy 500 Mario Andretti didn't go home and knit doilies."

"No. He goes out in the garage and works on his car. To be as good as Vollmer is, he's got to be obsessive. The man is a student of the culture. It is so much a part of him that he responds to the trauma of murder by ritualizing the act." She stood back from the table with a pleased look on her face, either for the explanation or the salad or both. "Now eat."

"Valerie would dearly love to have us believe there is an Ed Gein-type loose in the woods; she even mentions Gein in her story, but stops short of actually saying there's a man out there dancing around in another guy's skin." The salad was delicious even if the conversation was not exactly table talk. "What you're telling me is that Vollmer is nuts, thinks he's an Aztec."

"Not really an Aztec, but he understands the mythology of the rituals. He told you and you told me and then I read it again in Emily's textbooks. The Aztec were like the Romans. First they took over and then bastardized the culture they conquered. They picked up a whole set of beliefs that helped fill the gaps in the ones they already had. They took the old myths at face value and used sacrifice and enslavement as a means to political control."

"And Vollmer understood that as well as the foundation myths."

"Right. He killed the man and then he sacrificed Portilla's heart to atone for his sins, then flayed him as an offering to insure his own rebirth."

"You're not just some smart-ass college kid are you?"

"Right over there..." she pointed to the small brick and board bookshelf in the corner of the room, "...in that green textbook, it says the nobility used to do that all the time with slaves. The sacrifices were not done for the sake of the slaves, but for the sake of the nobility. Slaves were their stand-ins."

I stopped eating in mid-bite. "Vollmer thought Portilla was his slave?"

"In a way. The professor is the man in charge, the smuggler is his flunky. Everyone at the 'U' knows Vollmer is a pompous prick. He's just a brilliant one. Slave and master is a personality configuration people use in order to facilitate one another's existence under extreme circumstances. Psych 101. You use it with Mel."

"You are a smart-ass college kid."

"Only you're a pussycat, not some guy with visions of blood sacrifice and stone daggers floating around in his head. The Professor Vollmers out there do not live in our galaxy, Paul. Believe me, I've had three years of some of these guys and a lot of them ought to be locked up in their ivory towers come nightfall."

"And, you're a fuckin' encyclopedia."

"Encyclopedia's don't fuck, but if you recall, I do."

"I love it when you talk dirty."

"I'm not going to talk to you at all if you don't finish your salad. Besides, you got me going to the point where I forgot to open the wine; now you'll have to do it."

I'm good with corkscrews and opened the bottle of Chablis that had been hiding behind the milk in the refrigerator. While I was getting out a couple of mis-matched wine glasses from her cupboard she apologized for being a smartass and a know-it-all. She was only trying to help and that's what college did to you, make you think you know it all and then make you feel you have to tell everyone. Actually I was glad she went on about it. I guess I never would have come to that conclusion on my own. I told her she was beautiful and brainy as well. We finished dinner and toasted her beauty and brains.

"I'm glad I'm an art major. I get to use my heart more than my head. You're a heart person, too. You feel a great deal more than you let on. I know it. I couldn't love you otherwise."

We never did pick up the dishes and for all I know they were still sitting there when she left for work the next morning. Darkness had slipped in on us while we ate and talked; and while I didn't try to analyze all she said, I did let it flow over me and store itself in the back of my mind. I'd retrieve it later. We took our wine glasses with us and stood by the shore in the moonlight watching the waves break lunar reflections into millions of tiny silver pieces. The air was still warm; she let the hapicoat fall to the cobbles and let me unfasten her swimsuit top while she pulled off the bottom. Soon she had me undressed as well and shuddering with her touches. Valerie had not left her initials in my private places.

Later, resting quietly by my side she told me things I'd never asked to know. How her father died in an automobile accident when she was still in high school and how betrayed she felt when her mother remarried soon afterwards. The feeling of betrayal later turned to pity when her mother was diagnosed with inoperable cancer. Her stepfather took it the hardest. It was the second wife he would lose to cancer and that tragedy brought he and Marie closer in the final days. Her sister flew in from L.A.; the waiting was short. Her mother died three years ago. Her stepfather couldn't stand to live in Des Moines any longer; he worked in sales for a large aircraft engine manufacturer and soon put in for a transfer overseas. She understood he was doing well in Bombay and she had not seen him since her mother died.

The sister is back in L.A. and the roommate, Emily Baxter, is usually somewhere else. Marie devotes her time to art and almost exclusively sculpts in wood and stone, returning to a favorite family vacation area, Cache Harbor, for the past three summers to wait tables and try to save money for school. She'd be returning to the 'U' in a month and that realization made us both wonder what we would do about living and how we'd handle separation. I thought more about it as I drove home at three in the morning, and it left an empty hole in my stomach. I drove past Lisbeth Ann's house. No lights. The strange car parked in the driveway next to her old Volks made the hole grow larger.

Chapter Eighteen

By Tuesday morning, August 18th at 9:47 AM, Sheriff Ash Tucker had the answer to how he was going to dump the Jane Does case in my lap; henceforth to be known as the 'Erin Brantnober Case'. As soon as the detective from the Bureau of Criminal Apprehension hung up, Tucker was on the phone to my office. He got my answering machine and didn't bother to leave a message. Instead, he hove his large bulk out of his office and duck-footed it down the hall to the dispatch room where he had Ruthie find One Zebra One on the radio. I could feel his broad grin spreading out over the airwaves as Ruthie told me One King One requested a twenty at the SO, ASAP.

I signed off and went back to the fenderbender Mel and I were covering at the far east end of town. A thin, pale looking man and his thinner and paler looking wife were shaking their heads over what was left of their foreign compact car's left front fender. The local in the ¾ ton pickup was talking to Mel. The compact couple set about trying to re-tie down their canoe. Helluva way to start a vacation. I finished looking at the skid marks on the asphalt. Pretty clear to me the local was at fault this time; pulled out of a side street without looking.

Nothing was leaking all over the highway, so I assumed the pale, thin couple could get the fender pulled away from their right front tire and continue on their way. I gave my accident diagram to Mel and drove off to visit with Ash Tucker. The day was cooler and the forecast promised evenings and mornings would begin to feel a good deal more like fall. We'd still be on Daylight Savings Time into October, so the sun would set progressively earlier until my wrist alarm would chime 'Fur Elise' while it was barely light. In a month from now, the maple ridge above town would be in flames.

Voyageur Days was set to begin on Thursday. The carnival crowd had begun filtering in and would probably start setting up yet this evening. Ash Tucker loved to coordinate law enforcement coverage for the town's one big annual celebration. When the four days of fun were finally over, there was the Labor Day weekend, school starting, the leaves turning and then the tourists went home until the snow fell. New invasion from the downhill and cross-country ski junkies.

As soon as I walked into the Sheriff's office I knew this was not a Voyageur Days meeting. Sitting next to Ash was Jim Bledsoe, hotshot County Attorney. Tucker wore a smile big enough to wrinkle the loose flesh on his face all the way back to his ears.

"Sit down, Pauly. I got something for ya."

"Oh, shit."

"You got that right." He used the crooked forefinger of his left hand to push a file folder across the table at me. The nuns were right, left-handed people are evil shits and instruments of the devil. "She's all yours. Erin Brantnober, age twenty-six. University graduate student in anthropology, and best of all work study secretary for Doyle R. Vollmer, pee-haitch-dee."

I looked inside the file. There was one yellow sheet with Tucker's scrawled notes from his morning's conversation with BCA and several others detailing the discovery of the body and the department's subsequent questioning of the two fishermen, and the autopsy report. There were also over a dozen eight by ten photographs of the South Apple Branch Lake site. I closed the file thinking what a bastard Ash was.

"BCA make the ID?"

"Called me this mornin' as you can see by the notes. They checked with the University police, since anyone working in a department on a regular basis and authorized to handle over a thousand bucks of University funds, gets a rudimentary clearance check. They came up with a fingerprint match." He leaned back in his chair and reached for a cigarette. The courthouse was a no smoking government building. Tough shit, I guess. "She'd been Vollmer's secretary during regular classes for the past two years. Under the circumstances, I think it would be best if you sorta handled the two cases together, overlapping as they seem to do." He lit the cigarette, chuckled and blew smoke into the air above his head.

I watched the cloud curl above his jowly face. "Can't thank you enough."

"I knew you'd be pleased."

"And Voyageur Days? What about that?"

Jim Bledsoe broke his silence and bent his lean frame forward. "Fuck Voyageur Days, right Ash?"

"Fuck it! Right!"

"The thanks of a grateful peon, fellas." I aimed my response at the sharp, balding young man who considered himself a dynamite County Attorney, but whom everyone in local law enforcement considered a gross pain in the ass with a bad comb-over. "What else do I need to know?"

"Charges. We need charges," Bledsoe hissed rather than actually talk. "Everything I've seen so far is circumstantial – substantial, but circumstantial. All the evidence against this Vollmer guy makes me think he's up to his rosy red ass in both murders, but I don't see one solid turd floating in his toilet that I can use to make a charge stick." Bledsoe always talked this way. I'd heard him string twenty-five scatological references together in one sentence without repeating any of them. To Bledsoe, anyone who came in contact with his office in even a remotely criminal fashion, was a guilty piece of shit, a sleazy offal-eating dung heap...well, you get the picture. They were all born repeaters who would continue to suck up the public's money, his staff's time and space on the court calendar. I waited for 'Bledsoe's Law' because it always cropped up about this point in a conversation on charging a crime.

"We never prosecute a case unless we're at least eighty-five percent certain we can win." There it was, Bledsoe's Law. "We don't even want to worry about whether or not the asshole's guilty...we know he's guilty or we wouldn't be writing out a long form. What we want to do is cream his ass. To do that with this Vollmer, I only need one piece of solid evidence that will stand up in court. Just one."

"You know what I know, at least until I haul the Professor back down here for another questioning." First, I wondered how often I could do that before his pinstriped attorney would holler harassment; and second, it wasn't true Jim Bledsoe needed only one solid piece of evidence. He could fuck up a prosecution faster than anyone I'd ever heard of and usually did. He could blow a 'smoking gun.'

"The next time find a way to nail him." Bledsoe stood up and jammed his hands into his pants pockets like he'd seen some attorney do on television. His houndstooth sport coat hung loosely on the spare frame of his thin shoulders. "Arrest the cocksucker and hold him for questioning. He's gotta break down, there's too much here. I don't care if you screw his ass to the wall for skinning that poor Mex sonofabitch or for cutting up this Brantnober broad. If we can break him down on one charge, the other will follow."

Tucker sucked on his cigarette and spread his big hands in the air. "There ain't nobody else, is there?"

"Vollmer claims he's been set up, probably by someone who wanted Portilla out of the way. He claims the ritual killing and the convenient find of the victim's clothing were put together to finger him. But, he hasn't any real alibi for the night of the killing. Not solid enough, I know. I was thinking of getting a search warrant to look for the stone knife Vollmer claims was taken from his collection. I don't think anyone took it."

"You might get one, depending on how good a salesman you are with the judge. I think there's more to go on with the other murder. Prove the Prof has been fucking his secretary. Old guys do that all the time."

That comment elicited a side-eyes glance from Tucker, who was lighting up another cigarette. Every male in the courthouse lusted after Bledsoe's legal secretary. One of the reasons he was so disliked was because all those lusting males knew he was dipping his wick into the sweetest piece of action that roamed the three floors of Cache Harbor County Courthouse.

"If I were you, I'd arrest him, book him, beat on him – verbally – and make his shittin' life miserable for thirty-six hours. That creep got the Brantnober broad pregnant. He knocked her up. She drives up here to Cache to do Christ-knows-what, probably extort his ass off, and he kills her – and I might add, the fetus. That's another whole series of counts. You get me something I can charge and I'll make up so many fuckin' counts against this sleazeball, it'll fill your pants." Having delivered the Gospel according to Bledsoe, he sat down. Then he leaned forward and reiterated the central theme of his undoubtedly unconstitutional harangue: "One fuckin' piece of evidence that will stick! That's all!"

Tucker snubbed out his cigarette and reached behind his desk. He pulled out a sheet of cardboard with a piece of yellow lined paper attached to it. "Now, here's what I done for ya, already." He pulled away the yellow sheet, exposing a pen and ink drawing of the thin, wispy-haired man who was posed with Erin Brantnober in the Halloween Polaroid. "This is the guy dressed like a beatnik in the snap we found stuffed in the Brantnober woman's mouth." I'd only seen the photo once, but I could tell immediately who the rendering was supposed to represent. "I had Ben Duschaine, the high school art teacher, make me a drawing of the fella for distribution. I realize the beard and hairdo might be fake, but then again it might not."

I took the sketch and accepted the bent Polaroid he handed me at the same time. The likeness was nearly perfect; this came as no surprise, since Duschaine supplemented his teaching income by doing portraits of people's children and grandparents. Most police artist renderings are composites drawn together from several witnesses. They don't look like real people, their noses are always wrong.

"Ben did a good job."

"I figured that since the Brantnober woman didn't make any effort to disguise her looks for the costume party, maybe her boyfriend didn't either and maybe he looks just like what we got here – or maybe he looks that way part of the time."

"At least it'll give somebody something to look at," Bledsoe chimed in.

"I thought you were sold on Vollmer as the culprit."

"Just in case this little weasel is involved in it, we ought to talk to him. I mean, he obviously knows the victim, he's got his hand on her tit."

"What we're doin' here, Pauly, is handin' you a couple lines of questioning." Ash lit another cigarette. "We gotta show some activity on these killin's to keep the press boys happy."

"What press boys?"

"The ones from the 'I Team' flyin' up here in their big blue chopper right now as we speak."

"That fucking Richard Sarstadt."

"That be the one, Pauly. BCA gave me the tip this morning. I'll be sure Dogget sends them your way when they check in."

"I suppose I'd better get my ass in gear, then. Any more names in this file for me to contact?"

"That's it for now. BCA said they would send up what the University police have; but aside from her phone and address, that's all there is. They're checking for the next of kin through the admissions office in grad school, but so far they haven't pulled anything."

"Somebody's going to have to go down there and look around her place," Bledsoe added. "Talk to a few of her friends and shit like that. Could be something nails her murder right to Vollmer's ass. That's all we need."

"On the other hand," Tucker added optimistically, "the professor might just melt like sugar in your hot hand as soon as you start questioning him. Save us all a lotta crap."

"Wanna bet? You haven't met his attorney." When I opened the door to leave, there was Deputy Dog reaching for the doorknob.

"Hiya, Pauly. You got any asshole left?"

"They didn't ream out the old one, they just punched me in a new one."

"Look at it this way, Pauly. You get to have all the fun while the rest of us grunts hold hands with the tourists for the next few days." Dogget pushed past me into Ash's office.

"Oh, no. I expect to have the whole mess cleared up in time to pull my shift in the beer garden."

Dogget snickered through his adenoids and entered the office. "By the way, Duluth P.D. called. The 'I-Team' kids stopped to refuel at the airport. Should be along real soon."

Murphy's Law. Bad to worse. I pushed through the glass doors that led to the dispatcher's cubicle and asked Ruthie to raise Mel on the horn. She was blond, cute and wore large thick glasses that made her eyes look way too big for the rest of her face. She was also twenty pounds overweight. That had not made much difference to Mel a year or so ago; he had dated Ruthie before marrying Judy...or was Ruthie only ten pounds overweight back then, I couldn't remember. She raised Mel on the radio and he said he'd meet me back at the office right away.

"Valerie Hackney called from the newspaper while you were in with the boss. I told her I'd give you the message as soon as you were finished in there. Sounded like she'd hang by the phone until you called back."

I sat down next to Ruthie and dialed the Telegram-Herald number. One ring and I was talking to Valerie.

"I've got two things for you, Paul," she said breathlessly. "The TV people are coming up from the Twin Cities and I think I've found something in Portilla's file."

"I heard about the 'I-Team' invasion already and you can't imagine how it thrills me to know I'm going to have to talk to those camera jockeys in an hour."

"I understand Richard Sarstadt is in town and he works for the station."

"That's probably it, but they'd find out anyway."

"You mean from the Telegram-Herald?"

"Valerie? You did OK on the stories." There was a pause on her end of the line. When she spoke again, she had changed the subject.

"About Portilla. The file you loaned me showed he had been in Minneapolis three times within the last fourteen months. Do you recall when the first date was?"

"Not right off hand. I was concentrating on the last two."

"Halloween. Halloween as in the Polaroid picture Deputy Dog showed me. That could link Portilla, Vollmer and the dead woman from South Apple Branch." Big Pause on both ends of the line. "Is that any help, Paul?"

"Could be."

"I'm sorry if it makes it look like the two murders are connected – I mean, I know how you don't want that to be."

"Too late."

"What do you mean?"

"They're connected. Real connected."

"You found something? Can you tell me? Is it in that Polaroid? There's something in that Polaroid that bothers me, but I can't put my finger on it."

"Calm down, Valerie, and put away your pad and pencil. I have to go make an arrest."

Before I left the Sheriff's Department, I had Ruthie radio the airport. The tower had not yet been contacted by any TV chopper; but in case I was interested, Professor Vollmer had just filed a flight plan to the Twin

Cities. I swore a blue streak. Ruthie covered her ears. It would be twenty minutes before Vollmer and his passenger, J. Bentley Prudhomme, would be ready to taxi out. I told the airport manager to deny takeoff. Then I asked Ruthie to call Mel by phone at the office and have him meet me at the airport.

"Sirens?"

"Sirens."

Chapter Nineteen

Of course we really didn't need to run sirens and the light bars, but what the hell. Put the fear of God in 'em I always say, let 'em know you're serious; it might shake something out of their pockets...like a confession. It's a little heavy handed, and they don't expect that from rural 'Minnesota Nice'. I was tired of 'nice'; tired of Vollmer's excuses and dissembling and tired of having to think of alternative reasons for Sparky Portilla's death, when every morning my gut told me one thing: Vollmer. I was also tired of being Ash Tucker's scapegoat and having to defend myself against a snot-nosed little County Attorney. And, if some pantywaist part-time judge didn't like it, he could go hell right along with the rest of them.

I wheeled my truck full tilt around the entrance to Cache Harbor Municipal Airport, screaming and flashing for all I was worth. I saw Mel close behind screaming and flashing along with me. It was a sound and light show Vollmer and a whole bunch of stunned locals wouldn't soon forget. But, I had to admit, though I didn't want to in the midst of my moment of glory, most of all I was pissed off because Richard Sarstadt called in the 'I-Team', because Lisbeth Ann spent the night screwing him and everyone else in town was clucking their tongues at Marie screwing me. OK, I was really angry! I accept that. The cool thing about it was that I could dump it on someone, and I was about to dump it on Vollmer.

I drove right up to the nose of Vollmer's plane, Mel behind me. There's something surreal about hearing sirens die down while the light bar continues to go crazy. It's a nice touch of magic realism in an otherwise dull world. Maybe Mel didn't have to pull a screaming wheelie behind the plane to block any possible retreat, but it was a nice touch nonetheless. After all, Vollmer and company should not have been leaving without telling me. It all came down to this: let's see how much we can bark before we have to bite.

If Marie was right, Vollmer might be treading a very fine line between reality and something far more strange. That could push him over an edge...confession or turn him into a pit bull lunging for my throat. Watch your back, the man is good with stone knives.

Mel was younger and more athletic than me, so he was out of his squad and arguing with Prudhomme before I opened a door. Vollmer was standing on the sidelines letting his attorney do the talking for them both. I purposely slowed my gait. It's an old Army trick. Hurry up and wait. I hurried up to get there and now they would have to wait to hear what it was I had to say. Prudhomme was fussing about the way he and the professor were being treated by us country cops.

"Don't you think all this is a little dramatic? Lights flashing, sirens going off like we were a couple of criminals?"

"I don't know that you're a criminal. I don't carry a pre-conceived notion about attorneys. On the other hand, I'm not so sure about him." I nodded at Professor Vollmer, who tended to try and evaporate into the background. To make my point, I put on my mirrored sunglasses. The glasses really did cut down on the glare from the tarmac at mid-morning; they also hid my eyes from Prudhomme and Vollmer, and that was always a big asset in playing it tough.

"Are you accusing my client of something?"

"You bet." I stuck a piece of chewing gum in my mouth because I thought it might make me seem even tougher than the sunglasses. "Just where in the hell do you two think you're going? I thought I made it clear I wanted to know if you were planning a trip. Or didn't you tell your client that's what I meant?"

"And how did you think I was going to get back to the Twin Cities? Hitch hike?"

"Not in those shoes."

"After all, Chief, we're hardly fleeing a police officer...and, if I'm not mistaken, we're not under arrest."

"You are now."

"See here, Chief..."

"Not you, buster. You can start walking for all I care. But Vollmer's coming in for questioning. He's not free to leave for thirty-six hours, so that must mean I have him on hold pending charges."

"I think you're overdoing the prerogatives of your office, Chief. I believe this will make the fourth time you have questioned Professor Vollmer in relation to this matter." I counted back and made it three times, none of them in custody. "I suggest you don't have anything to question the professor about and that you are harassing him in an attempt to either get information or admissions without benefit of bringing charges. I believe the State Attorney General would agree with that."

"This is different. I believe the professor is acquainted with a young woman named Erin Brantnober." Vollmer blanched at her name. "Ms Brantnober has been murdered – the woman in the lake? The one you both got so excited about yesterday at our last questioning? I can understand why, since she's been the professor's secretary for two years. I'd like to talk with him about that."

"Is that a charge?"

"Come off it, Bentley, you're not dealing with a complete idiot here. I've got thirty-six hours to come up with charges before I have to let your man go. I intend to do some hefty questioning in the meantime and you, of course, are invited to attend all sessions. So, let's lock up the plane and grab our bags and get in the squads so I can start doing my job."

Prudhomme stepped in front of Mel as he attempted to escort Vollmer to his squad car. "I object to this shoddy tactic and I furthermore object to the sloppy way in which Professor Vollmer's rights are being dealt with."

"OK, let's make it formal." I way overstepped my bounds and arrested Vollmer. Mel immediately launched into a recitation of the Miranda Warning, after which I told him to drive Vollmer to the courthouse and book him, process his valuables and find him a cell. "Don't forget to take his belt."

"This is highly irregular! The man is a nationally respected scholar, this is not the way to treat..."

"Listen, asshole, I was willing to sit down and talk this thing through with the both of you...about Erin Brantnober and Sparky Portilla, but you kept telling me my job. If we can't sit down and chat, then we'll do it by the fucking book. It's not my fault your client is going to have to cool his heels in County lock-up – it was your idea." He blustered back at me. "And one more peep out of you, and we'll give you the room next to his and you can both be guests of the City."

"Don't you threaten me..."

"How about resisting arrest, fleeing an officer, obstructing justice? One of those oughtta do until you make bail." I gave Mel the high sign to put Professor Vollmer in his squad. "Now you've got about eight seconds to get into the professor's station wagon and follow us to the courthouse, or you too are going to be walking around without your fucking belt."

I turned on my heel and walked back to my truck, leaving Prudhomme standing there on the tarmac. Mel turned off his light bar and drove off the airfield. In the windshield reflection of my truck I could see Prudhomme hurrying over to Professor Vollmer's beat up station wagon. I hoped the keys were still in the ignition because I was damned if I was going to soften the impact of my threat by going back and helping to hot wire that heap just so Bentley could drive to jail and bother me with details for the rest of the day.

I had hardly driven off the airstrip before Ruthie was paging me on the radio. I was wanted at the library. A disturbance. No details. She signed off at eleven fifty-nine. I looked at my watch; time just had a habit of flying by when you were having fun. My stomach was growling, but I wasn't sure why...Vollmer, Prudhomme, two murders, having to see Lisbeth Ann or no breakfast. I had a habit of putting my mind into overdrive when events started crowding in too close; that way I didn't have to think, I could just trust to reflexes. Marie would say I was an intuitive who had all the important stuff already imprinted in the double helix of my DNA molecules – that way I didn't have to operate from my head, I'd just instinctively know what to do. I think Marie gave me too much credit.

Driving down the hill, I kept watching Prudhomme in my rear view mirror. I was also feeling the hot breath of TV journalists on my neck. Those guys would make a flashy entrance at the airport. TV chopper pilots usually had long hours of 'Nam duty or Desert Storm time, or whatever the current Pentagon fracas was, under their belts. They wouldn't just drop in at the pad on the far end of the field, they'd barrel in like the opening scene of 'Apocalypse Now', setting down in mid-strip, scattering dust all over the people who had shown up for flying lessons.

The reporter would be dressed like he was expecting Cache Harbor to be a trendy ski resort in Colorado; and he would bail out of the chopper on a dead run to a phone booth. The cameraman would be in blue jeans and tennis shoes, decked out in battery packs and coiled wires; his videocam would leave his right eye only at those times when he took nourishment – usually eighty proof. The pilot would sit in the airport waiting room and drink vending machine coffee until his bladder would damn near burst.

The TV station was going to spend at least ten to twelve grand for less than two minutes of airtime. The reporter was going to stick his microphone in the faces of half a dozen locals, ask them what they thought about the murders, emphasizing the gore. Then he'd close on camera with some stupid platitude about frightened people huddled in the clutch of mindless terror for fear of a slasher loose in the north woods. Oh, yes... somewhere in the report would be mention of the uncooperative local authorities. That would be me.

I radioed Ruthie my arrival at the library, she told me Mel was ten-eight. He had arrived at the jail with Vollmer and Prudhomme in tow.

A hand lettered sign was taped to the glass door of the library informing patrons it was temporarily closed – please come back this afternoon. Mertha spotted me just as I was about to knock on the glass. She hurried over and turned the key, her face showed worry, resentment and shock all at the same time.

"Thank God, you're here." She allowed me to squeeze in the door before quickly locking it again. "It started about forty-five minutes ago, just after she'd opened the building. I got here at my usual time, nine-thirty. She wasn't here yet, so I just went about my duties in preparation for opening at eleven." We were inching toward Lisbeth Ann's office, but I couldn't see anyone through the glass.

"She got here about quarter to eleven, and seemed all right, but she was quite late and I could smell alcohol on her." Mertha wrinkled up her homely face in disgust. I knew Lisbeth Ann didn't drink much, and I was sure Mertha would rather give herself to a motorcycle gang than be caught with booze breath. In fact, Mertha probably dreamed of giving herself to a motorcycle gang. It would be a good tactic for getting one of those gangs out of town that would merit remembering – the threat of a Mertha-bang.

"Then she went back in her office and I saw her bring out a bottle of liquor."

"What kind?"

"How would I know? Does it matter? It was a big bottle, at least a quart."

"A liter."

"It was half empty. It was brown liquor and she kept pouring it into a paper cup and drinking it just like it was tea."

So, I opened the office door and had a look around. I didn't see Lisbeth Ann or the brown liquor. "Where is she now, Mertha?"

"That's when I called 911." She removed her glasses and wiped the steam from the lenses with a corner of her sweater. Mertha always wore a cardigan sweater, even in August. "When she locked herself in the bathroom and wouldn't come out, that's when I called. I could hear her in there, she was screaming at the top of her voice and saying such things as I never heard before, even on television. Vile, awful things." Screwed up homely face, again.

"What kind of things?" I couldn't imagine Mertha knew any vile, awful things, whatever she watched on TV.

"I couldn't repeat them, Paul. Not in good conscience. They were awful things. Dirty things."

"Dirty things?" It wasn't like Lisbeth Ann to swear dirty things no matter how drunk she got. I assumed her super-ego would kick in and prevent her from venting filth, unless Mertha's definition of filth had a lot less latitude than my own. I had always thought Lisbeth Ann wouldn't say 'shit' if she had a mouthful. Mertha would probably suffer a stroke if she heard Jim Bledsoe's take on 'dirty things.'

"Yes, awful dirty things. I think."

I walked over to the staff bathroom and listened at the door, then tried the knob. Lisbeth Ann was sobbing inside, but when she heard me try the knob, she screamed out a rasping, slurred tirade.

"Get the fuck away from here you cocksucking sonofabitch, and leave me alone!"

I looked at Mertha, who after the first expletive had covered her ears. She nodded her head vigorously when I looked at her to see if this was the kind of language she'd been referring to.

"I had to close the library." Her hands still covered her ears. "I couldn't let the patrons hear that."

Mertha was right and I was wrong. Lisbeth Ann would say 'shit', mouthful or not. I got close to the door and spoke to the blue plastic plate on the door that read 'staff only.' "Lisbeth Ann? Can you hear me? This is Paul. We need to talk. Open the door and I'll come in and we can talk in private. It's all right, Lisbeth Ann. Mertha will take care of the library while you and I talk." Long pause. I thought I heard a sob. I steeled myself for another vile tirade – one she probably thought I had coming to me, and one I was dreading to hear – but it didn't turn out that way. I heard the lock turn instead. I thanked Mertha and asked her to wait out in the reading room. She uncovered her ears and placidly followed my instructions. She was obviously shaken by the outbursts of her librarian, plus I knew she didn't entirely approve of me and she probably figured part of Lisbeth Ann's behavior had to do with me, and frankly I did too. I opened the bathroom door.

"What's the bastard saying about me?" Well, it wasn't about me, it was going to be about Richard. She was standing tight to the far corner, the bourbon bottle was perched on the edge of the sink and I could see vomit dripping down the toilet stool.

"Which bastard?"

"Richard."

"Haven't seen him."

"You're the only one, then."

"What do you mean?"

"He's been up at Tuggy's ever since the bar opened this morning."

"I hadn't heard, I've been out arresting people."

"Bragging about last night. Bragging about his big conquest." She pushed herself further into the corner.

"Look, maybe I should take you home." But she shrank further into the corner and made shuddering gestures with her hands.

"Have you ever heard Richard brag about it when he gets drunk?"

"C'mon. No, I haven't. Let's go."

"He tells it all. Nothing left to the imagination. He'll tell them about what a great mouth I have and how I used my tongue on him...even what it looks like when it happens."

"Lisbeth Ann, let's knock it off. I'll take you home."

"He's a regular porno movie, Richard is." She stopped and slumped. "I got sick, Paul. I better clean it up." She tried to move out of the corner, but failed. She stayed wedged between the red tiles.

"We'll take care of that later."

"He's telling them someone ought to make shoe leather out of my cunt because you can't wear it out. Isn't that funny?" Her eyes glazed over and she slid down into a heap on the floor. I ran some cold water on paper towels from the washroom dispenser and patted her cheeks and forehead. She smiled at me and tried to focus. "You ruined everything, you know... with your sexy little waitress." Here it comes, what I'd been expecting. "I was ready to love you, to make us a real number in the social column. I was ready to set up housekeeping, wash your dirty socks, keep you warm this winter. But I can't compete with a kid." She glazed over again and I continued patting her face with damp paper towels and making reassuring promises about taking her home. "I hope you washed off the smell of my perfume before you went to bed with her. I hope you at least did that."

I eased her up on her feet and braced her against me with my right arm. Once we were out of the bathroom, I signaled Mertha to open the library as I guided Lisbeth Ann out the back entrance to where my truck was parked. I was pretty sure no one saw me lift her into the seat. She didn't need that on top of the rumors. I got in beside her and closed the door. Her body slumped over and her head made a cushioned thud as it bumped the window. She began to snore softly and her breath dried the yellow flecks of vomit clinging to the front of her blue silk blouse.

Chapter Twenty

There was one more detail I had to take care of before beginning evasive action with the press and questioning Professor Vollmer. I radioed Mel and told him to position himself along the main drag east of town, just at the city limits, and to wait there for my signal. Mel informed me Vollmer was being booked by Deputy Dog on behalf of the city and that Prudhomme was complaining at every opportunity.

So, I drove out of Cache Harbor east on the main highway to Tuggy's. The bar was a hangout for men trying to regain their lost youth. Richard Sarstadt made it his favorite watering hole before divorcing Lisbeth Ann, and was apparently continuing the old tradition now that he was back in town. Most of Tuggy's patrons had been high school athletes; when their prep days were over and life began in earnest, they discovered they had little aptitude off the playing field. Now most of them earned their money with their backs and tried to re-live their past glory through summer softball leagues and winter basketball tournaments. 'Glory Days' is what Bruce Springsteen named it and I was humming his song as I pulled into Tuggy's gravel parking lot.

The strange car in Lisbeth Ann's driveway last night was parked in the first rank at Tuggy's. It was almost one-thirty and the boys had fortified themselves for more drinking by downing quantities of mystery-meat sandwiches from the vending machine. Put in a buck, get a bun with something gray in the middle, leave it in the cellophane and pop it into the mic, set the dial on three. Have another, they soak up the beer in the bottom of your belly and make you burp; the burps leave room for more beer.

Richard Sarstadt was not drinking beer. He was sipping something amber colored in a glass filled with ice cubes; by the looks of him, he had been sipping for quite a while. He was hunched over the bar crosshatching plastic swizzle sticks in a pile as he talked to another man who was also hunched over the bar stacking folded paper coasters that advertised a Canadian beer. I guess nine pairs of eyes followed me through the gloom to the bar where I greeted Tuggy and ordered a Seven-Up. Then I took my soft drink and walked down the length of the bar where I interrupted the conversation between Sarstadt and the other hunched man.

"Richard Sarstadt?"

"Who wants to know?"

"Paul Tharp. Thought you'd like to know the chopper from your television station is at the municipal airport."

"Tharp. I remember. I was sorta in and out of town a lot when you came here a couple years ago." He finished off his drink and picked up the change from the wet bar top. "Real nice town, Cache Harbor. Lots of great attractions...course I expect you know that." He snickered and punched the other hunched man with the beer coasters. "Keep my seat warm, Smitty, old man, and I'll bring the boys back here for a few bumps."

He thanked me for being his errand boy and strolled out the door. I watched him go while I finished my Seven-Up. The change Sarstadt had scooped off the bar had amounted to $11.45. Unless the U.S. Treasury was printing fifteen dollar bills, Sarstadt had downed nine of Tuggy's ninety-five cent bar bourbons.

Outside, I watched Sarstadt pull out of the parking lot with a wide turn to the right. I got in my truck, nosed out on the highway and drove back into town. Sarstadt was driving thirty-six miles an hour as he crossed the city line. I called Mel on the radio and told him to stop the blue Olds, license number 'DICKEY'. Sarstadt would have his name on a vanity plate. The state allows it and it's a fine ego trip for a hundred bucks. It also has the distinct side benefit of alerting the cops and highway patrol to just which drivers are the biggest dipshits.

Mel's squad spit gravel as he turned on the highway, light bar flashing and siren wailing. He forced a pick up on to the shoulder as he pulled around, then cut in front of Sarstadt's blue Oldsmobile. I pulled up behind them and got out.

"What's the trouble, Mel?" I asked innocently as Sarstadt tried to pile out of the front seat.

"I clocked him doing thirty-five in a thirty zone, chief." His ticket pad was in his hand.

"Richard Sarstadt, here, is an important TV man on his way to meet a camera crew at the airport." I patted Richard on the shoulder; he looked slightly confused, but grateful for the intervention. "I don't think we should quibble about five miles an hour. Could be a speedometer problem, right, Mr. Sarstadt?" He nodded his head in agreement and said it was a new car and all and maybe it was mis-calibrated at the factory.

"Of course, I suppose as long as you've stopped him you might as well give him a routine breathalyzer test."

"What the hell does that mean?" He grabbed my arm.

"Well, after all you did come in to town from Tuggy's." I looked at him and then at the place where he gripped my arm.

"So, what's wrong with that?"

"Nothing, as long as you don't test positive."

"Test positive! Shit you can't have two fuckin' drinks in this state and not test positive, for chrissake!"

"You want to let go of my arm so the officer here, can administer the test?" I controlled the urge to cripple the sonofabitch right there on the main drag, but there was too much traffic. In this state, when it comes to driving while intoxicated, the law presumes you're guilty until proved innocent. Sarstadt refused to take the breathalyzer test and that meant automatic arrest for DWI. When Mel reminded him of that, he recanted and took the test. Of course, he failed it. His blood alcohol level was not up there with some of the better drunks in town, but it was close enough for my purposes. Mel impounded the blue Olds and stuffed its swearing owner in the back seat of his squad car. I radioed for a wrecker to tow in the vehicle. For what he did to Lisbeth Ann, I probably should of busted his knee caps with a tire iron or held his head under ditchwater for half an hour, but busting him for DWI was legal and had it's own satisfaction. Maybe Richard and I would talk about Lisbeth Ann later and maybe I'd beat the living shit out of him at that time.

Back in the office I found a sandwich on my desk with a note from Marie: 'I'm at your house cleaning. I'm going to stay there until you throw me out. Hope you like the new picture.' The small brass frame was standing by the answering machine. It was a head and shoulders photo, sunny, smiling. The one by the sculpture was gone.

I collected the files on Portilla and Erin Brantnober, played back through the answering machine, locked the door and left for the courthouse. I didn't like doing it, but I'd have to send Mel to the University to check on Erin Brantnober's apartment and talk to neighbors and students who might have known her. A man should be home with his wife and new baby, but with a lot of concentrated hoofing, Mel could have the job done in two days at the most. In the meantime, that left the Cache Harbor PD a little thin: me.

Lists. I hated making lists; against my basic nature to be organized, which is one reason why Marie felt compelled to clean my cabin. At the head of my list was to question Vollmer and make something stick, anything stick so Bledsoe had a wedge even if he would fuck it up later. Then, find a judge before he took off on a fishing trip to avoid Voyageur Days. I needed a search warrant to nose around Vollmer's collection while we was in lock-up. Then I'd deal with Richard, then the 'I-Team', and then if I was still awake, I'd forget this horseshit day and lose myself in Marie.

It was a good plan, but one destined to fail from the beginning. When I pulled into the courthouse parking lot there stood the broken down airport taxi parked illegally in the handicapped slot. That meant the 'I-Team' was waiting inside ready to leap on me as soon as I entered the door.

They were. They did.

Was I able to comment on the progress of the investigation? Only to the extent that both victims had been identified. (And why the hell hadn't either been claimed by a next of kin?)

Why was the city police carrying on both investigations when only one of the murders was committed in town? As long as there appears to be a connection between the two crimes, the city will head the investigation. (As long as Ash Tucker is sheriff, there will always be a connection between the two.)

Can I elaborate on the connection between Jorge Portilla and the second victim? Not at this time (At least they don't have her name yet).

Can I identify the second victim? Pending notification of next of kin. (Another mother finding out about her dead child through the wonders of the electronic media.)

Would I describe the condition of the victims? Sure, one was skinned and the other was halved. (You could read it in Valerie's stories).

They understood the second victim was a young woman and that she was pregnant, would I comment? No I wouldn't. (Where the hell did they learn that piece of information?)

Did the police have anyone in custody? I lied.

They understood the police had arrested a university professor, could I comment? Technically, holding for questioning due to special knowledge regarding the circumstances under which the victims died. (Vollmer was definitely safer in my jail than on the street among this pack of feral dogs.)

There is a fear that a maniac is loose in the woods. Confirm or deny? No substance to such a rumor. (The woods are probably filled with crazies, but they are not cutting up their neighbors)

Getting back to the method involved, the local newspaper claims at least one such death was carried out in the manner of an ancient Aztec ritual. Was I aware of any group in the area practicing those rituals and what the pregnant woman's death ritualized in the same way? No, no cults to my knowledge. No, the second victim's death was not ritualized. (Maybe the same weapon, but not in the same manner.)

Then why did my department insist there was a connection between the victims? Reasons largely other than physical. Beyond that I couldn't comment at this time. (Because the fuckin' lazy sheriff in this county says there is! And…if you'd get that goddamn microphone out of my nose, I'd get about the business of trying to prove a connection.)

I was giving it a valiant try, pushing my way past the reporter. I derived a certain satisfaction in noting I'd been right about the Colorado ski resort costume. And, as I'd correctly guessed, the cameraman was dressed in jeans and tennis shoes, wired umbilically to his equipment. I saw the helicopter pilot worm his way through the crowd and whisper something into the reporter's ear. She caught up with me before I could make my escape down the hall to Tucker's office.

"You've got Richard Sarstadt locked up, what's the deal?

"No comment."

"Whatta ya mean, 'no comment'? He's with us."

"No comment."

"Have you arrested our Northeastern advertising manager in connection with these murders?"

"No comment." Let them sweat this one out and give their fertile minds something to make compost out of. I pushed my way through the glass doors leading to the sheriff's office. The reporter and her cameraman stayed on the other side. Mel Swanson met me outside the dispatch room. I transferred some of the papers from the Erin Brantnober file to his clipboard, including the rendering of the bearded man I'd received from Tucker that morning. Then I clapped him on the shoulder and sent him on his way. In exchange, Mel gave me a note that indicated Portilla's body had finally been claimed by a shirttail relative in California. The relative had no money to fly out and back, let alone make funeral arrangements. Calexico PD secured a warrant to draw enough money out of Portilla's bank account to cover the costs. The flayed man would soon be on his way home, in a zippered bag and at his own expense.

I signaled Ruthie to let me through to the jail. The buzzer sounded, I opened the barred door and told the jailer to bring Professor Vollmer to the secure interrogation room. On the way down the hall I passed Richard Sarstadt being fingerprinted by a large deputy named Miller. Sarstadt called me a name denoting a classic form of incest. I waved and wondered if he actually told the boys at Tuggy's someone ought to make shoe leather out of Lisbeth Ann's privates because they wore so well. I wondered if the meat on Sarstadt's face would wear as well after a few dozen punches.

The only beating I was up for now, however, was the verbal kind at the county attorney's request: beating up Doyle Vollmer.

Chapter Twenty-One

"Describe again, if you would, your relationship with Erin Brantnober."

"He's already described it once." Prudhomme was taking notes almost as fast as the tape reel was spinning on Dogget's recorder. I was fifteen minutes into what promised to be a long questioning.

"Just so I can keep it straight in my mind, counselor. Now, let's go over that relationship again."

"She came to work as my secretary in the Anthropology department the fall quarter – that'll be two years ago this fall – and continued the regular fall, winter and spring quarters ever since. She also worked during the abbreviated summer session I held in the graduate school last summer."

"That's her work schedule, Professor. What was your relationship?"

"Our relationship was her work schedule. She was a graduate student secretary, that's all."

"Paid by a work program at the University?"

"Yes."

"How much?"

"I'd have to check in the graduate school office, there are formulae for that, I believe."

"Is it very much money?"

"I shouldn't think the University would pay handsomely."

"Did she ever mention to you she was short of funds?"

"Not that I recall."

"Did she ever ask you for money?"

"No. Even if she needed it, I doubt she would have approached me."

"Do you know *why* she was up here in Cache Harbor County the beginning of June?"

"No I don't."

"Did you know she *was* up here the beginning of June?"

"You don't have to answer that question," Prudhomme advised, but Vollmer waved him off.

"No problem, Lee. I didn't know it. There's no sense leaving a wrong impression. I do not know *why* she was in the area, nor did I know that she *was* here. This is a popular place for visitors, I don't see any special significance that she was here, just because I have a place here."

"Had she ever been up here in the past?"

"How would he know that? He's only known her for two years." Prudhomme splitting linguistic hairs.

"What I meant was, has she ever visited you at your summer home at any time in the past?"

"Never."

"Did she know you had a home here?"

"I assume so, I often mentioned it. My collection is here and I frequently visit even in the winter."

"You never asked her to accompany you?"

"He told you..."

"Even on business? As a secretary?"

"No."

"Do you have another secretary?"

"No, I don't."

"So, Erin handled all your secretarial work but never visited Cache Harbor where your substantial collection is housed? Never needed her to catalog anything? Answer inquiries?"

"What ever she did in those regards she did from my University office."

"Do you have any idea of how she happened to end up in South Apple Branch Lake?"

"You're asking some very leading questions, here, Chief..."

"Well, try to see it from my side, Bentley. So far the only person I know who knew Erin Brantnober at all well, is sitting right here. There's a strong possibility he may be able to shed some light on what she was doing here."

"I already said I have no idea what she was doing here."

"Or, I might add, that she was here at all." Prudhomme was off to confuse the issue.

"Really? Then tell me who is in the plastic bags?"

"Undoubtedly Erin Brantnober, but that doesn't mean she was ever here in one piece – excuse my harshness, Doyle."

"So you buy in with what the Professor said earlier about a conspiracy against him? Someone halved Ms Brantnober and hauled her up here, sunk her in the lake, all with the idea of having a couple of fishermen snag her body two months later."

Prudhomme made a smirking gesture with his mouth as if to suggest the conspiracy theory was at least on an equal footing with the one I was proposing.

"Ms Brantnober's private life was her affair, Mr. Tharp, not mine. You must realize it is unusual for a professor to have the same secretary for as long as Erin, Ms Brantnober, served as mine. I have never had a student secretary as long as she worked for me in the department."

"That's interesting, Doyle, I wonder why. Was there any special reason why she would stay in the department in that capacity for two years?"

"Other than the obvious one?"

"Which is?"

"She was a graduate student working in the department of her study and the job remained open to her."

"Why wouldn't it have remained open to another student in the past?"

"Let me say that perhaps my request and work load for someone in that position were not always to the liking of the young women who typically filled the position in previous quarters."

"What kind of requests, Professor? Where any of those requests sexual in nature?"

"You know I'm going to advise against answering that question, Chief, so why did your dirty little mouth even bother asking it?" Prudhomme waited for my answer with pencil poised over pad.

"Sexual harassment is not unknown between university professors and their students. The newspapers are full of it and this University has had its share. Furthermore, Erin Brantnober was pregnant when she died. That leaves any male she knew a suspect as far as I'm concerned." I of course had not told either of them beforehand about the finding in Eddie Loetz's autopsy.

"I'm sorry," was Vollmer's only response to the news. Not a big response from a man who had worked with the victim three to four hours a day for the past two school years. Of course, he could have been sorry and still killed her. He could have been sorry he did kill her. None of it cleared the air for me.

"Did you know she was pregnant, Professor?"

"No, of course not. She didn't show it."

"She didn't show it when you saw her last?"

"That's what I meant, yes."

"When exactly was that, Professor?"

"I'm trying to think. The spring quarter finished in June, but most of the graduate students had completed their work before that. I'm sorry to say the enrollment in graduate anthropology has never been large and it is even smaller now. I believe I stayed on a week or so after classes finished, as is my custom – to clear up whatever needs to be done before summer. I was not conducting a summer seminar this year."

"Did Erin finish at the end of the quarter?"

"Erin, Ms Brantnober, was only responsible for a thesis. She had finished her coursework."

"Did she finish the quarter?"

"Do you mean as my secretary? No." That drew a quick look from Prudhomme and he took furious notes as a result. "She did not report to work the last week of classes."

"Didn't that concern you?"

"Yes it did. I had a number of things that needed work and I had to ask a secretary in the Social Studies department pool to do it."

"Did you tell anyone that Erin was not reporting for work?"

"No."

"Why not?"

"There are certain confidences a teacher shares with students, an employer shares with an employee. Sometimes it doesn't seem like much, but there is room often for compromise."

"A minute ago you said you didn't know much about her private life, now you're admitting sharing confidences. Which is it, Professor?"

"I still don't know much about her private life, Mr. Tharp. What I meant was, that I was attuned to her as a teacher, advisor and employer.

She was upset about something and I could sense it. I did not expect to consider her thesis until at least fall quarter, so when she failed to come into the office that last week of school, I chalked it up to whatever it was that had been bothering her."

"Does knowing now that she was pregnant, shed any light on her behavior for you?"

"I've never been married, Mr. Tharp and I know very little about the complicated symptoms of pregnancy. I assumed she was having trouble with her boyfriend, whom I also understood to be her roommate."

"What's his name?"

"I have no idea. She always referred to the person as just her roommate. In fact, I didn't realize it was a man until last fall."

"How did you find out?"

"Something of a fluke, I suppose. A number of graduates in the social sciences organized a costume party at Halloween last year. It was also to be something of a good-natured roast of instructors within the departments. I attended and caught my share of barbs. That is when I met her roommate."

"Did she mention any name for this person when you were introduced?"

"He already told you he doesn't know the person's name." I guess Prudhomme figured he'd been quiet too long without making an objection.

"It was only a passing introduction and she referred to him only as her roommate."

I reached into the file and took out the crumpled Polaroid of Erin Brantnober and her stringy haired companion, Vollmer confirmed it was the person he met at the Halloween party, that they were dressed that way when he met them. Was the roommate in the department? A student? Had he been seen by Vollmer before? The answers were all negative. Dogget yawned and told me to stop the questioning for a minute while he flipped the tape reel.

"Let's get back to Erin's absence the last week of spring quarter. Did you try to contact her at all?"

"I suppose I phoned her once or twice, but I did have other things to do."

"So what I'm supposed to believe is that you were not all that concerned about the absence of a woman who had worked as your secretary for two years, a woman whom you had advised as a graduate student and a woman who had been a frequent pupil of yours. This is a woman in her mid-twenties, obviously attractive, skilled in secretarial work as well as a good enough student to continue graduate work at the University. You even went to parties with her! Did you know any other women as well as you knew Erin Brantnober?"

"Please, Chief, this is badgering the witness."

"He's not a witness, Bentley and this is not a courtroom. I think it's a reasonable question to ask, for chrissake. Unless he's living with an old maid sister or has a mistress, Doyle spent more time with Erin Brantnober than with any other female acquaintance, and I'm supposed to buy the idea that he doesn't care where she is for a solid week?"

"I told you I attempted to call at least twice."

"But you didn't contact the University Police. You apparently didn't drive over to her apartment to see if she'd injured herself and was unable to answer your calls. You didn't alert anyone else in the graduate school. You didn't ask about her roommate or try to find him. In other words, you acted exactly like you knew where she was."

"That's not true!"

"Even in two pieces I could tell this woman was good looking. Do you mean to tell me you were not attracted to her?"

"See here, Chief..."

"That no one else was attracted to her either? That no one inquired where she was?"

"This kind of questioning has got to stop..."

"How did she get pregnant, Professor? From a toilet seat?"

"For God's sake, Chief, the man has already told you she had a live-in boyfriend..."

"Was it you, Doctor?"

"Chief! I insist!"

"No!"

"Was it Jorge Portilla?"

"What are you saying?" Vollmer was sweating and Prudhomme was out of his chair.

"I'm saying Portilla's parole officer puts your smuggling friend in Minneapolis over Halloween and again at the same time Erin Brantnober disappeared from her desk in your office."

Vollmer raised his hand and indicated Prudhomme should sit down, then in an even voice he addressed me. "Not all men, particularly men my age, have the same sexual drives as you, Mr. Tharp. If you are suggesting Jorge Portilla had an affair with Ms Brantnober, then I suggest it was a very interesting one, biologically. I can assure you Ms Brantnober did not fly out to California during winter quarter to become impregnated by Mr. Portilla. She never missed work until that last week of spring quarter. With that in mind, if she was three months pregnant at her death, and the last time Jorge Portilla was in Minnesota was over Halloween, either a new gestation record has been set or they were having intercourse by mail."

When I glanced up at Dogget, he was wetting his forefinger and making a score for Vollmer on his air blackboard.

"Furthermore, Mr. Tharp, since you insist upon linking me with these deaths, I'll tell you something that is probably none of your business. I've been sterile for years."

Prudhomme stuffed his mechanical pencil into the breast pocket of his suit coat and announced that the brave statement by his client should close the questioning down for good.

"Not exactly."

"Why not, Chief? You've been accusing the professor of intimacies with a college student for the past half hour. The man has just told you he is incapable of making any female pregnant. Surely that's easy to verify."

"He said he was sterile, not impotent. Had you been having an affair with Erin?"

"No."

"It's possible she could have seen Portilla at some other time, unknown to you, then tried to pin the pregnancy on you."

"Not possible."

"She confronts you here at your summer home and you kill her because she can ruin your reputation. Portilla, not wanting to be responsible for a kid, joins in."

"No."

"Which one of you jabbed at her with the stone knife? She was slashed with a rough blade. She ran away, out into the woods. You and Portilla followed. She was bleeding and finally you found here, dead or unconscious from loss of blood. You finished the job by cutting her in half and sinking her in South Apple Branch Lake."

"This is absurd. I demand to speak with a judge." Prudhomme tried to leave the room, but Dogget shoved his foot across the door.

"When Portilla came back here a few days ago, he'd had time to devise a method for extorting the bejesus out of you. You argued and then you killed him. Either because of who you are or because of some cockamamie scheme to make it look like you were framed, you cut out his heart, burned it as an offering and flayed him out to finish the picture. Now isn't that just about the way it plays, Professor Huitzilopochtli? Only this time the hummingbird can't fly away; his feathers are too matted with the blood of his sacrifice."

Dogget was staring at me with his mouth open. Prudhomme was staring in the same direction gritting his teeth. Vollmer was red in the face and sweating but his voice was even and controlled.

"I see you've been studying your Aztec mythology, Paul, but I'm afraid you're wrong about me. I don't see you've one scrap of evidence to hold me any longer. I want you to know that I don't blame you for pursuing this matter the way you have. I admit much of what you say would appear plausible. I can't blame you for following that line of reasoning. I rather admire you for it. You're a bright fellow. But you have no evidence, all you have is a reasonable scenario."

Dogget dropped his foot from the doorjamb as Vollmer rose from his chair. Prudhomme opened the door and allowed his client to precede him. The door swung closed of it's own accord. I looked at the wall, then at the floor, then I sat on the table.

"Better see to it he's released, Dog."

"You fuckin-A couldn'ta done better than you did with what you got. You even had me goin."

"I'm not finished."

"No, I guess not."

"No retreat, baby, no surrender."

Chapter Twenty-Two

So, I closed the file. Put Jorge Portilla and Erin Brantnober to bed. Put the case in an "out" basket. Nice try. No brass ring.

It was close to five and I needed my gun and leather back around my waist. I didn't want to kill anyone – I just wanted to know I could. I'd collect the hardware from Ruthie in the dispatch office, then see what Marie wanted to do about dinner, then maybe sleep a year. I was walking past the long row of white barred cells.

"Tharp!" Richard Sarstadt had not sobered up in four hours. "Tharp! When the fuck am I gonna get outta here?"

I detoured past the last cell in the unit. Sarstadt was agitated and pacing back and forth like the caged animal I'd hoped he'd transform himself into. "Tharp, you sonofabitch, that's entrapment. I'll have your ass when I'm outta here."

I stopped in front of the cell. If I had been inside with him I'd have torn him to shreds, just on principal. But I was outside, so I waited.

"You can't make this goddamn DWI stick and you know it."

"Why don't you tell me about Lisbeth Ann? Why don't you tell me about all the things you said to her? All the goddamn promises? All the fucking lies?"

"What's to tell? She loves me. She wants me back. She thinks you are a two-timing shitface for fuckin' some little waitress. I mean, man – she is pissed at you. She has your number and I'm on the flipside." His face pressed against the cream colored bars; the paint job had been recent and perhaps the last barrage of petty crooks had spent their days painting ecru latex on inch and a half iron bars. "She only fucks for me, now."

At that I reached in between the bars and wrapped my sizeable right hand behind Richard Sarstadt's neck; grabbed the base of his skull and pulled forward with all of my might, which magnetized his face to the iron. His features were meshed into a barred pattern that pushed his front teeth and lips into an apish grin, his cheekbones into a flattened smile. His eyes dimmed at the contact.

I held him for a while then walked out of the cellblock past the jailer who had his feet resting on a desk.

"Better check on cell one. I think the occupant passed out and hit his head on the bars. Could look bad if the corrections inspector came through."

Marie was asleep on my davenport when I opened the door to the cabin. She was still wearing her waitress uniform. The house was spotless. I had never bothered much with housework. No wonder she was tired.

"Chicken" was the one word she spoke without opening an eye. I agreed it sounded like a good idea. She was too tired to cook and probably would refuse to eat anything creative. I dropped my files on the dresser and went into the bathroom to wash my face. Even the toothpaste cap had been wiped clean.

She again mumbled something about chicken and I assured her I'd understood. Outside the cloud bottoms had begun to waffle. It would rain soon. By the color of the horizon, it would rain a great deal. On my way back to the café, I had to admit to myself that punching out Richard Sarstadt was probably a stupid idea. It couldn't set things straight between Lisbeth Ann and me and it could cause a great deal of trouble with my badge.

The TV newsmen had left. I'd release Sarstadt tomorrow, but I'd pull a computer check first, just to see if the DWI was aggravated, in which case I'd take it to Bledsoe. That would mean Sarstadt would have to come back to Cache Harbor and either stand trial on a gross misdemeanor or plea negotiate his way down. I'd almost rather drop the charges and send the pain in the ass home after he dried out...but then the whole thing would look like the planned vendetta it really was.

The town appeared quiet as I drove to the Outpost Café. The calm before the storm of Voyageur Days. If it was going to rain, best that it do it now before the celebration started...but it would rain during the four-day event anyway, it always did. In fact residents of the North Shore could barely string together three dry days even during a normal summer.

When I walked in, Reefer Carlson was sitting alone eating something with a lot of gravy on it. I sat down with him and gave my chicken-to-go order to a new waitress who wore the name 'Kathy' on a plastic plate pinned on her uniform.

"Now that the paper is out, everyone in town is talking about the murders. By tomorrow everyone will have read it. Should keep that answering machine of yours busy."

"You have the thanks of a grateful police force. Actually, the stuff isn't too bad. You'll be happy to know I even told Valerie that."

"Yeah, she shouldn't have done that...given you the copy before it was published." He cut into a piece of leathery roast beef and considered it in its pool of gravy.

"I considered that a real courtesy. Besides what could I have done about it if I didn't like it?"

"Nothing. It's the idea of the thing. By the way, those TV boys even interviewed me. I don't know whether they'll use it or not."

"Why you?"

"Well, you know, me being the publisher and all. I sort of reflect the feelings of the town...or they figured I was supposed to have my finger on the community pulse."

"But Valerie wrote the stories."

"Technically, the paper wasn't out when they were here, and besides I think they were looking more for impressions than for anything else. Probably will sensationalize the hell out of it."

"Still, you would have thought they would have wanted to talk to the reporter who covered the story." A sinking feeling started to crawl into my stomach. "By the way, were is Valerie?"

"Around." Reefer filled his face with the remainder of the hot beef sandwich and gravy. He stopped in mid chew and looked at me as I looked back with a look I hoped would convey that this answer didn't go down as easy with me as the mashed potatoes. "Around the University."

That was what the sinking feeling was all about. I just rolled my eyes at the ceiling and slumped back in the booth. "That's the last fucking time I work out an agreement with that woman. Or with you, for that matter."

"Take it easy, Paul. Val isn't going to screw up your goddamn case any. From what I understand, you could use a little help."

"No, she won't screw it up. Maybe she and Mel could go door-to-door together, holding hands and asking questions in unison."

"Probably not. She left before Mel did."

"Fine. That means by the time Mel questions they will have already talked to Valerie. Creates a hell of an impression of this police force."

"No one down there is going to have a hell of an impression of this town, anyway, Paul. If you're gonna get mad, get mad at me. I'm the one who let her go."

"Was that because of some inflated idea of journalistic responsibility or did you just want to give your cock a night off?"

"C'mon, Paul. Easy does it. It's our story and we chose to go after it. You already admitted she did a good job on what's in the paper. Give her a chance. She won't get in your way, or Mel's either. What's a few more questions? Once the Brantnober woman's friends or neighbors know she's been killed, they'll be glad for all the interest paid."

"There are just a few technical things wrong with that idea, Reefer." I took his unused water glass and drank from it. "First, I haven't released Erin Brantnober's name for publication and neither have I released her address."

"By the time our next edition comes out, her name will be public and as for the address...well, next time don't leave murder files lying around on your desk."

"So now it's breaking and entering?"

"She went to your office and you weren't there. Your girlfriend brought you a sandwich and while she was fussing with some photograph in a frame, Val happened to look at the Brantnober woman's file. She came back to the office all hot and bothered about going to Minneapolis. So I let her."

"I suppose she took a copy of the artist's rendering along."

"Sure."

"Shit! Don't you realize we're dealing with a murderer, probably a double killer? And you send your honey off to the University to knock on doors and show people a picture of a suspect. What if she knocks on the wrong door, Reefer? What if a wispy-bearded guy opens the door and pins her to the wall with a butcher knife?"

"That's not going to happen, Paul and you know it. You don't think there's some hippie down there responsible for these murders, you still think it's Professor Vollmer, and so do I. The only thing Val is going to find out is more about Erin Brantnober and maybe, just maybe, the evidence that will forge the final link in the chain around Vollmer's neck."

"Nice speech, Reefer, but that's why Mel Swanson is down there. That's his job, not some wet head reporter from the north woods. How to get that information is part of what he learned in four years of schooling. I have to be able to build a case from that information. It has to be gathered properly and given to Bledsoe ironclad. That's hard to do even when you know how."

"Whatever Val finds out, we'll give you."

"If it's not damaged in the process."

One of the waitresses had turned on the color television that sat on a shelf above the counter. It was only used to watch reruns of high school sports events that were taped and broadcast over the local public access cable channel. Tonight, however, Cache Harbor was going to be on TV. Reefer and I broke off our argument as the waitress turned up the volume on the early edition of the news.

"The citizens of this small north shore community will not sleep easily tonight..." The ski resort reporter was standing on the harbor with the town spread out behind him. He gave the viewers a brief outline of the facts of the two murders, getting the time of death wrong in both cases. He played up the Aztec sacrifice angle for both murders, which was also wrong, and then he talked to three townspeople, none of whom had the foggiest idea of the facts. An older gentleman, who said he was a tourist, claimed it reminded him of the Ed Gein killings. The man was from Wisconsin and so was Gein. A local woman I recognized as working at the electric cooperative said she was keeping her doors locked and the kids inside after dark. To cap off the interviews, a local grease monkey with a socket wrench in his hand told the camera that he and his girlfriend thought there was a maniac loose in the woods. The camera switched to Reefer standing in front of the Telegram-Herald office. The graphic under his picture read 'Carl Carlson'. Reefer assured the reporter there was no panic and everything was under control. Then they spliced in some of the questions thrown at me in the courthouse interview. I was identified as 'Paul Thorpe' and most of the footage managed to paint me as a living color asshole, uncooperative and unwilling to discuss the cases – and probably unable to cope with the seriousness of the crimes. The best that could be said, I guessed, was that at least I looked official.

I paid for the bucket of chicken with coleslaw, smiled at the smart remark the waitress at the cash register made about the way I looked on TV, and then drove back to my cabin. Marie was up and seated in front of my small television screen where the weatherman was pointing to a map filled with cute little clouds and telling northern Minnesotans to batten down the hatches for a doozy of a storm. I never watched Twin Cities television news even though I could get it on cable. I preferred the stumblers in Duluth. Less polish, more sincerity and very little happy talk. Marie was wrapped in a light quilt, her uniform laid out on the back of a chair. She said she was starving, then told me how impressive I looked on TV and what an idiot the reporter was. Pretty, but an idiot. I sat down beside her and she opened the quilt, enclosing us both in the wrap. Her naked body was warm against me.

"First things first." I struggled to set down the barrel of chicken.

"Oh, no. We eat first."

"That's what I meant."

"They say you shouldn't make love on a full stomach."

"They also say you shouldn't go swimming for an hour after a meal."

"This has nothing to do with digestion. They say people's sexual desires are dulled after eating and that sex on an empty stomach is hornier."

"We could make an experiment of it. Once before we eat and once after, just to see which was better."

"Nope. I'm too hungry."

"Well, you brought it up."

"Just as a point of information. Did you get coleslaw, too? Do you want a beer?" I slipped from beneath her quilt and she re-wrapped herself as I found my way to the kitchen. "You be the waiter and if you do a good job, I'll give you a terrific tip."

The tip had been terrific, but I couldn't help think there may be something to making love on an empty stomach. Maybe it was because I was dog-tired and depressed as well as full of chicken and beer, but I didn't seem quite as motivated. It was still pretty athletic and Marie certainly didn't complain, but I was weary, worn down by my inability to solve the two murders. Maybe the TV reporter was right to leave the impression that the Cache Harbor cops didn't know exactly what they were doing, that it was too much for them, that the BCA or someone should take over and let Chief Tharp pass out traffic tickets during Voyageur Days instead.

"So you had to let him go?" Her head was resting on my lap and I was sitting up in bed with the sheet over us. The air was chilling and soon I'd need to reach for the quilt. It was still early evening and the promised rain was a few hours away.

"Yes, I had to let him go. He had an answer for everything, not that I believe him. But it's my word against his and that's not good enough for Jim Bledsoe and a jury."

"What do you have?" The vibration of her voice made my groin tingle.

"A corpus delecti."

"You have two, what more do you need?" She rubbed her nose in the sheet claiming an itchy nose meant someone was talking about her.

"No, not another body, but a body of facts that hangs together. I hope once Mel gets back from the University, we'll have something besides air that ties Vollmer to at least one of the murders."

"Was he pretty smooth? He struck me as being pretty smooth." The vibrations from her voice on my groin were making me excited all over again.

"Very smooth. He didn't even need his stout attorney. Vollmer knew what he had to say and how he had to say it. He only slipped up a couple of times. I'm sure around his office he called her 'Erin', but he wanted me to think he only addressed her as Ms Brantnober."

"Hmmmmmm."

"Do that again."

"Hmmmmmm. Hey, what's happening down there?"

"Wait a minute."

"Actually, I thought you'd rather wait a couple of hours."

"No, not that!" I had begun to slip down in the bed, but now I straightened up with a jolt. "It just dawned on me that Vollmer talked about Erin being three months pregnant."

"You told me she was."

"But I didn't tell that to Vollmer. I just said she was pregnant when she died. He made a point of it by saying that if Erin and Portilla had been having an affair, it would have been sex by mail…or something like that, because Portilla was in the state over Halloween and not again until Erin was killed."

"What makes anyone think the professor wasn't responsible, that seems far more likely." She reached for the quilt.

"He says he's sterile. That's one of the things that might show up on his medical record. Mel is checking that out. Another thing, now that I think about it, he wasn't very surprised to see that Polaroid picture of Erin and the hippie. He doesn't know who her roommate was, but I would have expected a little more reaction at seeing the picture. He didn't even ask where I got it, like he knew all along."

"You know, that seems kinda odd to me." She pulled up the sheet and quilt and settled down next to me. "I mean, that's another one of those clues you keep talking about…the ones that seem a little obvious? Why would somebody do what they did to that poor girl and then drop a piece of evidence in her mouth? They must have gotten rid of everything else – no clothes or anything."

"My only guess is that they hedged their bet. In case she was found, we'd all go looking for the guy with the wispy beard. I'm sure Vollmer didn't anticipate killing Portilla back when they murdered Erin."

"And that's what's happening. You're off chasing the guy with the wispy beard while Vollmer remains free." It wasn't meant to be anything other than a statement of fact, and her voice didn't carry any trace of scorn, but I felt the barb nonetheless.

"I'm requesting a search warrant tomorrow. It'll take some doing, but if Vollmer is missing one of those Aztec knives, there may be something to his claim of being set up. If they're all present and accounted for, which I suspect is true, then I'm one step closer to nailing him."

"Couldn't he just hide a knife or toss it?"

"Hide it maybe, but not toss it. His collection is too large a part of his life."

"I don't know, Paul, that doesn't sound like much. What you need is to find another Polaroid in his desk drawer, letters or something like that."

"What I need is a miracle. Maybe Mel will come up with one."

"Miracle Mel. That's cute. I hope he does, then I'll call him that and it'll really bug him."

"Or Miracle Val."

"Don't tell me that bitch is down there!" She sat up straight, the covers falling to her waist. I nodded and drew her close to me. "What business does she have doing that?"

"She was going through the file, apparently while the two of you were chatting in my office this afternoon."

"Not exactly chatting. More like spitting."

"What's the problem?"

"Being catty, I suppose. I brought you that frame and another photograph I like better. She insisted upon looking at the old picture and I wanted to get back to work. Then she asked a few personal questions that I didn't think were any of her business. It wasn't much, but I guess you could say we spit at each other a couple times. She makes our relationship sound like hers and Reefers." She turned in my arms and kissed me hard on the mouth. "And it's not like that. Not at all, and I think she's jealous of us."

I don't know, I couldn't think of Valerie Hackney as the jealous type, but I could see where she may have picked up a few lines from Reefer's script and tried them out on Marie to see if she could get a rise out of her. She obviously had.

Marie did not slip back to my side, but kept her mouth close to mine. She ran a cool hand down my chest and stomach, twined my pubic hairs in her fingers. She kissed me again and began to stroke me until I was hard. I pushed my head back into the pillows as her tongue probed deeper into my mouth and her hand worked faster. I was wondering what she had in mind when our mouths uncoupled and she began kissing her way down my body. When her mouth reached my pubic hairs, the telephone rang.

I climbed out of bed, penetrating only the darkness. The phone was clattering in the other room. Marie followed with the quilt enclosing us both against the cooling night. I picked up the receiver. It was Mel calling collect.

Chapter Twenty-Three

"Saw you on TV just now. You looked great."

"Yeah, I was on the six o'clock news too. I probably aged by the ten o'clock spot." My phone is mounted on the wall and I was standing there in my all together.

"Those guys don't get much right, do they?"

"They're famous for it, but they've gone now and I hope they don't come back."

"Don't bet on it. The longer this thing drags on, the more apt they are to do some investigating of their own."

"You mean like Valerie Hackney."

"You know about that, then. That's one of the reasons I'm calling. She's everywhere, but the University police won't give her the time of day. They've been real helpful to us, in fact I'm calling from their office."

"Burning the midnight oil?"

"I guess, but not much is coming to light."

"I was afraid you'd say that. Nothing much happened with Vollmer, either." Marie was starting to act up. She was inching herself around my body from back to the front.

"This Brantnober woman is a hard one to trace. It seems the University is the only one has any information on her and darn little at that."

"I know you got there late, but have you been to her apartment?" Marie had worked herself around and began nipping at my chest with her front teeth.

"Yes. So had Valerie."

"Shit!" There goes the evidence." Now she was giving me a hickey on my stomach.

"I wouldn't say that. The place was clean. According to the building super the rent had been paid through August, but sometime in June everything was moved out. He was on vacation at the time and didn't see who did the moving. I'm checking on that, though."

"I suppose he told the same story to Valerie." Marie gave up on the hickey and moved to my erection.

"Yeah, in fact he was kinda pissed at having to go over it all twice. He lives in an adjoining building and didn't appreciate having his TV show interrupted."

"What's Valerie doing?" When she heard the name she began working with her mouth in earnest.

"Talking to the neighbors is about all I can tell – and the super. The 'U' cops won't release any information to her and neither will the grad school. I should have some stuff on Vollmer for you to look at tomorrow."

"Anything on the roommate?" I was having a hard time concentrating on the conversation and I was betting Mel could tell something was going on.

"Not much. The super said he didn't know anything about any roommate and added that all the students sleep around so much, it's hard to tell who's rooming with who. The guy's kind of a prude about that. I do have one lead on the fella in the Polaroid, but it'll have to wait until tomorrow. I should be back around two."

" Good work, see you then." It sounded more like a croak than a sentence. I put the receiver back on the wall cradle and reached for Marie's hair. I think thunder rumbled down the shore.

My mind was not on the two carnies who insisted upon standing in the pouring rain arguing over who was going to put up which dart toss, where. I was thinking of the phone message left on my recorder. The carnies had been arguing since eight that morning, and finally the girlfriend of the younger man stopped me on the street and brought me to the carnival site. She said she was afraid someone would get hurt. I was going to say I was clean on Voyageur Days duty, but what sense would that make if her boyfriend was about to get himself knifed, or knife someone else. I went through the motions of settling the argument, but I kept thinking about the message from Valerie: three in the morning.

"Damn funny time to call, I know – 3AM – but these college kids really know how to party. By now you should be over being pissed off at me for being down here. Nothing against Mel, but he's not going to drink beer with kids getting ready for fall quarter. I'm calling now, because I know you'll check this damn recorder first thing in the morning, and I want you to be careful. I believe there's more to all this than Professor Vollmer. The key to it could be 'Sheepie'. Be careful, Paul. Watch your back. I'll see you this afternoon. I've got to get some sleep." Click.

The carnies finally finished their argument after I'd asked a woman who sold posters of rock musicians if she would consent to placing her tent between the two dart games. I didn't see what real difference it made since all their efforts were going to be mired in mud for the next few hours.

The city issued its officers latex-coated anorak parkas for this kind of weather; dark blue, very waterproof and being plastic, very hot. I hurried up the street to the Outpost Café, ducked inside the vestibule, removed the slicker and went in for a cup of coffee.

"Jeez, Paul, watcha doin' about that killer fella loose in the woods?" The question came from an earnest old fellow named Vince. Reefer was right, the answering machine was going to be busy – the human one as well as the mechanical one.

"Don't you worry, Vince, we've practically got the guy behind bars."

"The TV said he was a maniac." Vince's eyes were either bleary from lack of sleep or no lack of drink. I knew which.

"No maniac, Vince, you'll have to take my word for it. Those TV fellas – always getting it wrong." That seemed to placate the old timer, so I ordered a cup with no cream from Marie. "How do you look so goddamn good in the morning?"

"I slept like a log. It was you tying the sheets in knots."

"It's not fair."

"Of course not. It's not supposed to be. I'm prettier than you so I'm supposed to look better in the morning. You're supposed to have bird cage mouth and look like hell...don't you watch TV?"

"Valerie called last night."

"I didn't hear any phone."

"Early this morning at the office. Left a message. Been to a beer party with a bunch of college kids. She sounded funny, but I guess she would. Said there was more to this than just Vollmer."

"Did she say what?"

"No, there's only about a minute on the recorder, so she cut it short. Said she'd be back this afternoon. Said I should watch my behind. Said the key was something or someone named 'Sheepie.'"

"Sounds like she's writing a crime novel."

"Pretty cryptic, I agree. I think what it was, was a few conversations with Erin Brantnober's friends, a few beers and maybe a little Acapulco Gold. Valerie thinks she has a Pulitzer going and is doing me a favor by dribbling it out."

"Valerie is getting to be a pain in the ass."

"Maybe she's jealous."

"After last night, what do you think?"

"I think the control factor is a joke. We got off all rounds in the chamber with no control on the trigger finger."

Marie tended to her waitressing and I drank my coffee. The rain fell just like the weather lady predicted. There were severe thunderstorm warning out for the shore and small craft warnings for the lake. There were no U.S. Weather Service warnings for me. Why should I be careful? What had Valerie smoked to give her that impression? Who or what was 'Sheepie' and why was he, she or it so important? The weather lady couldn't answer those questions by pushing her laser pointer at the little rain clouds dotting her map.

"Was the fella on TV right?" Gert Bushmiller sat down next to me at the counter. I hadn't seen her since the day she discovered the flayed man in Palmer's barn. I asked her how she was doing, but she wanted an answer to her question, so brushed it aside.

"Gert, it's been a week. It would take a week just to type up the paperwork. It'll be over soon."

"Got an angle, eh Pauly, Boy?" She slapped me on the back. If only I did, Gert. If only I had an angle. "You cops, just like on TV. You got the best goddamn job around. Must be the most fun, anyways."

"It's a riot, Gertie, a goddamn riot." I paid for my coffee at the register. Marie took my change and smiled. "You're place or mine?"

"I got a letter from Emily, so I better do some cleaning and packing at my place. I like your bed better, anyway. See you at supper, this time on me."

"Do I have to leave a tip?"

"Wouldn't that start the tongues wagging."

I took my anorak off the hook and threw it over my shoulders. It was only a few steps to the truck, but the downpour continued; it was what the locals called 'a soaker'. I drove off to the county courthouse where Richard Sarstadt was waiting his release and a judge was waiting for a search warrant request on Vollmer. Jim Bledsoe was also waiting to ask why there was no long form complaint replete with charges against the good professor.

When I pushed though the glass doors to the Sheriff's department, I spotted Lisbeth Ann sitting on one of the oak benches opposite the record secretary's office. Her blue trench coat was wet on the shoulder tops and sleeves where the rain had pounded down on her. She stood up when she saw me come in.

"Did you do it for me or your pride?"

"He'd had nine drinks and he was driving."

"He says you set him up."

"Everyone claims everything is set up these days." I walked over to the rack of cubbyholes fixed to the wall. All the cops and deputies had cubbies with their names taped to them. Vollmer claimed he's been set up, too, now so did Richard. And he had been, of course. There was a slot for Cache Harbor P.D. and Richard Sarstadt's driving record printout was there. One glance showed three priors in five years. I shook the printout at Lisbeth Ann. "Gross misdemeanor DWI plus an aggravated count. If the goddamn judges did their jobs, Richard would have been in jail or a mandatory treatment program instead of a bar."

"He's gone through treatment." She sat back down on the bench. "After we separated."

"Apparently he needs to go through it again." I sat next to her and she didn't try to move away. "Look Lisbeth Ann, between you and me, I guess I did sort of set up Richard. I mean, I went out to Tuggy's with the idea of finding a way to arrest him. I wanted to get even and I wanted to make sure he didn't come looking for you again last night."

"His TV station manager called me. Wanted to know if Richard was being charged with murder." Her eyes were wide and wetter than usual.

"You didn't tell those reporters that, did you?"

"Reporters sometimes draw their own conclusions based upon what they see. Cause and effect thinking can be misleading. My intent was to let Richard dry out and then let him go. I can't do that now, not with this report. He's going to need an attorney."

"Regardless of what you think happened the other night, Paul, I'm not going to fight Richard's battles for him." She stood and adjusted a rain hat over her blond hair. "I didn't come down here just to see poor Richard. I came to gloat. I also hoped to see you. Now that I've accomplished both, I'll go to work." She leaned close and kissed me lightly on the cheek. "Thank you, Paul."

Well, I looked at the floor and felt more confused than ever, embarrassed, too.

"Thank you for helping me at the Library. I made a fool of myself, but you know why. I've explained it all to Mertha and she was surprisingly understanding. Also, thank you for being honest with me about Richard. It was wrong, you know, but I can't say I'm unhappy you arrested him." She walked to the exit and I opened the first set of doors for her. "He's such a bastard. I'm such a fool."

"I think you called me a bastard, too."

"If I did, I'm sorry. I'm apparently more of a territorial woman than I thought I was." She paused at the door. "Your library card hasn't expired, you know." The smile was faint and blurred away from me in the rain.

"Chief?" Ruthie called me from the doorway. "What do we do with your prisoner, it's been fifteen hours."

"Well, Ruthie, you saw the printout. I guess I'd better fill out a complaint and see the county attorney."

"You want to see the prisoner?"

"No need."

"Says he fell against the bars yesterday. He's got a pair of great looking shiners."

Ash Tucker's search warrant philosophy was a practical one, especially if you were looking for drugs, illegal weapons or kidnapped babies. You showed up at the back door at 4AM, knocked once and walked in. Nobody is awake at four in the morning except bakers and baking is an honest profession. Tucker maintained that if you were really looking for something, you'd most likely find it at four in the morning.

That however was not going to be my approach with Vollmer. You don't break down doors in the wee hours and go rummaging through a collection of Pre-Columbian artifacts. Marie was right. The premise was thin and the likelihood of finding anything, thinner. On the other hand, I had to try something to move this case off dead center. The judge would see me in a half hour. In the meantime I filled out a complaint against Richard Sarstadt and gave it to Bledsoe's legal secretary. I understood why all the courthouse boys tripped over their tongues every time she walked by; but I had a college girl in love with me and a librarian who had not given up. I also had two dead bodies and Jim Bledsoe wanted all my attention.

"Dogget said you did good in there with Vollmer."

"I didn't win"

"I understand you're going for a search warrant."

"I'm grasping at straws."

"Frankly, yes, but maybe the Prof will slip up and you'll get lucky." He looked at the complaint form his secretary had given him. "What's with this little shit?"

I gave him the Sarstadt briefing, he bitched about judges who wouldn't throw the book at drunks. It's the same gripe everywhere. The cops and the prosecutors bust their asses and the judges look the other way. Before I left his office, Bledsoe asked if I needed any help with the murders, which I took to mean there would be a lot of help soon if there were no arrests. I couldn't blame him. The BCA would come sweeping into town at short notice and I'd save face by working with the Bureau. It would look like a big time operation to the public, but to the other cops it would look like I'd fucked up big time. And they'd likely be right.

Failure is a way of life. The judge refused the search warrant. Come back when you're ninety percent sure the murder weapon is collecting dust in the Professor's display case. There's no such thing as a search warrant for just looking around. Call him up, the Professor's a nice man. Maybe he'll show you around without a warrant.

The rain didn't improve my spirits. I switched on the wipers in my truck and turned on the blower to clear the moisture from the windshield. What I had was a wet, soggy day that promised to drag on forever. Two flamboyant murders with clues that led nowhere. A prime suspect who was smarter than me and a county attorney who had run out of patience. I had a fledgling officer trying to root out information in the big bad city and a highly motivated newspaper reporter getting in his way. I had an alcoholic ex-husband who could probably make big media gashes in my career and a forgiving librarian who sounded like she was trying to make a couple out of us again. I had a college-aged lover keeping me thin, but at the same time packing to go back to school. All this and that fucking Voyageur Days started tomorrow.

I also discovered, driving back to the office, the media had not gone home. I now had two TV news teams in town this morning. Murphy's Law.

Chapter Twenty-Four

Listening to what Mel had dug up in the Twin Cities made it seem as though Erin Brantnober existed only on the University campus. She had her entire identity there; off campus she disappeared. No one by the name Erin Brantnober held a driver's license or state identification card. No one by that name had charge accounts at major department stores... no Visa, no Mastercard. No junk mail showed up at Erin Brantnober's door and she never had a telephone according to Northwestern Bell. What she had was a Social Security number, a bank account, a file full of paid student fee slips and a record of grades that had kept her above the 3.5 grade point average through six years of college.

Between the time I'd discovered two TV I-Teams roaming the Cache Harbor streets, and Mel walked in the office door suffering from automotive jet lag, Murphy's Law continued in full operation... everything that could, did go wrong. At least it seemed that way. There was another fight at the carnival grounds, this time it was alcohol and stolen girlfriends. Then there was a call from an attorney who said he was representing Richard Sarstadt and another who was complaining about the way a traffic accident had been reported. I also managed to speak face to face with both teams of TV reporters and told them nothing new that they could not have reported from last night's competition. I received a report from the US forest Service that no abandoned vehicles had been found in the last week. I opened a letter that told me my personal auto insurance had elapsed; I had forgotten to tell the company that my personal car had lapsed into the junkyard last month. Finally Reefer Carlson stopped in to see if I had heard from Valerie. I hadn't. If he didn't like her giving me advance copy of stories, then she certainly wouldn't want him to know she had called me at three in the morning, slightly buzzed.

"From the graduate school office, I got her grades, her work record as Vollmer's secretary, a wage statement of earnings, her medical plan details and a few other things." Mel tossed the file folder on my desk.

"How did all that check out?"

"Good student, no so hot wages. Only used the medical plan once and with the exception of her absence that last week of Spring Quarter, a very good work record as Vollmer's secretary."

"What about the University Police?"

"Nice bunch of guys, but since Erin Brantnober was never in any trouble, they didn't have much. They were a big help in getting me connected to the Grad School and finding out some other things, but they only have a record of her because they have her prints on file. She apparently was responsible for some departmental expenses, but there were no discrepancies in the money handling.

"Did she ever file a complaint of any kind against Vollmer?" I knew the answer before I asked the question."

"Nothing. The only indication they even knew each other was Vollmer's quarterly performance reports on her and they were all marked excellent."

"What about other people she worked with?" I figured these waters had been muddied by Valerie Hackney.

"I talked to two other part-timers in the Social Services division; remember classes haven't started yet and there aren't all that many students around. The two I spoke with said they knew her slightly, and she seemed like a nice person. Not much."

"What about the guy who took care of her apartment building?"

"The Super? Aside from what I told you last night about his attitude, he couldn't offer much else. Erin's was toward the end of a big four-story unit, one building over from where the Superintendent lives. The rent had been paid with a check dated Saturday, May 30 – that was Memorial Day and was for 700 dollars – June and July. He had not received the rent for August, so went ahead and advertised the apartment. A week later he got three hundred and fifty dollars in cash with a note from Erin apologizing for the past due payment. He told me he had not seen Erin at all in June or July, but when the August rent wasn't paid, he checked out her place and found everything had been moved. He said he left it as he found it. He was surprised when the rent came in the mail, but money is money as far as he's concerned."

"Postmark on the envelope?"

"Zero. He thinks it was mailed locally but can't remember."

"What about the neighbors?"

"Mostly upper division students. Three fifty a month is a little heavy on rent even for working grad students. No one had occupied the apartment adjoining hers during June. The Super rented it in July. For what it's worth, there was a doorway between the rooms. Apparently it could be used as a large double for multiple roomers, but with the Superintendent's attitude toward loose living college students, I doubt he rented it that way."

I thought about loose living college students and recalled the phone message from Valerie. I also thought about Marie going back into that environment. I didn't want her hanging around with students…I wanted her hanging around me."

"A neighbor on the other side of Erin's apartment said she had moved in the building in May. The best she could do was tell me the girl in the place adjoining the Brantnober apartment had a lot of stuff when she moved out. No names. No positive ID."

I played Mel the recording of Valerie phoned in at three that morning. "You pick up anything on a guy by that name?"

"Only that maybe she was living with someone. One of the secretaries I spoke with in the Social Sciences Division? She'd been at the Halloween Party in the photograph. She thinks Erin was there with someone answering the description of the guy with the wispy hair and a beard, but it was her impression the beard wasn't real. She didn't mention any names."

"Could she place Portilla at that party?"

"No. Only Professor Vollmer, but there were a lot of people there, and most of them in costume."

"What about Vollmer?"

"I guess that's where I'd disagree with what Valerie said in that phone call. I think the story is Vollmer, at least there are a few things I found that don't jibe with what he's been telling us."

"Like?"

"Like a lot of what's in his collection doesn't belong to him. It got there because Portilla has been hauling the stuff across the border by the truckload. Vollmer isn't the only one buying either, apparently."

"What did you do down there, talk to the FBI?"

"Better than that, I found a jealous colleague. Another PhD. His specialty is similar to Vollmer's and he's trapped by it. He doesn't have the tenure and he basically believes Vollmer's scholarship is firmly grounded in greed. He wants Vollmer's position in the worst way and was ready to badmouth him the first chance he got."

"Sometimes the disgruntled employee syndrome can backfire." I looked over the file Mel handed me and picked out the medical records from the University.

"I think he gave me enough so you can go back to the judge with a search warrant request, but with a little different angle."

"Bledsoe says we do anything we can to break him down. Apply pressure. If we don't, I'm convinced he'll apply the Bureau of Criminal Apprehension and we're back to ticketing the Dickey Sarstadts of the world." There appeared to be nothing in Vollmer's medical records indicating sterility. I kept on looking.

"Well, according to Dr. Ben Mastroianni, the departmental snitch, Vollmer has been collecting the property of the Mexican government hand over fist for ten years. He really got going when Portilla came on the scene. Mastroianni says it would not be difficult to obtain a list of known artifacts stolen or presumed smuggled. The Mexican government publishes such a list annually. All it would take is someone on this end to match Vollmer's collection to the Mexican want list. We request the list, get the search warrant and Bingo!"

"I could have used that 'Bingo!' a couple of hours ago when the judge threw me out of his chambers." I found another medical report, this time for health insurance. Bingo! Vasectomy eight years ago. "According to this, the Professor's been shooting blanks for eight years. That means that if Erin Brantnober was pregnant, it wasn't by Doyle R. Vollmer, PhD."

"That's another thing Mastroianni claims. Vollmer was something of an ass-bandit around the graduate school. A few female anthropology students, so he claims, were passing classes on their backs. He said Vollmer's attendance at parties like the one given last Halloween was common."

"And of course this Mastroianni doesn't diddle the students." I noted one or two ailments Vollmer had been treated for, but nothing that couldn't be explained by creeping middle age.

"If he does, he doesn't allow himself to be used or trapped. According to Mastroianni, Vollmer had on several occasions in the past, actually paid for sex with young students by giving them passing grades. This was mostly on an undergraduate level. He also claims Vollmer was not beyond fixing up friends with some of the choice students."

"Tell me it was one friend in particular."

"You got it. Mastroianni didn't know the name, but the description fits Portilla. Also, that list of visits logged by Portilla's parole officer is apparently pretty incomplete. Mastroianni remembers seeing Portilla many more times than we have documented."

"So, the Professor is buying hot artifacts with a combination of money and sex for grades. Portilla has the genuine hots for Erin Brantnober and is sneaking up here to see her in violation of his parole. In the meantime Erin is getting straight A's and Vollmer is paying bargain basement prices for Pre-Columbian art. Erin turns up pregnant and threatens to blow the whistle on the scheme; Portilla or Vollmer panics and kills her. Portilla shows up a couple of months later with a sweet little feather amulet. There's no more Erin, so the price is up where it should be. Vollmer argues with Portilla, who probably threatens him with Erin's death, and the professor kills him." I whistled and claimed I'd not been too far off all along. Vollmer must have been burning up during yesterday's questioning. Gotta hand it to him, he's a cool character. We danced all around this story yesterday and he never budged.

"Once classes start again, it shouldn't be too hard to find a couple of students who will testify to Vollmer's tactics. By that time we could have the artifact deposition sheet from Mexico and a search warrant as well."

"It means cracking Vollmer, and that won't be easy." I recalled his clam exterior under questioning.

"But we can charge him with receipt of stolen property and conspiracy to smuggle. That puts him in jail...and it's an international crime, as well. High bail and high visibility. If anything will break him down, that should. I mean, without credibility, what has the guy got?"

"So what do we do about this 'Sheepie' character?" The thought crossed my mind that Valerie should have popped into the office long ago.

"Maybe Erin talked to her boyfriend about it. Maybe Valerie meant this guy is the key because he can nail Vollmer."

"Why should I have to cover my ass?"

"An end run by Vollmer?"

"I don't know, maybe Vollmer is a psycho. Marie thinks he floats in and out of this world and one that existed two thousand years ago. Maybe he'll try to put an end to our investigation by taking a look at the underside of my epidermis."

"Maybe I can go home and see my wife and baby?" Mel stood and stretched his car-cramped legs. "In the file there is a number to call for a Telex to Mexico City and the artifacts division of the National Museum. Tell them you want the complete artifact deposition list. Mastroianni says you might win a trip to Cancun or a year's supply of nachos."

I glanced at my watch. Four thirty-seven. "Drive by Valerie's house on your way home and see if her car is there. I'll check at the Telegram-Herald office. In this weather, I wouldn't blame her if she parked at some motel for the night."

My phone call to Reefer's office caught the girl who took want ads at the front desk. She was closing the place and about to leave. Reefer had been tied up with the television reporters for the past hour. No, she had not heard from Valerie. Could she please get home before it got dark? She believed what she had read in her own paper about crazies in the woods with bloody daggers.

Mel's voice crackled through the radio base station in my office. Valerie's car was not parked in her driveway. I checked with the Zenith number for highway patrol information. No accidents involving a Valerie Hackney, but the weather was so rotten, she'd be better off sitting it out in a truck stop.

It was well after five when I completed my Telex to Mexico City. I dialed Valerie's phone number and let it ring eight times. Then I locked up my office and threw the anorak over my head and hurried out to the truck. It was only two blocks away, but the trip to the Outpost Café was slow. The sewers were backed up with flooding rain and I stopped to help a tourist family of five get their car started.

Inside the Café, Reefer was eating again. No problem. A nice lady from a motel fifty miles south of here had called. Val was safe and sound but bushed. She couldn't drive on. Not to worry, if the rain let up, she'd be home tonight. If not, tomorrow.

Sitting there with Reefer, I remembered tonight's dinner was on Marie, so I only ordered a cup of coffee. My pager beeped. An accident west of town. A TV news van collided with a lumber truck. State patrol was on the way, could I cover? Fuck 'em. They deserved it for missing the six o'clock deadline; now they'd miss the ten o'clock as well.

I wheeled out of town and hoped it wasn't a messy accident. I hoped Mel's theory on the Vollmer collection was on target. Most of all I hoped Marie would keep dinner hot. Then I thought about love on an empty stomach.

....

If life was a stream...a stream of consciousness, as someone wrote, then my banks were caving in. It was almost eight o'clock when I opened the door to my cabin and the rain was dripping off my anorak as I looked at Marie who was dripping back at me.

"My goddamn car quit! Right in the middle of that damn low spot at Zabel's corner."

"At least it quit in front of a service station."

"The water was right up to those things at the bottom of the door."

"Rocker panels."

"Whatever. Zabel pulled it out, but the engine was too wet and I had to walk here." Her hair was hanging down her back in long black slippery streaks. Her raincoat was not as waterproof as the label claimed and her jeans were soaked from the running shoes up to her knees. "I just got here and I haven't fixed dinner and I'm wet and cold and want a shower."

"So do I." I stripped off my parka and unlaced my boots and she did the same. We laughed at the squeegee noises the nylon and leather made and the way the rubber soles would squawk on the wet linoleum. Her pout was gone and the banks of my river seemed to be shoring up.

I guided her to the small bathroom where we peeled off each other's clothes. She was wetter than me, but by the time we had finished touching and holding and undressing I was equally wet.

"The first time I saw you like this, your hair was just as wet," I recalled Bullpen Lake.

"I always want it to be like this, you and me." She turned on the shower and the water was almost immediately hot. "I got real depressed today packing up Emily's things. I couldn't think about packing my own.

I don't know what to think about going back to school. I want to finish my degree, but I don't know how I'll manage not being with you."

"I don't even want to think about that."

"I can't think about it anymore today, either. I just wanted you to know I was, and that I don't know what to do." She held me close as the hot shower needles beat on my back. I turned her around so the water shed off her head in long rivulets down her black hair. I began to gently shampoo and caress her scalp at the same time. Soon we were lathering each other's bodies.

"Have you ever made love in a shower?" She wiped the shampoo from her face.

"Can't be done."

"You know, I've just been considering that and I think you're right." She hit the cold water handle and a piercing shot of ice slammed me in the middle of my back. She giggled and stepped out of the stall while I cursed trying to find the water faucet.

"One thing I meant to tell you." She was drying off in front of the full-length mirror and inspecting herself as she patted dry. "When I was packing today, you know? Well, I read some more on the Aztecs."

"No more Aztecs, not tonight." I shut off the water and opened the curtain.

"That name is pronounced 'Shee-pay', not 'Sheepie.'"

"You mean the guy Valerie thinks is important?"

"Also, he's not a guy. It's spelled 'X-I-P-E' and he's a god. The Flayed God."

Chapter Twenty-Five

Some men create goddesses of their women; some women set their men up as gods. The Greeks seemed to have the best of both worlds, since the Olympian ones intercoursed with the mundane. But in this century, and probably for the several past, gods have not been known to roommate with mortals – at least to my knowledge. Marie said she didn't think Erin Brantnober was living with a god either, but she was studying at the feet of her mentor, Doyle Vollmer, the one man who knew more about the Aztec gods than anyone else in the neighborhood.

I tried to make light of it by saying that I thought living with a guy who walked around in another man's skin must have been a little messy, but Marie didn't think that was funny. She told me that she'd read in one of Emily's textbooks that in the purest sense, Xipe was the god of rebirth and that the shucking off of one's skin signified the giving up of the old for a new life. The book referred to him as the Lord of Liberation: a robust metaphor, she remembered it said, of the painful freeing of the light that is within us...freed from its terrestrial loneliness.

I was having trouble getting past the blood and gore, the screaming pain and unimaginable suffering to come anywhere close to seeing how that kind of activity freed the light within me. Maybe I'm just not a very religious guy. I get nervous in a Catholic church, too. I have problems with excessively bleeding gods hanging by iron nails.

Marie seemed to understand the metaphor better than I did. She thought Erin Brantnober was truly in love and that the nickname she had chosen for her lover was the most robust one she knew, the Flayed God himself.

Then, who was her lover and did he kill her? Did he kill the interloper, Portilla? Was it the professor, the smuggler or the man in the phony whiskers? Murder is hard enough to solve, hard enough without making it even more complicated: murder by metaphor, for crap sake.

I was squeezing out our wet clothes in the sink and Marie was sitting huddled in the corner of my big old davenport, a quilt wrapped around her. The rain was pounding on the windows and a candle sputtered uncertainly from the middle of the empty dining table.

"I have a light inside of me, and I'm so alone."

"No you're not. I'm here." I wrapped a bath towel around my waist and re-entered the room.

"I'm not alone now, I'm alone next week, next month. I'm afraid of the loneliness of not having you, of having to go away."

"I thought we weren't going to talk about that tonight." I sat next to her and she kissed me lightly.

"Does that mean we can stop time? If we don't talk about it, will it go away? Will we be suspended in space and never touch down? How much does love liberate and how much does it confine?"

I had no answers to her questions. We just held each other as the thunder rolled ceaselessly through the lightning flashes and I could smell the ozone smells of electric sky fire. Then the sound of the telephone forced its unnatural tinny mechanical intrusions into these wholly physical moments.

The old woman's voice was filled with panic. There was someone in the church screaming horribly. Pastor Mark and his family were gone and she lived right next door to First Immanuel Lutheran. She apologized for bothering me at home, but she was sure someone was being killed.

I dressed and was in my truck cursing the weather shortly after she hung up. The scare had started, the urgency increased, they needed immediate attention, immediate answers; it wouldn't do to just leave messages on a recorder anymore, they were starting to call at home – killings, maniacs and rain-drenched imaginations.

First Immanuel dominated the corner where it stood. A large church with iron flying buttresses after the fashion of what a modern architect thought was the look and feel of a medieval cathedral. I dipped my truck down the sloped driveway into the flooded parking lot and stopped. Near the rear entrance stood a small car and a minivan. I recognized them both: Reefer's van and Valerie's hatchback. I gunned my motor and skidded around the outside of the van, hit the breaks and was out in the rain in an instant. I ducked under the church's brick canopy and tried the door. It was unlocked. Pastor Mark had told me once there would always be an open door at First Immanuel. There were few if any real church thefts over the past several years, and even if there had been, the good-natured pastor would still leave his church open for those who might need its sanctuary, especially on a cruel and sodden night like this.

I edged open the door. No sound, no tortured screams the old woman had so graphically described over the phone. I pushed the light mode button on my watch, it read 9:38::44 PM/WED 19. The dim overhead lights stayed on throughout the week as a soft welcome to any of the faithful who wandered in for whatever reasons they carried with them. I stepped out of the hall into the narthex. The rain beat steadily on the vaulted roof and echoed up the aisles into the nave. The hollow beating drew my attention to the sanctuary. A large polished brass cross dominated the back wall over the altar, a marble table resting on two carved stone legs. In gold lettering etched deep into its white and gray-laced surface were the inscribed Gothic letters of 'Holy Holy Holy'.

A thin red line of blood dripped down the last 'Holy' and filled the first letter of the word with gore. Elsewhere on the altar blood was drying into the more porous veins of the marble. On the flat table surface, soaking into the fringed lace runner was a splayed naked body. I walked cautiously up the center aisle where the dim overheads playing softly on Valerie Hackney. She had been ripped open from her navel well to the base of her neck; her bare breasts fell away from the gashes that followed the line of her lower rib cage. A large dark hole had tried to seal itself after her heart had been cut out and the life violently pumped from her body. Now it only seeped red and pale yellow fluids. Her eyes were wide open and her mouth gaped. The final instant of recognition on her face – what was happening and that there was no escape.

I moved counter clockwise around the altar. In the small stone baptismal fount was a black obsidian knife lying in a pool of coagulating blood. Her sightless eyes watched as I reached for the knife. She had been diminutive in life, but now she seemed even smaller in death. I think all things look smaller dead, without the gift of animation that makes them seem large. A moaning cry broke through the hum in my head and the rain tattoo on the roof. I spun around and focused on the narthex and stairs to the choir loft.

"Reefer! It's Paul. Reefer! Stay where you are." I ran to the end of the pews and took the loft stairs three at a time, unsnapping the leather keeper on my holster as I went.

Reefer Carlson slowly stood up at the far end of the choir loft. "I can't find it, Paul. If you'll help me, maybe we can find her heart and put it back. If we put it back in time, everything will be all right. I've looked everywhere Paul, but I can't find it. Help me Paul."

The next words wailed out of his mouth like a tornado siren. He screamed for help, any help at all and now I could understand the fear in the old caller's voice. There was someone being killed in First Immanuel. Valerie's death happened in shocked silence, Reefer's life was being ripped from him in long protracted screams of disbelief and leaving him a hollow shell with eyes as vacant as the woman he loved. I took him in my arms and turned his face away from the lighted altar below. The siren shrieks melted into heaving sobs when the screaming turned deep inside. I felt the cries seep up my throat like bile from a hangover and infuse themselves into the tissue of my pounding brain. My screams spread out into a silent high-pitched wail as I felt the flesh-shell that was my friend fight to shudder itself back to reality.

He looked up at me, eyes wide as Valerie's. "I don't suppose it would do any good if we found it, would it?" He broke into such a heavy sob, I thought he'd choke on his own saliva. After a few moments, I eased Reefer's shaking frame to the stone floor. I stood up and rested my hands on the choir railing. Below and far to the front of the sanctuary rested the draining body of Valerie Hackney. 'Holy Holy Holy' Lord God of Liberation. World without end. Amen.

The first day the twisted story of ritual murder began – a week ago, it was – I remembered turning the corner by this very church and wondering what its jovial pastor would make of a blood religion like this. Now that blood could never be washed from the lace or the marble pores, from the gold inlaid carving of 'Holy Holy Holy'.

Twenty minutes later everything was business. Mel had cordoned off the area, Pastor Mark was on his way back from a visitation, Reefer was being treated by a night duty nurse and Eddie Loetz was examining the body. Two paramedics stood by looking at the ceiling and trying to avoid the corpse; they were volunteers, but they hadn't volunteered for murder.

Even Dogget was on hand to help with the dusting of the obsidian dagger. We lifted several good prints and committed them to a sticky plastic tape. Neither of us for a moment believed they belonged to anyone but Professor Doyle Vollmer.

"You better have a back up." Dogget folded a hard case over the print tapes.

"Ten minutes. Just give me ten minutes, then you can back up."

"Why take the chance?"

"He'll be waiting for me and there won't be any trouble. I know it." I dropped the obsidian knife into a plastic bag. Dr. Loetz pulled a plastic sheet over Valerie's body – a shroud over Reefer's happiness, a veil away from the mystery and a body bag over Vollmer's alibis.

From the truck I radioed the airport. What time had Vollmer returned from piloting his attorney back to the Twin Cities? The answer was Vollmer never returned because he never left. Prudhomme booked out on a private charter. Vollmer's Beechcraft remained in the hangar after we had taken him in for questioning.

I hit the siren and light bar. It would keep me company for almost fifty miles and drive out the need to think, the need to understand. I put my brain and my truck on cruise control and raced toward a rendezvous with a murderer; smashed through a curtain of rain for a meeting with the Flayed God.

The driveway to Vollmer's summer home was riddled with rivers of rain; the gravel had been channeled deep and the ruts caught my tires, jerking the truck from side to side as I sped up the road. The house was dark and my headlights illuminated the deck where we had first met. I killed the motor and stepped out into the downpour. My anorak was still in the truck and I was immediately soaked. I unsnapped the keeper and placed my hand on the butt of the .357 magnum. Lightning broke open the sky, casting blue shadows against the whiteness of its voltage. A tree fell in the forest by the lake, the leaves of a nearby maple hissed in the deluge. I walked up on the wooden deck past the table where Vollmer ate his breakfasts on mild mornings. I suddenly stopped by the topside railing. Something touched my arm. I turned and looked at a pair of shoeless feet swaying in the wind, then another shot of lightning illuminated the body and face of Professor Doyle R. Vollmer dangling from a heavy extension cord looped over a maple branch. His face was dark and his thick pink tongue protruded from between clenched teeth. No one ever hangs himself properly – never a broken neck, always slow strangulation with a very long time to consider how wrong the decision had been.

No need for a search warrant now and placing the Telex to Mexico City had been a waste of time and money. I stood up on a wooden seat built into the deck and looked into the bloated face of Doyle Vollmer. I spread open the lapels of his suit coat. Minus the shoes, he was wearing the same clothing as when I'd last questioned him. Inside his left breast pocket was a rain-wet envelope with my name on it. I stuffed it inside my shirt and hurried down the deck stairs to my truck, trying to keep the paper from dissolving. It was already soaked, but maybe if I dried it properly, it could be read and saved. I placed it on the truck seat and watched the flashing lights of two squads turn up the driveway, their reflections bouncing off a million pounding raindrops. I put the truck in drive, waved as I drove by and headed back to town.

I wound up the small hair dryer cord. Vollmer had typed the letter neatly, folded it and put it in a hand-addressed envelope, but he hadn't expected it to rain so hard. Marie had suggested spreading the letter out on an oven rack and using the hair dryer. The typing was dim, but readable.

> *Dear Chief Tharp:*
>
> *By the time you read this you will have, I'm sure, put together an admirable case against me. There is little benefit in carrying this charade further. I choose to end it now.*
>
> *You were very close to correct when we last discussed the matter. I was only able to keep from giving in to you because I knew it would come to this, my death.*
>
> *By now you know of the grades-for-sex game I played with some of my students. You also know I used

the girls to keep down the prices I was asked to pay Mr. Portilla. It was not my intention that he become infatuated with Erin Brantnober. She, I'm certain, was not as infatuated with him. Her interests lay elsewhere. But the fact of the matter is she took a few days off to visit her father in Iowa. Portilla followed her there and that apparently was the time she became pregnant. She confronted us both in June, as you guessed. I cannot minimize my role in the matter. It was Portilla who killed her, but I was a willing participant. He would not stand for blackmail, I could not tolerate exposure. After she was dead, we shared equally the guilt of disposing of her body.

So, it appears I am an accessory to murder. My crime is greed and what follows – not outright murder. Perhaps my death will bring to light that travesty as well.

—Doyle Vollmer

I put the dryer back in her travel case. Her uniform was laid out ready for the morning breakfast club at the Outpost Café. She was asleep on the davenport. I sat down in my tattered easy chair, kept for comfort not for looks. I was asleep in an instant and then in another instant I heard the echo of my wrist watch alarm. Marie was already serving coffee and listening to the horror stories circulate among the booths and tables. I wondered who spent the night with Reefer and where. I hoped Loetz and the RN took him to the hospital and sedated the hell out of him. I wondered what Pastor Mark thought and whether or not he could explain any of it to the kids in his youth groups. I wondered if the church custodian would ever be able to scrub the blood from the marble altar or soak the stains out of the lace runner. I wondered if there would be a Telegram-Herald this week and if I'd see the TV I-Teams again. I tried to wonder about everything, everything except whether last night really ended the case.

I dragged myself out of the easy chair and went to the bathroom, tried to clean up my face and hair and sat on the stool a very long time.

There wasn't any food in the house worth eating and my stomach was rubbing against my backbone. The last place I wanted to go was the Outpost, but the thought of a bag of gooey sweet rolls from the bakery started sympathetic acid indigestion.

I opened the cabin door and looked out at a clearing sky. The rain had stopped and there was a gentle wind blowing from the west. Downtown Cache Harbor the tents and canopies would be fluttering to announce the opening morning of Voyageur Days. Soon the town would be filled with people playing cheap games and buying bargains they didn't want or need. Each day's list of events was posted all over town on bright yellow sheets of cardboard printed at the Telegram-Herald. I slipped into my truck and wondered if there would be any Voyageur Days photographs in next week's paper, and who would take them.

I parked in front of the café. If people wanted to rag at me about last night's events, they had a right to know where I was. But it wasn't like that inside. People must have figured I'd had a rough night and left me pretty much alone. I smiled weakly at Marie, who also looked tired. Toward the end of my meal, old Vince shuffled over to my booth.

"I'll bet you're glad it's over." He stuck out his liver-spotted paw for a handshake.

Chapter Twenty-Six

"Things got a little out of hand last night." Jim Bledsoe closed his office door behind me.

"No kidding." I collapsed into one of his plush office chairs and stretched out my legs as far as I could without pulling them out of their sockets. "Don't take it personally if I nod off occasionally."

"Hell of a way to close out a murder case. Looks like you had that puke Vollmer pegged all the way." Bledsoe rummaged around in his desk, finally finding a pack of cigarettes.

"Yeah. One victim shy of nailing him."

"Sometimes that can't be helped." He lit up and blew out a cloud of acrid smoke. "Nobody said the legal system was on a fast track."

"A little tough on the last victim." My socks were wet and my feet were starting to itch, I was tired, ornery and generally shot to hell.

"I don't mean any disrespect, but if that broad hadn't been doing other people's business for them, she might be crawling out of Reefer Carlson's sack this morning instead of being zipped up in a body bag of her own. She was way over her head, Paul, and got too close to the wrong guy."

"Maybe. That's the way it looks."

"Well, correct me if I'm wrong, but she was hauling her ass all over the University asking questions and maybe even getting answers…enough answers to make her cocky and that got her blasted. She confronted him with what she found – like a Monopoly game: do not pass 'Go', proceed directly to Professor Vollmer's on 'Park Place' and try to buy him out. Except she wasn't packing a .38 so she goes directly to the morgue."

"I can't figure out why she did that, why she bypassed me – or Reefer for that matter – and especially after calling and saying she was holed up during the storm."

"Grandstanding, Paul, it happens all the time with amateurs. No glory if the cops do the pinch. You can tell by reading the stories she ran last week. It was her cake and she could taste it. She set everybody up and then fucked the finale."

"Wanna buy a newspaper?" I was trying to scratch my feet through my running shoes and succeeded only in making them itch more.

"Don't bet on that, either. I'm sure Valerie was more than a casual piece of ass for Reefer, but he'll snap out of it." Bledsoe rubbed out his cigarette.

"I used to think like that, too, Jim, but you weren't with him last night and I was. That was not a man who lost his girlfriend, that was a man who had a piece of his existence chopped out. He could snap before he snaps out of it."

"Maybe you're right. I shouldn't be such a hard ass, but that still doesn't alter the fact that the broad did a dumb shittin' thing by going after Vollmer without the rest of us."

"Recognizing she did something dumb, won't make it any easier on Reefer."

"Doing dumb things, Paul, is the main reason people like her disappear. Cops are paid to go after murderers, hick reporters are not. If it wasn't in such lousy taste, I'd use her as an example in every talk I give to high school kids or senior citizens or the League-of-Women-fucking-Voters."

"Somehow I don't picture you speaking to any of those groups without getting arrested yourself."

"I'm a Dr. Jekyll and Mr. Fucking Hyde. Paul, that could'a been you on the altar. Think about that. He had plenty of reason to punch out your lights. You were a pussy hair away from putting him in the tank for good." Bledsoe lit up another cigarette and pulled out a yellow legal pad from the same drawer where he kept his mentholated habit. "Now let's get the official story straight. I have to say something about all these dead bodies, so feel free to chime in if you think what I'm releasing is way off the path or a piece of shit."

I pushed myself deeper into the chair and pried off my right shoe with my left toe and then my left shoe with the soggy sock of my right toe. I was going to leave wet footprints on his carpet.

"We give all the usual shit about names and ages, dates and causes of death, then make a statement to the effect that in our opinion the murders of Portilla, Brantnober and Hackney were all related to the suicidal Dr.

Vollmer. The Prof had been involved with smuggling art objects and was using a combination of money and sex for the payoff. Brantnober's pregnancy jeopardized the operation, so she was double teamed by Portilla and Vollmer. Portilla returned the favor by boosting his prices back to extortion levels, and Vollmer returned that favor by killing the bastard – ritualistically, because Vollmer was not a well man exacerbated by guilt and pressure – great word, exacerbated, I use it whenever I can. During the course of the brief investigation, Vollmer had been questioned several times by Cache Harbor police, however the independent questioning by Telegram-Herald reporter Hackney unfortunately resulted in her death, also at Vollmer's hand, and also in a ritualistic fashion. Vollmer was found with a note of admission after committing suicide by hanging at his summer home approximately fifty miles from Cache Harbor, etcetera, etcetera, blah, blah, blah. That about right?"

"That's neat and it closes the case." I'd been listening with my eyes shut and didn't open them with the answer. My feet were finally free and happy.

"Yes, it's neat and it closes the case, so what's so fuckin' bad about that? I know you have some reservations about this scenario, but unless the finger prints on the knife that killed Valerie don't match Vollmer's, I think we can put this baby to bed in spite of your reservations." Bledsoe laid down his yellow pad and crushed out his cigarette.

"For the record..." I opened my eyes.

"Nothin' for the fuckin' record, Paul. *This* is the fuckin' record, what I just told you. That is a plausible explanation and it fits the facts. It also closes the goddamn book on the whole shittin' mess." He stood up and jammed his hands into his pants pockets. His hounds tooth jacket flared out at the hips and his thin shoulders hunched forward and he glared at me. "I'm listening."

"Closing a case is a matter of everyone covering their own asses." I watched the county attorney move to the window where he concentrated on the parked cars two stories down.

"Shit, I know that. This one is cast iron underwear. All our asses are protected."

"Maybe, but first of all, the note I found on Vollmer is not a confession to three murders. He claims complicity in Erin Brantnober's death, but says Portilla did it. He doesn't mention killing Portilla, in fact the note sounds like he hopes his own death will lead to solving that one. As for Valerie – nada."

"OK. Let's agree on one thing: Vollmer is a psycho."

"Vollmer was a troubled man, filled with vanity and guilt, fear of exposure and a whole lot of other baggage, but I'm not sure that makes him a psycho."

"Paul. Any asshole who participates in cutting a pregnant woman in half – with a sharp rock, no less – and then dumping those halves in a lake, is a certifiable psycho and I can make any jury believe he was capable of anything after introducing that fact. How many little bobby-soxed legs have spread for a passing grade in Anthropology one-oh-one? Do you think that would be hard to prove? Do you think it would be hard to prove the professor was up to his cheeks in smuggling? Good reason to chop up his Mexican buddy when the heat turned up. As for Brenda Starr, girl reporter, that's easiest of all. By this time the professor is loony as a naked camper in black fly time. He's walking the edge and she pushes him over." Bledsoe turned from viewing the parking lot. "But he's still a professor and he's smart and he still wants your ass for bringing the whole thing crashing down around him."

"I don't understand that, Jim."

"Vollmer is a gold-plated sonofabitch and he wants to go out the underdog. He wants us to feel sorry for him – poor guy hung himself out of guilt and frustration like you said, didn't he? He admits to being dragged into Brantnober's death, but he says the other guy did it. Pity ploy number one. Then he denies killing the Mex, says he was framed – we got that on tape – look someplace else, it wasn't me, I'm really not that bad a guy. In fact it doesn't even cross his mind to mention it in his suicide note. Pity ploy two. And Valerie? Valerie who? Ploy three. Where does that leave us? More importantly, where does it leave the academic community? Feeling sorry for the asshole, that's where." Bledsoe had delivered his logical tirade leaning forward, fingers spread out on the top of his cluttered desk. He looked at me hard, then bobbed his head and returned to the window and the parked cars below. "Don't think guys won't protect their innocence – especially narcissists like him – right up until the time the warden throws the switch. They will and they do, all the time. 'I'm a poor little lamb who has gone astray and the cops hounded me until I did this to myself.' To paraphrase Shakespeare, methinks Vollmer protesteth too fuckin' much."

"The note was wet."

"It was raining fuckin' cats and dogs." He spun around from the window. "What? Was he wearing a plastic suit?"

"But if you were going to hang yourself, would you write a note and pocket it where you knew it would get soaked and possibly turned to mush in the process? For that matter could you just as easily throw a cord over a rafter in the basement?"

"Less dramatic."

"It's also more certain the note will be found and the explanation interpreted the way you say he wanted it read."

"When a man decides to kill himself, especially after coming off a number like the one he had just performed on Valerie, I doubt that he's thinking whether or not his suit coat had been waterproofed. I doubt he's thinking much at all. The psycho factor, Paul. The psycho factor for chrissake.

"Why isn't there any skin? Portilla's? Why did we find Sparky's heart partially burned and can't find Valerie's anywhere?"

"You don't need a search warrant now." Bledsoe's shoulders sagged and he turned back to his desk and sat down. "Look in the professor's freezer, in his fuckin' microwave. There are bound to be a shitpot full of unanswered questions in a case like this. All the players are dead. Short of a séance I go with the facts I've got. But, let's just suppose Vollmer didn't kill Sparky Portilla. If it was a set-up like he claimed, whose doing the setting-up? The mob? Now I don't know about you, but I'm not in the mood to go down that road looking for hired guns from Chicago or Detroit – not when I've got a perfectly workable case here at home."

I bent over, struggled with my wet socks and wet running shoes. Bledsoe got up and walked around his desk and perched next to a pile of manila file folders.

"The party's over and all the revelers are dead. You ask good questions, I like that about you. Good cop. But in my business it's Occum's Razor. It's a science; the simplest answer is the one that usually works. Let's not fuck up the experiment with extraneous details. It stands on its own. We don't need all the answers, just the ones that make it work."

Bledsoe was pragmatic to the end. If it worked, it was the truth. I wasn't as sure about that line of reasoning, but I had to admit most of the pieces fit together. You rarely get all the pieces; he was right, rarely get all the answers. Maybe on TV all the ends get tied up into a neat package. Usually the unanswered questions have to do with what snapped inside a person that either made him or allowed him to kill another human being, often someone he knew. People do strange, violent things to one another for reasons buried deep in the folds of their brains. Electrical impulses that coalesce and transform themselves from energy to reason.

I had a college instructor years ago that insisted most murderers have a roadblock in their heads, a detour that keeps them from heading down the road they want to travel. Once the detour is removed they can function again. Unfortunately the detour is another person, and just as often the murderer genuinely doesn't know why it's wrong to remove the roadblock. A wife, a parent, a friend, an employer, maybe the checkout girl behind the counter who doesn't hand over the cash fast enough. Roadblocks: people you know. Even rapes. I know you but I lash out against you.

Hate I can understand, fear and self-preservation, too. The ballgame is more orderly that way and I could explain Vollmer's triple using all three. But that didn't remove the gnawing feeling that kept signaling something else beneath the surface. Other voices, other motives. If I could just remove the obvious, the facile explanations, peel back the skin of the flayed man and look into the musculature concealing those tiny chemical and electrical impulses that moved a whole body. Not just why he murdered, but how it was allowed to happen. What combination of substances and impulses failed, and at what point? Where was the weakness? Would I have to split genes to find that answer? Against all reasonable odds and a long life of scholarship, Vollmer carried with him the tendency, the capacity to kill. Hundreds, probably thousands of people had met him, known him, liked him, disliked him, and even loved him. If they had looked closely, deeply into his eye could they have detected the chemical imbalance, the electrical short circuit, the mutated gene that would someday fail when presented with the choice to kill? I'd get nowhere fast thinking like that.

I pushed open the glass doors of the sheriff's department and waved to Ruthie in the dispatch booth. She pressed the buzzer that unlocked the hallway door leading to Dogget's office. If I had that buzzer maybe I could unlock the door to Vollmer's molecules, but if Jim Bledsoe was right, nobody would care. What worked was the truth and what Bledsoe had, worked. The public just wants to know 'who dunnit' and about thirty seconds of 'how come', which is why the public keeps generating more killers, crooks and creeps. They don't look for the short circuits.

"Knock, knock." I entered Dogget's office where he sat nursing coffee and looking tired.

"I'm no print expert, but Danny Peck is. He was on the early shift, so I pulled him in this morning to look at what we lifted last night. The slides are being flown down to BCA as we speak, but under the microscope even I could tell they matched the set we pulled off Vollmer when he was our guest in the lockup. Coffee?"

"Any other prints?" I accepted a stained cup and declined my usual cream.

"No. Couple of smears on the baptismal whatchamacallit..."

"Fount."

"...fount, like he had tried to wipe it clean."

"Why do you suppose he'd do that and leave clear prints on the knife?" Dogget's coffee was weak and hot.

"Don't nit-pick. It isn't often you get a chance to use fingerprints as evidence at all. Vollmer had just killed somebody and he wasn't functioning well at the time. Maybe he was trying to get caught. Maybe he ran out of time." Dogget poured himself more coffee. He was one of those people who have mouths impervious to scalding hot liquids, and cast iron throats to match. "What's biting you anyway?"

"Bledsoe says I'm trying to find all the little answers to all the little questions, when the only thing I need is a few answers that explain the big question...or something like that."

"Maybe you don't want it to end." Funny how sometimes the biggest slobs could be the ones with the biggest insights.

"You mean I've lived and breathed it for a week and now that it's over, I have to give it up...and because it's been such a big part of my life for a lot of hours and I'm so used to it, that I can't and won't let it go? That what they teach you in deputy school?"

"Because it's so often true." He leaned back in his swivel chair. "Maybe what you need is a good dose of Voyageur Days duty. Take your mind off the whole thing, put you back in the real world. Keeping kids outta the beer garden, hustlin' drunks outta their cars, answering complaints about crooked carnies and directing traffic."

"I suppose that was the deal. We're off the celebration to solve a murder and now that's over so we're back on the crew. When do we sleep?"

"If you can keep your hands off your girlfriend long enough, you'll go to sleep."

"Thanks for the advice. I've got paper work to do and a trip up the trail to look around Vollmer's house. Then when I get the autopsies, I should be able to lock it up. Put me down for Saturday beer garden duty and Mel for Sunday parade." I set the stained coffee mug on Dogget's desk. I felt like a zombie looking for a nice warm grave to lie down in and sleep into the next century.

I drove home to change my wet shoes and socks. When I awoke I was lying on my bed with one dry sock in my hand and the other on my foot. It was two o'clock in the afternoon.

The drive up the trail to Vollmer's summer home was punctuated with calls back and forth on the radio between myself, Mel, Ruthie and Dogget. Holes left in the day due to my unscheduled nap had to be plugged. I swung into the rutted driveway at three-fifteen. The extension cord still hung from the tree where the paramedics had taken down Vollmer's body. A cool August wind blew in off the small lake. The forecast was a good one for the Cache Harbor city fathers. Voyageur Days would be a climatological success. Plenty of sunshine, cool nights, good junk food, funky bands, spent money and more gossip than had been available in years.

The gossip would be about the man who had owned this house and I couldn't help wondering what would happen to it and its valuable contents. So far we hadn't turned up next of kin, and we hadn't had much more luck finding anyone related to Erin Brantnober, either. She still only existed on the University campus. I walked up on the deck and did a tour of the outside looking for possible vandalism. I looked out over the rippled lake at the docks jutting out from the north shore. How did the cabin owners on that side of the lake feel about the man who had lived on this side? What did they see, what did they know? Asking those kinds of questions could drag out this case forever; and why bother? Bledsoe said it was closed. Finished. Kaput. I walked around to the front where Mel had sealed the door. It was unlocked; I broke the seal and went inside.

Before my first visit with Vollmer, I'd expected the place to look and feel and smell like a museum, but for the most part it was really quite ordinary. Vollmer had not used his collection for interior decoration. There was a lot of un-matched older wicker furniture. Pictures on the walls were mostly photographs of archeological sites in Mexico, black and whites of Vollmer with this scholar or that at a convention, at this head table or that podium. Vollmer would be missed by quite a number of people, not to mention some of his students who will undoubtedly have a tougher row to hoe with Dr. Mastroianni in charge – Mastroianni, one of the few who won't miss Vollmer a bit.

Off the main room was an area that had been built to serve as a dining room. In it and two of the three bedrooms of the house was Vollmer's collection of Pre-Columbian art. He had installed track lighting throughout the three rooms and widened archways between them where doors had been. The walls were white and the floors were parquet. This was the museum and stepping into it was like stepping into another world – the real world for Professor Doyle R. Vollmer.

The articles were all coded, numbered and briefly described on small typed cards, pre-computer era. Were these cards that Erin Brantnober had scrolled through her electric typewriter?

[Colima – 615. Red ware jar. Late Classic?] I looked through a plexiglass box at a fat hairless dog standing on three legs; the left front was lifted as if waiting for a handshake from its master.

[Colima – 013. Mixtec Cholula Polychrome pottery. Post Classic] The yellow bowl was molded to a stand almost as wide as the opening.

There were pale green and red geometric designs on it and a green and red hummingbird perched on the lip.

[Oaxaca – 018-023. Mixtec stone. Post Classic] Inside the plexiglass box was an arrangement of five figures carved from various colored stone. They looked like idols I had seen in a National Geographic story on Hawaii. The little men all faced ahead with slitted eyes and held their arms across their chests, fingers pointing at each other. They all appeared to be smiling at me.

I continued looking through the display until I stopped in front of a life-sized stone mask. The face was supported on a plastic tripod and was almost a perfect oval. The ears were large and pierced at the lobes. The hairline was carved into ropes and pulled back from its stone forehead. The nose rose only slightly from the expanse of face, the eyes quarter moon slits. The mouth was a circle without an indication of lips. The card simply read [Xipe]. This was the Flayed God and I could imagine human eyes peering out of the moon slits and human lips behind the open mouth – moving and forming my name. Fashioned in stone, a representation of the dead leathery flesh slipped on over a live face and body. Xipe slipped on his costume, dressed in another person's skin.

Enough of that. I quickly looked away from the mask toward a woman's face. Pale, cream colored pottery that reminded me of Marie's complexion. Her sculptured eyebrows carried a thin brown color and the eyes were closed, but lashes had been carefully painted on in a resin color that matched the brows. Her nose was fine and straight, the lips full and parted; a small cleft was marked in her chin. She wore an elaborate headpiece like a crown. I bent closer to examine the details of her face, squinting my eyes to frame her silhouette against the white wall. There was a familiar cast to the lips and chin. Then I noticed a fine hairline that circled the mouth and two more that circled her eyes, barely etched in the pale clay surface. [Tlazolteotl, female version of Xipe]. I reached out to touch the plexi box, the wind outside picked up slightly and whispered past a half-opened window.

I jumped a foot when a loud ringing shattered the room's silence and for an instant I thought I'd set off an alarm. I jerked my hand back from the box as another ring split the room, then silence. It was Vollmer's telephone hanging on the wall next to me. I grabbed the receiver to keep it from screaming at me again; my heart was pounding in my chest. I spit out my last name to the caller. The voice on the other end belonged to Dr. Eddie Loetz.

"They told me I could find you there, Paul. Listen, I think we've got a problem. Two problems to be exact. I did the autopsies. I haven't really finished Valerie, but I can tell she was killed like the other fellow."

"Portilla."

"Yeah. Heart cut out, but of course, she wasn't skinned. That's not the problem, though. Vollmer is the problem. I did him first because he didn't look right to me, you know what I mean?"

"No, I'm afraid to ask."

"Yeah, well he looked too dead to be dead only a little while. I can't be sure without more tests, but I don't think the professor died last night, Wednesday. Valerie probably died in the late afternoon, early evening. Vollmer, on the other hand probably died the day before, Tuesday—more than likely in the afternoon is my guess. Asphyxiation was the cause, for sure. He hung himself from the light cord and I'd guess it took quite a while by the looks of the scratch marks on his neck where he tried to loosen the knot. Paul? You still there?"

"Right. What's the other problem?"

"Reefer Carlson. I checked him into the hospital last night and had him treated for shock. It was a squirrel cage in that room until they got him sedated. We made the mistake of letting him get at some of Valerie's personal effects. What it was, was her tote – one of those canvas and strap affairs that holds a week's supply of everything. The RN accompanying Reefer to the ER found it in the parking lot by Valerie's car, picked it up and took it to the hospital to give to you. This afternoon while Reefer was walking off the sedative, he apparently spotted the tote bag at the nurse's station. He took it back to his room, got dressed shortly afterwards and walked out the door."

"Do me a favor, will you Eddie? Get hold of Mel and tell him to try and track down Reefer. Hold him by force if necessary." I hung up and once again felt the cool chill of the August breeze come in off the lake. Bledsoe was wrong. Shit! Now I wished he'd been right.

Chapter Twenty-Seven

So, I helped myself to the professor's expensive sipping whiskey and sat in one of his big white wicker chairs with a sun-faded flower design on the seat cushion. The living room was spacious and ended in tall glass patio doors that opened out on a short expanse of redwood deck; from that point, the lake spread out in front of me. The sun was casting long slanted copper shadows across the yard and boathouse to the east; to the west the sun's deep orange ball filtered through a tangle of red pine and cedar branches. Little smallmouth bass were jumping near the stubby dock that jutted only a rowboat's length into the water. The breeze had died to a mere whisper.

There was a very good chance Reefer Carlson was not aware of Vollmer's death. There may have been talk in the hospital corridors as the stunned editor walked up and down trying to wear off the sedative's grogginess and to adjust to his new life without Valerie. Likely as not he hadn't heard. Even walking out the hospital door and into the town still might not have given him a clue to the rest of what happened last night. He would avoid contact with others and use the Voyageur Days crowd to keep from the police. I was betting Reefer would soon find his way up the trail to this summer home with murder on his mind.

On the other hand, and equally plausible, Reefer may have found his reporter's notebook in the tote he removed from the nurses station. Those notes may have incriminated Vollmer, or maybe not. She had left me the message saying there was more to the story than the professor. In light of the autopsy, of which Reefer knew nothing, that surely would seem to be the case. Sheepie was the clue, she had said, but that was Xipe the Flayed God. If Marie was right, the nickname might carry deep connotations of love and dependence. Whoever or whatever Xipe was certainly was responsible for Valerie's death. But the fingerprints belonged to Vollmer and Vollmer had been dead a day before Valerie's lights went out.

The question remained: who was Reefer looking for and who was I looking for? I was still betting Reefer would soon find his way up the trail to this summer home with murder on his mind. I'd wait to see.

I reached over to a stack of files I'd retrieved from the front seat of my truck. I fingered my way through one and pulled out the small, bent and faded Polaroid of Erin Brantnober and her costumed friend. The photo had not changed; if pictures change at all, they just fade leaving the subjects less distinct versions of themselves. But sometimes the way you look at pictures can change. Erin was still smiling at the camera and the roommate still held the jack-o-lantern. Erin was still dressed as a gypsy – headscarf, golden earrings and a sash. The sash looked familiar. Maybe I had seen it in another photograph. I squinted closely at the wispy-bearded hippie seated close to Erin. I tried to cover the bearded face with my thumb and look only at the eyes. Then I searched the files for a copy of the artist's rendering of the suspect's face. I covered the bearded portion with the flat of my hand – thumb along one side of the face, forefinger along the other. The eyes in the drawing were unfamiliar and those in the Polaroid were indistinct.

I took a sheet from the Portilla file, the list of cities the tile salesman told his parole officer he was visiting. Minneapolis, Chicago, Denver, St. Louis, Des Moines. What was it Vollmer had told me? There were Pre-Columbian artifact collectors in those cities, but he was not aware of any collector in Des Moines. The jealous professor Mel had interviewed said that Portilla had visited the University many more times than what he apparently reported. That may not matter, except for arithmetic. If Erin were just three months pregnant by the first part of June, then she would have conceived in middle or late March. The file told me Portilla had been in Des Moines the last two weeks in March. Vollmer's suicide note read: 'But the fact of the matter is, she took a few days off to visit her father in Iowa, Portilla followed her there…' In the sentence before that, Vollmer had also written: 'She, I'm certain, was not as infatuated with him. Her interests lay elsewhere.'

I finished the whisky and walked out the patio doors into the gathering evening. I could hear the purr of either a motorboat or a car down the lake. The familiar feeling began to roil around in my stomach. I'd had it before earlier in the week and I knew it was tied to dread and fear. I made my way down the path to the lakeshore where the small boathouse stood. There was no lock on the plank door, and I pushed it open without effort.

In the fading light of sunset I saw familiar objects. Books and a pile of boards and bricks that had once held them against a cabin wall. There were some other things as well, but without closer inspection I knew they all belonged to Emily Baxter. Emily Baxter, Erin Brantnober. The initials were the same. Erin did not exist off the University campus and this was the reason why. There were also no next of kin because the BCA was looking for someone named Brantnober.

I closed the boathouse door and walked slowly back up the path to the summer house. There was no sense in waiting for Reefer any longer. The ball of dread erupted in my stomach and I ran the last few steps to the house. The man in the photograph, the man with the wispy beard was not a man at all. The woman came from Des Moines and there was no one there to identify the body because the next of kin was not in Iowa, but in Bombay.

I remember reaching for my drink glass to drain whatever few dregs were there and hearing the whisper of wind in my ear. My teeth hit the edge of the glass and there was a dull echoing thud at the back of my head. The pain spread up into my brain for just an instant and then there wasn't anything anymore.

....

In the blackness, even the black of unconsciousness, half formed images appear skirting the edge of mental sight, flowing in and out of existence. Sometimes they are only lights, sometimes they surface momentarily as people, real or imagined. And there are emotions, too, just like those felt in a particularly vivid dream. Joy, wonder, great excitement, bottomless longing and despair, fear and loss.

Just before I felt my body being lightly plied and kneaded, I became dimly aware of the restraints. I couldn't move my arms or legs. Then I felt the fingers sliding over my body and I slowly became aware of my own nakedness.

I opened my eyes to the faint glow of remaining sunset, and looked into Marie's soft face.

"You're awake," she whispered.

Chapter Twenty-Eight

I felt the pain start at the base of my skull and then shoot around to my temples to meet in a crackling throb just above the hairline of my forehead. A slight movement of my arms confirmed they were tied down and so were my legs. The rope felt tight around my ankles and wrists and I sensed something like ridges running up my back and buttocks. A light breeze played over my exposed body.

"How does your head feel?" She was massaging my chest.

"It hurts. What are you doing?" I could smell the sharp scent of insect repellent as she worked her hands around my rib cage.

"I'm sorry I hurt you my darling, but I was afraid you wouldn't understand." She continued the massage for a moment, then paused to drip more repellent on my stomach. "Just relax while I finish this."

"Finish what, Marie? What are you doing this for?" Her face again appeared above mine, but there was something wrong with what she was wearing.

"I have to leave you here while I prepare the temple. I couldn't bear the thought of the mosquitoes and flies biting you. If there was any other way, I'd do it, dear…" Her voice trailed off. "Just try to relax."

"Relax! For chrissake, Marie you've got me tied down. How can I relax?"

"Please Paul, don't struggle. I'm trying to cover your body so the mosquitoes won't torment you while I'm gone." She moved her slippery hands down the sides of my legs. I tried to sit up but could only manage a slight bend at my waist. I choked at what I saw.

Marie bent over my abdomen spreading oily insect repellent around the tops of my legs. She wore no clothing, but hanging loosely around her shoulders and far down her arms was a mantle of copper colored skin. The arm skin had been laced together with leather strips and fitted over her own like sleeves The larger severed hands of Jorge Portilla hung limply at her wrists. The dried hands had curled into claws and one of them brushed against my groin as she applied the repellent to my genitals and between my legs.

The sheet of skin hung open down her front and as she moved I could see her firm breasts alternately covered and exposed by the dusky leather. Her rich brown nipples caressed the inside of Portilla's flayed chest. I couldn't make out the details of her legs, but the skin appeared to hang down, waiting to be laced around her calves. As she moved her hands down my legs, she turned her head at right angles to my eyes and I could see the loose flesh of what had once been Jorge Portilla's face draped down her back like the hood of a cape.

"Marie. I think you'd better let me go." I tried to force the panic from my voice, but I'd done a poor job of it.

"Paul, we'll soon be together after I prepare the temple." She continued to massage down my legs.

"I don't understand any of this, Marie. Please untie me." I strained at the ropes and she continued patting repellent on the tops of my feet and between my toes.

"Of course you understand. There is no other way for us to be together than this way. You know they won't let me live with you now." She finished by rubbing the remaining repellent on the bottoms of my feet. "Falling in love with you was not a part of my original plan. But I've been so happy."

"What was the original plan, Marie?" I was hoping to work the ropes loose while she talked to me. My hands and arms were slippery from the insect repellent, but for the effort, her bonds dug all the deeper into my flesh.

"Emily was my half sister." She put down the repellent bottle on a picnic bench. She stood framed against the last wisps of sunset and I could see we were on a small hill overlooking the lake. The professor's summerhouse must be close by. "We met for the first time at mother's deathbed. I tried not to lie to you too much, darling, but I had to tell you my sister was in Los Angeles and that Emily was a roommate away most of the time. I couldn't let you know Emily and Erin were the same person."

"Why did there have to be an Erin Brantnober at all?" I finally realized I'd been tied to a slatted picnic table and the more I struggled, the tighter the ropes held and the deeper the wooden surface bit into my back.

"Emily had a bad experience with a man when she lived in Los Angeles, so when she came back for the funeral, she changed her name. We stayed together at the University and we loved each other deeply."

"You were telling me the truth when you said she could have found such a liberating experience with a lover, that she could have called that person Xipe."

"I was Xipe. I never thought I could have found as deep a love as we had, but then I met you." She brought up a naked leg and set her foot on the picnic bench next to my head. Then she slowly began to lace the torn edges of Portilla's ankle and calf skin over her own. He had been taller than she, so it had been necessary to cut away his feet. "At first I paid attention to you just so I could be close to your investigation...until that afternoon on the beach when you could have taken me but didn't."

"You killed Portilla?" I watched as she continued to lace the long leather strips through holes in the dead man's skin and draw it close over her leg.

"I had planned it for a long time. Ever since I knew they had killed Emily. We were coming up here to work and study, but that pig Portilla forced himself on Emily. When she discovered she was pregnant and told him, he and Professor Vollmer killed her. It was Vollmer who I really wanted."

I slowly began working my ankles and pulling the ropes with my oily feet. One binding seemed looser than the other. Marie had laced one leg all the way to her crotch. It was hard for me to hold myself partially bent to watch her moves.

"It was the professor's fault that Emily got into trouble and it was his fault that pig killed her. I stole the stone sacrificial knife from his collection. When the professor left the pig at his summer home while he flew back to the University a little over a week ago? I drove up to the house and got him."

"You mean killed him." I kept working the loosening ropes at my feet as Marie laced up the other leg.

"I used the same hammer on him as I did on you and Valerie."

"Then why am I alive and they're not?"

"I'm a sculpture student, dear. I know the correct force to chip stone or trim off a leaf of wood." She stopped lacing the skin to her leg. "I tried to get you to accept the clues I left. You just didn't seem to want to believe it was Professor Vollmer who killed that pig. I had several more ideas planned that would point to him, but then they discovered Emily and I thought for sure that would put Vollmer in jail. It would have, too, if Valerie hadn't gotten involved." She began lacing the skin again. "Darling, sometimes you were so frustrating. I just couldn't seem to lead you in the right direction. It was going to work, though. The problem was I didn't have enough time to think through Valerie's death."

Now I was certain I was going to be Xipe's next victim. "Valerie saw the photo on my desk, didn't she. She recognized the sash you were wearing as the same one in the Halloween Polaroid. She also learned about Xipe and that the roommate was not a man." I began to feel the pressure on one ankle begin to ease.

"She also re-drew the sketch you'd made...without the beard and beret. It looked very much like me and that's why I had to kill her. You were gone all day. I called Reefer and told him she was staying at a motel because of the weather, but she was already dead." Marie finished lacing her leg. The dead man's withered penis hung to one side of her dark pubic hair, dangling against the hollow sack of his scrotum. She pulled together the gaping cut of his chest wound and began lacing it closed over her bare breasts. "I wanted her to be alive when I cut out her heart, it's better to have a beating heart to sacrifice...but I hit her too hard. When I found you asleep on the bed this noon after work, I left and went back to the cabin and burned her heart there."

"What are you going to do with me?" I hoped she would not see that one foot was almost out of the rope loop.

She finished lacing up the skin and acted as though she had not heard the question. I could see the bulge of her breasts against Portilla's skin. He had been larger than she, but his flesh had shrunk even though she had done something to keep it from drying out completely.

"How did Vollmer's fingerprints get on the knife that killed Valerie?" My eyes were finally getting accustomed to the dark and I caught sight of my clothes and hers piled together at the base of a birch tree.

"I sculpted the knife I used on the pig and Valerie. I knew the dagger I'd taken from the professor's collection had his fingerprints on it. I kept them from becoming smeared because I thought I could use the knife as a clue. I almost did after you released him from jail. But, then there was Valerie." She bent down beside me and took something from beneath the picnic table where I was tied. She stood up and raised the stone dagger for me to see. My heart began to thump harder and I squirmed against the rough boards of the old picnic table.

"If you love me so much how can you kill me?"

"I'm not going to kill you, darling, I'm going to give you eternal life along with me." She placed the ceremonial knife on my chest and I shut my eyes waiting for the blade to tear a jagged cut through my flesh, and to know finally what thousands of ancient slaves learned at the moment of death – what it felt like to have your beating heart slashed from your breast. "But I must make the temple ready." The knife lay cool on my chest. I opened my eyes.

"What temple?"

"The Temple of the Burning Water. I have to start the professor's house burning just like Quetzalcoatl when he burned his house. It became the temple of his resurrection. Then I'll come back for you, my dear. Together you and I will do what he did. I will take your heart with me into the flames. We will be consumed and rise to heaven. There we will live forever with the feathered serpent and shine with him like Venus, and at last understand the mystery of the burning water."

"Marie, I don't want to die this way. I don't want to die at all and I don't care about understanding the burning water. I want you to let me go. I can see that you'll get help." I pushed my foot harder against the circle of rope and felt it give a little more. She had not seemed to hear. She looked down at me with great tenderness, then reached behind her head and pulled over the cowl of Portilla's eyeless, mouthless face, fastening a thong to a length of skin through a hole under the chin. She knotted the lacing and bent over my face. My reaction was to try and force my body back into the wooden planks to which I was lashed. I could see her eyes glowing behind the open holes in Portilla's face and her full mouth protruding from where his had been.

I could feel her breath on my face. "I will save your soul and carry it to heaven. I am the bearer of repentant souls. Together our hearts will keep the sun alive forever." She bent closer and I instinctively tried to avoid her, but her lips found mine and she kissed me long and lovingly. As her tongue penetrated deep into my mouth, I could feel the rough scraping of Portilla's dried flesh against my chin and upper lip. I was afraid I'd gag and choke to death lying on my back. But just when I'd thought I could detect the smell of the dead man's skin, the kiss ended, she picked up the obsidian knife, and she was gone.

I lay still for a moment, then tried to sit up. The terror settled in and knocked the wind from my lungs. I'd been too busy thinking how to get loose to know the depth of the fear that finally hit me. I was sweating; the insect repellent glistened and rolled along my body. I could not see her. I didn't know if she was still there or had left me – and if she had, how soon would she return?

I called her name, then yelled it. I struggled against the ropes and tried to free my left foot. I had been screaming her name, but wasn't aware of how many times until I suddenly stopped when one foot came free. I heard the multiple echoes of my voice booming down the shore of the lake.

I worked on the ropes of the other foot as I had done this morning in Bledsoe's office. Removing wet running shoes. There was nothing casual about this however, it was a matter of life or death. The ropes must have been wound around each foot and then tied, because in a matter of seconds the other foot was free. But you can't untie your hands with your toes. The ropes binding my hands were tied down around the edges of the table and then together behind my back. I was not just strapped to the planks, I was tied to the support grid bolted to the top. If she had just tied my hands together with the table between my arms and back, I could have slipped along the top and eventually inched my way free. But she had tied them to the cross supports and nothing was moving.

With my legs free, I walked my buttocks down the table until there was no slack left in the ropes. My feet and legs hung over the table edge enough to act as ineffective pendulums. I began swinging them, rocking the table forward and back. Then with a final thrust, the table tipped ahead and I was standing upright on the ground with the table's wooden legs pointing out from my back.

I was standing in a small clearing that had been used for picnics. Besides the table and benches, there was a fire pit and a small stock of firewood pieces. I hobbled from side to side and was able to slowly turn to see where I thought Marie had gone. Suddenly behind me, an orange light had flared up and cast my shadow against the trees to my front. I turned around, struggling to keep my balance. There was a sharp drop of maybe fifteen to twenty feet ahead of me; below that was part of the driveway and beyond – the length of three football fields – was Professor Vollmer's house going up in flames.

I screamed her name again and as I did two white lights swung around the corner of the driveway and illuminated the road below where I stood tottering under the weight of seventy-five pounds of old wooden picnic table tied to my naked back. The van belonged to Reefer Carlson and it was heading towards the burning house.

I took a step toward the van as it moved away from me. I called out Reefer's name, and then tumbled over the edge of the twenty-foot drop. The table with me as its captive human cargo hit short end first where my head would have been had I not worked myself down into a standing position. The whole thing flipped the other way and rolled down the bank. My arms were still tied around the table edge and they took a beating on the stony trip downhill. I landed face first in a brush pile.

I reached for my left elbow which had taken the first brunt of the fall. It was at that point that I realized the pounding trip down the embankment had broken the under supports on the table and I was free to slip out of the ropes. It took a few moments, but when I scrambled out from under the table, by hands were no longer tied.

I stood at the edge of the driveway and did a spot check of my body to see that no parts were missing, then scrambled back up the hill. The summer home was completely engulfed in flames by now and I could see Reefer's van silhouetted against the bright orange sheets that pushed skyward, fanned by the light breeze.

I stopped to put on my clothes but at that instant the entire impact of loosing Marie hit me in the pit of the stomach. I reeled in self pity, but the sagging jolt of defeat lasted only long enough to make my eyes tear and turn my vision of the burning house into a wild, blurred painting. Then the panic struck.

I ran naked down the hill. Thorn bushes dragged at my legs and my feet ached with rock bruises. There was still a chance for Marie – not for a life together, but at least I could try to save her from total destruction. I'd seen it before, read about – the rehabilitation. Not that the people she killed would ever know or care, or that she might ever be free of confinement, but at least she could sculpt and I could visit her on warm Sundays and rainy fall afternoons.

I ran up the driveway toward Reefer's van. I had to stop him from committing the revenge I knew burned in his heart. I had to stop yet another killing. I had to save Marie. Reefer's name burst from my lungs as I saw his shadow dance in front of the swaying flames. I cut the distance between us in half but still had a football field to run.

Reefer turned to see a naked man charging full speed toward him, the call of his own name fading into the rushing noise of the fire, but he knew I was screaming at him. He drew a long, thick bladed Bowie knife from its sheath and moved toward the conflagration. Then I saw a figure emerge from the boiling red-orange heat and Reefer held out the knife in both hands.

I stopped short when I saw Marie run from the house, a naked torch, her long black hair streaming in flames behind her as she rushed toward Reefer's outstretched arms. I was only a few yards away from them when I yelled at him to put the knife away. But Reefer steadied the long blade at the point of his left hip and when the burning shrieking thing lunged at him he was ready. Her face was covered in a blackened film of crisp skin and shards of another man's flesh dropped away from her as she flung herself at Reefer, hair a blazing mass. I shouted again for him to help her, instead he set his legs wide apart and met her ragged body with an upward thrust of both hands. He lifted her two feet off the ground when the soft flesh of her abdomen met the foot-long blade. The upward thrust split her heart and she died hanging on the steel as they fell backward together in a fiery heap.

EPILOG

It was Pastor Mark's idea to meet together after the funerals. He didn't exactly call it counseling, because I wasn't a member of his congregation. He called it 'closure'. Closure seems to me to be one of those catch-all words we use these days instead of something more to the point, like "dealing with it" or "figuring out how to continue on continuing when continuing seems pointless as hell and you don't want to anyway."

But I appreciated the gesture. He needed to deal with it, too. He said he realized I'd lost a lover and a friend. I said I realized his congregation's need to 'renovate' the sanctuary – a nice way of saying they were going to tear out the bloody altar and re-configure the whole area because it was all too awful for Protestants to deal with.

The funeral services had been subdued and in good taste. Reefer died on the way to the hospital; Marie had died before she hit the ground. I felt like I was dead from the asshole both ways. Portilla, Vollmer, Erin-Emily, baby, Valerie, Marie, Reefer. Fuckin' lucky there was anybody left in town breathing.

"Why are our religions so violent and bloody?"

"Oh, I don't know that that's the case so much any more. I don't think it would be fair to classify what went on here as a religion. After all, with due respect, this was an ancient belief system, one that died out before it had a chance to be modified. I doubt that the natives in central Mexico still adhere to these same beliefs.

"How do you explain the Crusades? The Inquisition? Salem witch hunts?"

"I'm not saying there weren't mis-interpretations in the past. What I'm saying is that today, we don't follow that eye-for-an-eye logic. I can only speak for my denomination and what I believe to be the practice in Christianity today."

"Nobody burned at the stake?"

"No, the message is one of peace and understanding, love and compassion. It's actually harder to live by those rules than it is to kill and torture out of righteousness."

"What about crucifixion? That seems a pretty violent and bloody way to accomplish salvation and for that matter, many of the same things the Aztecs were after."

"The cross in this church is empty. The symbol of the risen savior."

"And down the street, that church is filled with bleeding hearts and hanging Christs on bloody crosses."

"I can't presume to speak for another's beliefs. Besides it's all symbolism anyway."

"Xipe, too?"

"I can't say. All I know is we don't dwell on blood and violence, sacrifice and pain in this church. And I think you'd do well to put that behind you, too. Compassion, Paul. We need compassion for them all. And prayer. God is all loving and all forgiving. There's no blood lust here, not any more."

I thanked him for his words and assured him I'd be fine. The city council had given me the month off to 'regroup', as they put it. We shook hands and he invited me to attend services any time I was ready. I could have furthered the discussion and brought up communion: bread and wine turning to flesh and blood. I'm not sure if he'd call that just 'symbolism'.

I walked back through the empty Wednesday halls of First Immanuel. Late afternoon light was filtering through stained glass fractures of the round sanctuary window. I became aware of the choir beginning practice for Sunday's service. I reached for the door to go outside to my waiting truck and caught the words of their hymn.

> *In Jerusalem flows a river of blood*
> *Let from Christ's own vein;*
> *Sinners baptized in the flood*
> *no longer wear the devil's stain.*
> *Sinners baptized in the blood*
> *no longer suffer in his reign.*

ABOUT THE AUTHOR

Jay Andersen has written for and edited two community newspapers, as well as served as News Director/Producer for a community public radio station. He has also authored, and seen performed, numerous stage and radio plays. When not writing he has been a non-profit arts administrator and consultant.

All of these activities have taken place in Minnesota, where he continues to reside with his wife.